Kay —
Appreciate you
supporting me —
Thank you!
I hope you find value
in my words in some way.
In gratitude —

Eyes Wide Open:

Learning to Suffer

JASON L. SHARP

Dedication

For My Unbreakable Family

To my father and my late mother, whose choices may not have always been the best but whose unwavering determination kept us alive in the heart of Chicago. Your struggles taught me resilience, and your love laid the foundation for the person I am today.

To my sister Jodi, the guardian angel who took care of us during those years on the streets. Your strength, selflessness, and fierce love held us together when everything seemed to be falling apart. You are the embodiment of courage, and I am forever grateful for your unwavering support.

To my three incredible sons, Xavier, Quincy, and Nathaniel. Xavier, my eldest, you have stood by my side through thick and thin. Your unwavering loyalty and unwavering belief in me have been my guiding light. Watching you grow into an amazing young man fills my heart with immense pride.

Quincy and Nathaniel, my youngest, I regret the nights and weekends missed while bringing this book to life. Know that every sacrifice was made with the hope of building a better future for you. As you embark on your own journeys, I will be there, cheering you on every step of the way. Your potential is boundless, and I cannot wait to see the extraordinary lives you will lead.

To Yael, the angel who stepped into my life and saved me. Your compassion, warmth, and unconditional love transformed my world. You embraced me as your own, providing the support I desperately needed. I am eternally indebted to you for the kindness you have shown me.

To my greatest mentor, Brian Galarza, who taught me how to navigate this complex world and become the man I am today. Your wisdom, guidance, and unwavering belief in me pushed me beyond my limits. You saw my potential and nurtured it, molding me into the person I always aspired to be.

To everyone out there who played a part in my journey, who offered a helping hand, a word of encouragement, or a glimmer of hope. Your collective influence has shaped my path and filled my life with immeasurable love and support. I am forever grateful to each and every one of you.

To my extraordinary family and cherished friends, this book is a testament to the love and resilience that binds us together. You are my foundation, my inspiration, and my reason to strive for greatness. Your unwavering presence in my life is a constant reminder of the power of love and the beauty of human connections.

Finally, to my love and my anchor, Nayeli, whose unwavering support has been the bedrock of my journey and whose love has been my guiding light through every peak and valley. This book is as much a tribute to our bond as it is a testament to our personal growth.

Through the waves of joy and sorrow that swept us along, you stood beside me, a steady presence in a world of uncertainty. Your unwavering belief in me fueled my spirit when doubt threatened to consume me. In those moments when I chose to write instead of sleep, you reminded me to nourish my body and my soul.

You have been my pillar of strength, my unwavering cheerleader, and my anchor in the stormy sea of life. Your unwavering faith in me and our shared dreams has propelled us forward, transforming obstacles into opportunities and challenges into triumphs.

Every word penned in this book carries the essence of our love, the resilience of our bond, and the profound impact you have had on my journey. It is a testament to the unwavering support and love you have shown me every step of the way.

As we celebrate the victories and reflect on the hardships, let this dedication serve as a reminder of the profound gratitude and immense love I hold for you. Without you, this journey would have been incomplete, devoid of the meaning and purpose that your presence brings.

To my rock and my sanctuary, thank you for loving me unconditionally, for walking by my side when the path grew treacherous, and for always believing in the power of our shared dreams. You are the embodiment of love and the reason I dare to reach for the stars.

With heartfelt gratitude and boundless love,

Jason

Acknowledgments

Writing a book is a journey that no author embarks upon alone. It is with immense gratitude and a full heart that I acknowledge the many individuals who have played a significant role in bringing this book to life.

First and foremost, I extend my deepest appreciation to my family, whose unwavering love and support have been the foundation of my creative endeavors.

To my siblings, your constant encouragement and belief in my abilities have been a driving force behind my success.

I am forever indebted to my editors, whose keen eye and invaluable guidance transformed my words into a work of art. Your dedication, patience, and insightful feedback pushed me to refine my ideas and craft a story that resonates deeply.

To the team at Elite Books, thank you for believing in the potential of this book and for the countless hours of hard work dedicated to bringing it to fruition.

To my friends, thank you for your support and understanding during the countless hours I spent immersed in writing. Your encouragement, late-night coffee runs, and uplifting words have kept me motivated and inspired.

Finally, to my readers, thank you for embarking on this journey with me. Your enthusiasm, feedback, and support are what make this whole endeavor worthwhile. It is my greatest joy to share this story with you and to touch your lives in some small way.

To all those who have touched my life, whether mentioned here or not, I am eternally grateful for your presence and influence. Without your support, this book would not have been possible.

Table of Contents

Preface

As a person who has faced multiple challenges in this life, I've come to understand the true nature of suffering and how it shapes our lives. Over the years, I've been inspired by the words of William Ernest Hensley's poem *Invictus* and have taken its message to heart. It is the idea of being unconquerable, undefeated, and unbroken in the face of adversity that has driven me to write this book, *Eyes Wide Open: Learning to Suffer*.

Out of the night that covers me,
Black as the Pit from pole to pole,
I thank whatever gods may be
For my unconquerable soul.

In the fell clutch of circumstance
I have not winced nor cried aloud.
Under the bludgeonings of chance
My head is bloody but unbowed.

Beyond this place of wrath and tears
Looms but the Horror of the Shade,
And yet the menace of the years
Finds, and shall find, me unafraid.

It matters not how strait the gate,
How charged with punishments the scroll,
I am the master of my fate:
I am the captain of my soul

My journey started with surviving the streets of Chicago, then Ranger School, and later, cancer. But it wasn't until I met Johnnie Blue Hands in February of 2018 that I truly felt inspired to share my message. I realized that my purpose was to help others understand what happens when you learn to suffer with your eyes wide open.

The human condition is defined by suffering, and it is something that we all carry with us in one form or another. We all carry emotional baggage that can bring with it fear, hurt, guilt, and insecurity. But these challenges are what shape us as individuals and leaders. They teach us about resilience, mental toughness, and how to stretch the boundaries of human potential.

In this book, I will take you on a journey through my life, sharing the lessons I've learned about suffering and how they have shaped me into the man I am today. I will explore what suffering can teach us about life, leadership, and our individual concepts of happiness. I will also delve into the role of the human condition in our development as leaders.

In the first part of the book, "The Suffering," I will define the human condition from my perspective and explain how it shapes us as individuals. I will delve into what suffering can teach us about character, compassion, and empathy and how it helps us develop resilience and mental toughness. In the second part, "The Path Forward," I walk you through my journey of self-discovery and the mindset that has carried me through this stage of my life.

The third part, "Executive Function Beyond the Classroom," is targeted at business leaders, educators, and non-profit leaders. This part is near and dear to my heart, having spent many years as a youth mentor. I will explore the practical applications of these concepts, focusing on individuals, parents, schools, and organizations. I will focus on the importance of executive function skills and evidenced-based programing, such as Social Emotional Learning (SEL)

This book is not only about learning to suffer, but it's also about leadership. It's about finding and delivering purpose and direction and how to generate it even in the face of adversity. It's about exploring the drive that propels some individuals to succeed far beyond failure.

Through my personal experiences and lessons, I hope to reshape perspectives on the topic of suffering and provide a roadmap for staying vigilant with your eyes wide open.

Introduction

I decided to write this book after many years of contemplation. Initially, I thought I was ready to write sometime after surviving Chicago. Then, I thought I was ready to write after surviving Ranger School. Some years after, I thought I was ready to write after surviving cancer. Then on a random cool day in February 2018, I met Johnnie Blue Hands. He was the driving force compelling me to wield my pen. My motivation soared as I realized my path was to deliver this message: What happens when you learn to suffer with your eyes wide open?

Ever wondered what it might be like to live a life without trauma and suffering? Me too. Many a night spent bursting with tension, fear, and a tomorrow unknown. "It's a fantasy," most would quickly say as they respond to my question. I agree with them, and I am sure you do too. Separating fantasy from reality delivers the true nature of the human condition at this moment if you take the time to think and reflect deeply on the concept.

In "Through the Fire," Emily Smith surmised that "we all carry around emotional baggage of some kind – baggage that can bring with it fear, hurt, guilt, and insecurity… [these] pose serious threats to finding meaning in life…shattering our fundamental assumptions about the world – that people are good, the world is just, and our environment is safe…." I argue that the true nature of the human condition *is* suffering. Most people, at best, live a life of trauma, setback, failure, disappointment, and struggle. Along that agonizing road, we make every valid attempt to find happiness. Fighting through thick layers of chaos and suffering in hopes of a peaceful ending, we lose sight of the here and now. We lose sight of the precious time in this moment from which our circumstances are created.

"I've always been buffeted by circumstances because I thought of myself as a human being affected by outside conditioning. Now I realize that I am the power that commands the feeling of the mind and from which circumstances grow."

Bruce Lee was one of my greatest heroes growing up, and he delivered a decisively important message to us: ownership of your life. If not you, then who? The journey I will take you on throughout this book will tell my story, lessons learned, and how to apply those to your life.

Even in the context of suffering, this writing is, in every sense of the word, a book on leadership. How do we find and deliver purpose and direction? Do we always have to find it? Or can we generate it? What drives the few to succeed far beyond failure?

Despite how taboo the label has become in recent years, I will explore non-cognitive skills, or as I call them, executive function skills, and why they're so critically important to our development as leaders, teams, and organizations. Further, we will explore the novel concept of social-emotional learning (SEL) and some evidence-based programming for young people.

In closing this introduction, what I am about to write would typically be a BLUF statement, Bottom Line, Up Front. In this case, it will be how I will begin Part 1.

The human condition is suffering. We all suffer in different ways, from emotional trauma to physical pain. The glory in it is yours to seed. Why can't something beautiful grow in spite of the embattled seeds handed to you? We simply need to tap into the depth of that opportunity and learn to generate meaning and purpose in the face of our suffering and adversity.

Most would agree with the cliché that hindsight is 20/20. Steve Jobs would say, "Connecting dots is easiest when looking back on your life." As I drew my lines, I realized I used my emotional baggage as a platform to launch my life. As fuel for existence and purpose. A driving force in who I became.

I decided at a very early age that no one would dictate my life or mental state. With this mindset, what can a man really do to me? Sadly, many of us lack the ability to transform our lessons in suffering and trauma into actionable, useful tools from which to navigate life. We collectively have a moral obligation to face this reality and develop a path forward. It is time for a long overdue executive session with ourselves. We need a gut check.

This book will focus on what I have come to understand as suffering with my eyes wide open. That is, what happens when we face our trauma and pain straight on, and make the executive decision to remain undefeated by it? Have you ever been punched in the face? It's ok if you haven't. Most will never know the experience (but you should try it!). Just imagine it for a quick second. What would you do the moment that fist is hurling toward your face with the inevitable end result of smashing into your flesh?

Most would twitch, squeezing their eyes shut, head down, and brace for a beating. Now imagine if you stared at that person with your eyes wide open. Owning the moment, undefeated by it, in fact. Taking the punch and standing tall. What can that punch really do to you at that moment? Cliches are cliché, yes, but in this case, it works. As a kid, I loved watching Rocky Balboa, and I learned that it isn't about how hard of a hit you can take but rather about how hard of a hit you take and keep moving forward. We're only able to move forward if we keep our eyes wide open.

This was a mentality I could build upon. This would make me stronger and more resilient than I could have ever imagined. The goal is to interpret what happens to you in life and apply it directly to your future success. This is where you force something beautiful to grow in spite of whatever seeds were planted.

What will you take away from this book? You must decide that as it unfolds, but my goal is that you redirect your mental state to own the outcome of your life. To face forward and forge ahead with your eyes wide open.

A Tribute to Johnnie Blue Hands

On February 25th, 2018, I boarded the Southwest Chief as I usually did, escorted by my good friend George from the Metro Lounge of Chicago Union Station. I was heading to Kansas City. Simply put, George is an amazing person. Charming, sincere, and a true no, bullshit kind of guy. He will tell you exactly what he thinks at the exact moment you need it, or he thinks it, whichever comes first.

I had another fantastic weekend in Chicago with Xavier, and as usual, I hopped the blue line from my brother's apartment near Cicero and Irving to Chicago's Union Station. There was nothing, particularly special about this day except, of course, my time with Xavi. I arrived at the Metro lounge early, enjoyed a cup of coffee, relaxed a bit, and read some before boarding time. 2:15 PM rolled around pretty quickly, and George called my name to board, "Where's Pitbull!?" Still don't know why he gave me that nickname, but it's stuck with me.

We were on our way, navigating the chaos of passengers by the hundred, all on their own journey across the country for every reason known to man. I pack light on these short trips, so I'm not encumbered by extra bags and nonsense. Because of this, I usually offer my help to those in need. There are so many people who've never traveled by rail before, so they're totally clueless by no fault of their own. And plenty of elderly traveling unassisted. I usually end up standing, passing/loading bags, and helping wanderlust travelers find their seats until the train actually departs. My thought here is: first, people do need help, and if I am capable and available, there's no reason I shouldn't. The bonus is we have a happier group of people on our train car, and I did my part to help the train depart on time as scheduled.

Needless to say, by the time I arrive at my seat and actually sit down, I am either sweaty, tired, or both. On this particular day, however, I sat down next to a large, solid-looking, well-kept elderly black gentleman. He was a large person, so I was worried we'd be cramped as I am rather large myself. He immediately introduced himself, "Hi, I'm Johnnie, but my friends call me Blue Hands." He was probably in his late 60s or early 70s, if I had to guess, but as I said, well-kept and squared away.

We immediately began talking. Well, he did, at least. I, at first, was ready for a nap, which is usually how I start my train rides once seated, of course. Our conversation was rich from the very beginning. We spoke deeply about life and the various paths we all take. I described mine, and he described his. We engaged back and forth about the very experiences that shape a person's soul.

Johnnie said to me, "Hey, don't worry, I won't burn up all your time. As soon as they scan my ticket, I'll find myself in the viewing car working for the day." I replied, asking what he did for work and if that's why he was on the train. He went on to immediately describe his purpose in life.

First, he was working on a book about his life experiences, and second how he got his nickname. "They call me Blue Hands because of the chalk, you know," he said with a raspy voice you only get from those who've endured a troubled life, thick in rich layers of experience.

You can easily tell the difference between a raspy smoker and raspy Blue Hands. He slowly turned over his hands to reveal his rough, marbled palms, and as odd as this may sound, I could see a very subtle, hazy tint of blue.

"I've been riding these trains since I was 13 years old", he said, "traveling the country by rail playing pool in every bar in America." I was immediately taken aback, in a state of awe and wonder. At that moment, he earned my undivided attention. He continued on to describe his life experiences while I exchanged mine in return. I talked about Chicago life and what it was like visiting my father in prison and managing our drug-addicted mother. I went on to talk about the Army and my experiences in Ranger School before getting my cancer diagnosis.

I asked him if he considered himself to be a true nomad, a vagabond of sorts.

"No, I most certainly do not. I consider myself to be in the right places and at the right times."

We carried on this way for a bit longer, and eventually, he did, in fact, find himself yearning for the viewing car. As he got up to continue his journey, he started to walk away but briefly turned back and said, "You know, we probably won't see each other again, Jason." His voice was captivating. It reminded me of classic raspy southern blues.

"You're the kind of person who lives the words I'm writing," I asked him quickly about his book and what he meant by that. He wouldn't go into more detail except to say that his writings were about his life experiences. He turned again, muttering as he walked away, "You've learned to suffer with your eyes wide open."

It was as if a lightning bolt had struck me, and I was in total shock. I began taking some notes in my journal and slowly drifted away to sleep. I woke sometime later and went to seek Johnnie out in the viewing car, but he was nowhere to be found. Turns out, after a conversation with the conductor, he departed the train somewhere in eastern Iowa. I never saw him again.

Heading for Kansas City aboard the Southwest Chief, I found myself in the viewing car, pen to pad, cranking out thought after thought in deep reflection of my short time with Johnnie Blue Hands.

Part One: The Suffering

In the depths of hardship and adversity lies the crucible that forges resilience and strength. Life, at times, deals us a hand that forces us to confront our deepest fears, endure immense suffering, and overcome seemingly insurmountable challenges. It is within these crucibles that we discover our true capacity for growth, adaptability, and the mastery of vital skills that enable us to navigate the complexities of life.

In Part One, we lay the foundation for understanding the transformative journey that awaits us in the chapters to come. We delve into my personal experiences, where I've confronted and triumphed over extreme poverty in the unforgiving streets of Chicago, battled through the crucible of Ranger School, and waged a fierce fight against advanced stage three cancer. These experiences, like fiery trials, have forged a profound understanding of the human spirit and the power of perseverance.

Prepare yourself to embark on a transformative expedition through the crucible of suffering, where you will witness the indomitable spirit of human willpower. Through this exploration, we shall discover that even in the most harrowing circumstances, there lies an opportunity for growth, and within the depths of suffering, there resides the potential to emerge stronger, wiser, and more resilient than ever before.

CHAPTER 1— An Executive Session

The Gut Check:

This first chapter is meant to be an initial lens from which you experience the next few chapters. My goal is to provide a brief framework for you here so you might better understand my message in Part 1 of this book. In full transparency, my journey and the story of my life kick off in the next chapter.

We have difficulty assessing our abilities and who we are as human beings. Why is that? Fear of failure, maybe fear of judgment. Nonetheless, the first avenue of approach to owning our future and our impact is knowing who the hell we are deep to our core. We can explore many factors, but I'd like to address several that have impacted my life over the years.

Subjectivity: Bottom Line Up Front (BLUF) is that we are subjective in our self-assessment. This means we tend to evaluate ourselves based on our internal perceptions and biases rather than objective measures. This can lead to a wildly inaccurate and useless gut check. Rather, you should seek mentors and coaches who will give you no bullshit feedback. These are the people you love, trust, and admire the most. I remember saying, "No shit, I can do that Ranger Physical Fitness Test, no problem'. Famous last words, of course, because the first time I tried it, I fell flat on my face (literally) and felt like my lungs were filled with acid, ready to explode.

Social Comparison: We often compare ourselves to others, which can distort any executive session you embark on. We may overestimate our abilities when we compare ourselves to people who are less skilled than us or underestimate our abilities when we compare ourselves to people who are more skilled than us. A proper gut check helps you get past this by taking a close, hard look at what you are really capable of and not focusing on the attributes of others. While I compared myself to others, I focused on my mentors whose shoulders I would stand on to learn and grow.

Fear of Failure: As many of us know, this leads us to avoid situations that challenge us or make us feel vulnerable. "Challenge" is the operative word in any goal tied to learning and growth. I firmly believe that a human being only grows when we leave our comfort zone. Growing up on the streets of inner-city Chicago, I learned at an early age. When it comes to failure, I think of David Brinkley's words, "A successful person is one who can lay a firm foundation with the bricks others have thrown at him or her." Take the bricks and embrace failure.

Self-Fulfilling Prophecy: Our beliefs about ourselves can become self-fulfilling prophecies. For example, if we believe that we are not good at something, we may not try as hard or practice as much, which can lead to poor performance and reinforce our belief that we are not good at it. Educators, mentors, and coaches exist to undue this self-inflicted damage. My mentor ensured I never held back despite my internal perceptions about my capabilities.

The Complexity of Identity: Our identity is complex and multifaceted, and it can be challenging to understand and integrate all aspects of ourselves into a coherent self-concept. This can make it difficult to assess our abilities and who we are. How would you introduce and identify yourself right now? Go ahead and write it down. My name is Jason—I am a husband, father, soldier, author, and business leader. I exist to serve my friends and family and help people grow into exceptional leaders.

Knowing yourself and what you're capable of is a very complex process. It involves many factors, and it isn't always easy to accurately assess our abilities and who we really are. However, by being aware of these factors above and actively working to overcome them (make a plan), you can walk away with a seriously practical executive session knowing you can deliver a gut check worth acting upon. This is where you open your eyes and intentionally decide to own your outcome.

Now that is ownership at its deepest level.

The Premise of Extreme Ownership

The premise of extreme ownership seems hardly original. As a matter of fact, it draws inspiration from a quote by the famed subcontinent politician Mahatma Gandhi:

"Be the change you wish to see in the world."

During my introduction, I shared my favorite Bruce Lee quote about how we command the power of the mind from which our circumstances grow. That lesson was my first-ever exposure to the concept of owning every outcome of my life.

That said, the concept has been popularized by an ex-Navy Seal named Jocko Willink, whose TedX talk gained insane popularity over the internet. In fact, Jocko Willink co-authored the book with Leif Babin, whose central premise is leadership.

Furthermore, Jocko stipulates that the concept assumes complete ownership of everything responsible for the mission's success and other indicators.

While the philosophy applies to individuals, too, Jocko's book is more targeted toward teams who can benefit from it the most.

When things begin to go wrong, the status quo begins to point fingers at everyone else. However, this strategy is nothing but counterproductive and resolves nothing. This strategy is not viable for any individual or organization seeking growth.

So, instead of opting for the finger-pointing approach, look inward and have that gut check we talked about. Your goals and objectives must be crystal clear to both yourself and everyone around you.

Owning our failures can make us competent and better leaders. Secondly, it also inspires those around us to step up their game and breed a culture involving progress, productivity, and steering clear of cutting corners. People around you will begin to own their failures too.

The core premise of Jocko's book is the same: To become a stellar leader, one must own everything. No one should be blamed. This is the entire premise of extreme ownership.

Principle of Extreme Ownership

A leader assumes complete and categorical responsibility for everything that happens in their personal and professional lives. So, to this end, they can develop a concrete plan and secure the resources which enable successful outcomes. They are leaders of their world and must assume the mantle of responsibility that comes with it. No one else is to blame for the outcomes of your life.

Implementation of Extreme Ownership

Before we get into the depths of my story, I want to make sure this concept is clear out of the gate. Again, it is important to have this framework before reading the next few chapters and even more so when we explore what it means to learn to suffer.

We will take the instance of an individual in an organizational setting to explain the full-on application of extreme ownership. The premise of extreme ownership implies that the individual is agile and successful. In doing so, he is a leader in his own right. Such a person never makes excuses and prefers to take responsibility for his role. They believe in the bigger cause and can address questions regarding why with an answer couched in personal accountability.

Furthermore, ego and arrogance have no place in their work ethic, so the concept has strict implications and beneficial outcomes.

So, a person who adheres to extreme ownership within a team will look for productive answers and ask productive questions. They will pinpoint areas that require their attention and needs addressing right off the bat.

When a person has the issue(s) highlighted, they will look for ways to resolve the situation and assume complete ownership of the failure.

A Lack of Extreme Ownership

We will once again take the instance of an individual in an organizational setting where shortcomings can occur:

- **A lack of trust in a team setting:** A person should protect others when things go south. This individual must assume responsibility for their mistakes which will inspire others to follow suit.
- **Lead by example:** The individual cannot follow the rule of being above the law since it reflects poorly on others. He must set an example for others to follow.
- **The issue of egocentrism:** This common goal is bigger than everything else. If egos take precedence, then it means that extreme ownership will be challenging to apply.
- *A lack of action-oriented plans: The results will be lackluster when there are no answers to why and how. No one will fill in the blanks, and the results will be below standard.*

- **A lack of communication:** The individual must communicate clearly and more frequently. Sometimes, others may not know the bigger picture, so they must be in the loop. As is the case, clarity in communication takes precedence.

The Case for Resilience

We often feel stressed out, challenged to the maximum, and traumatized by certain life events. After all, life is not a bed of roses, so it certainly has its fair share of ups and downs. Each of us is en route on a different path, as one may kickstart a small-scale business while another individual recovers from an illness.

Resilience is a crucial and necessary tool that can assist in managing these challenging circumstances, recovering and readjusting from their effects, and thriving later on. Thus, one can say that building resilience is of paramount importance as it leads to happiness and overall well-being.

Before we proceed with our discussion, let's define resiliency and how one can go about it.

Resiliency

First things first, how resilient is a person? This depends greatly on a person's life experiences and the tools available to them to manage stress and trauma. Some people can bounce back quickly from a failure or setback. It can be more challenging and cumbersome for others, however. Why? What gaps do these people have that others don't? Why?

Ordinarily, people fall into two categories with no middle ground in between. Let's look at the two cases:

- When a person encounters a setback, will the person come back stronger and adapt to the circumstances?

- When a person encounters a setback, will they be overwhelmed and question their skill and confidence in the face of insurmountable odds?

Resilience is an intriguing concept that is equally hard to define as it is to describe. Resilience, from my perspective, is either mastered through life experience with an absolute need for survival or through life experience with a mentor or leader, adding tools to your toolbox for tactical deployment when consciously triggered or necessary. As is the case, there is a reason one individual weathers the storm when times are hard while others may be in shambles. Here is where we initiate true growth. Later in the book, I will describe what that looks like and how to open your eyes and learn to suffer.

This reminds me of a leadership seminar I sat in where they described how a buffalo runs into the storm as opposed to how cows run away from it. Storms generally approach from the west and travel east. They say that when a storm approaches, buffalo run westward into the storm while cows run eastward to try and get away from it. What happens is the buffalo endure the immediate effects of the storm, but this is short-lived as the storm passes overhead. In doing so, buffalo make it through the storm more quickly and enjoy the fruits of the storm on the other side, including water and new vegetation. As the buffalo run into the storm, cows run with it to escape and ultimately end up enduring the storm for much longer, resulting in more suffering and little energy on the other side to capitalize on the fruits of the storm.

Buffalo are generally well-suited to handle harsh weather conditions, especially storms. Their thick fur coat and strong muscles make them better equipped to handle cold, wet, or windy weather than many other domesticated animals. Cows, on the other hand, are generally

28

smaller and less robust than buffalo, and their coat is not as thick or well-suited for cold or wet weather. If a buffalo were to run into a storm, it might be because it is trying to reach a specific destination or objective, such as a source of food or water or a place where it feels safe or comfortable. I want you to develop a thick coat and a strong mind capable of not only weathering the storm but running right into it with your eyes wide open. Coming out the other side, having learned to suffer and ready to enjoy the fruits your storm has offered.

This could be due to many factors, which are mentioned below:

- Learned capacity expanded over time through experience
- Environmental factors
- Natural traits
- Explored and known triggers
- Developed tools to manage known triggers

While the ability to bounce back strong from setbacks and obstacles is vital, your goal should be to bounce back even stronger.

This section will dig deeper into the premise of resilience and its elements. Learning and exercising resilience involves a process that should be followed to learn and perfect.

Resiliency implies managing challenges, recovering quickly, and growing from those experiences. This results in a different form of learning, fortifying the ability to take on these challenges head-on. The ability to run into the storm.

This is the key that pushes a person forward despite enduring setback after setback: a tough breakup, missed promotion, or for some, a missed meal or an absent parent. Resilience is the key to looking at these obstacles and setbacks as a chance for a better opportunity or overcoming the stresses of difficult events.

The Importance of Resilience and Notable Aspects

As is the case, people may survive the most grueling and challenging circumstances and thrive. However, they could be massively unaware of *how* they endured that challenge.

Inner resilience is quite an important soft skill that is nothing short of a recipe for success in the outer world and the basis of good mental health.

Incidentally, resilience can also be defined as the ability to come back stronger than before, which is why it is used in physical sciences more. For instance, a resilient material can return to its original form when stretched or pulled forcefully. Consider a suspension bridge spread over a wide river, maintaining its integrity despite the climatic changes and strong winds exerting weight over it. The instance of a flower growing and blooming regardless of the concrete surrounding it also works well in this context.

So as far as resilience is concerned in the human context, it can be best described as an ability to remain flexible in our feelings, thoughts, and behaviors when faced with disruption in life or periods of major change. Periods of difficulty and intense pressure may persist, affecting the person differently, which is when resilience plays an important role.

It is because of resilience that a person has an opportunity to emerge wiser, stronger, and far more capable than before. A calm sea has never produced a good sea captain, after all.

Psychological Resilience

Different people have different coping mechanisms and ways of handling stress. As a matter of fact, stress can exert a physical, emotional, and psychological weight on a person over time. Take a cup of water and hold it in front of you. No problem, right? Now hold it there for the next two hours, then four, then six and eight. See what happens. Your body can probably do it, but it will be your mind that quits first.

Understanding your true capabilities while mastering psychological resilience can safeguard people from the disastrous effects of stress and boost their ability to exercise a certain sense of control despite challenging circumstances.

Resilience has several definitions. Though it is generally believed to be a multifaceted concept, typically involving the ability to handle tough times well and respond flexibly to them. I always picture a tennis ball and its ability to bounce back immediately. Incidentally, resilience comprises three essential factors:

- Recovery: This involves a return to normalcy or the pre-stressor degree of functioning.
- Resistance: It involves next to no disturbance following any or every stressor.
- Reconfiguration: This implies returning to a different state of mind and recovering stability per the changed circumstances.

Dissimilar to resistance or recovery, reconfiguration is a key component of the transformation process, especially when returning to the original path seems unlikely or unthinkable. If you don't like something, what do you do? You change it. What if you can't change it? The only answer is to change the way you think about it.

Resilient individuals are adaptable and always open to new challenges and experiences. They also adopt a healthier perspective on life, especially when they see setbacks as new opportunities to learn and grow.

Certain external factors can play a role in strengthening resilience in an individual. Some factors governing the resilience in a person involve the following:

- Good parenting
- Effective schools
- Self-regulation skills
- Community resources
- Mindset

- Knowing and fully understanding triggers

Resilient people often benefit from these factors, especially if they are embedded into their systems from an early age.

Mental Toughness

This could be defined as a personality trait that assesses a person's ability to perform consistently despite pressure and stress. Mental toughness is closely related to soft qualities like grit, resilience, character, and perseverance.

As a matter of fact, resilience is a part of being mentally tough. However, not all resilient individuals are necessarily mentally tough. Think of it as a metaphor for a moment: Resilience is a mountain, whereas mental toughness is among several mountain climbing strategies. If we look at surviving vs. thriving head-to-head, resilience drives survival, while mental toughness enables a person to thrive.

Mental toughness begins when a person takes notice of specific and unique thoughts going through their mind. However, they do not personally identify with those thoughts and feelings, so each thought is new and scary at times. And secondly, the person still has optimistic thoughts regarding these thoughts and underlying situations. In Chapter 3, I will expand more on Mental Toughness and a model to build this strength.

The Case for Self-Awareness

Everyone goes through the phase of life where they question their existence and purpose for living. A person who feels like this may embark on a journey to find out who they are and how they can answer some pressing questions regarding themselves. I truly believe this starts with an executive session and a gut check.

Some people exercise a strong sense of identity and understand who they are, which helps them discover their true selves. However, many others don't and have to intentionally understand their true self.

Those who are unsure of themselves and in search of their true self may undergo a process of shifting identity. They may see themselves trying new personas and ideas to see which fits the best. Maybe they may change themselves based on the response they field from others.

This section will discuss the essentials of self-discovery and analyzing who we are and why it can be difficult for people to understand themselves clearly and where they wish to go.

A stronger sense of self and personality will provide a clear standing regarding strengths and weaknesses. It will also help a person analyze who they are, which is when the journey will truly begin.

Everyone wants to be happier, wield considerable influence, and become a better decision-maker. We all crave relevance. Who does not wish to see themselves as a leader? I distinctly remember an image in an old Sergeant Major's office of a twisted and contorted fork alongside a row of pristinely shined forks. My interpretation of that was simple. Just because you are unique doesn't make you useful. What make's you useful? What makes you relevant? All this and much more come from self-awareness, an important non-cognitive skill one can develop. Self-awareness provides the keys to the kingdom and helps one become the best version of oneself and an effective leader.

Self-awareness can have as many benefits as there is a person. For instance, a higher influence, better perspective, and better relationships are all hallmarks of self-awareness.

In chapter three, we will revisit this topic in detail to explain the ins and outs of self-awareness alongside certain related concepts necessary for discussion.

Conclusion

As I said, Chapter 1 was meant to be an initial lens through which you experience Part 1 of this book. My goal was to provide a framework for you here so you might better understand my message in the following chapters and take us into Part 2.

All roads to success begin with knowing oneself. People are often unaware of their true potential and how much they can make of themselves. The key is self-realization, self-awareness, and honest assessment of oneself to take things forward. Remember, the future holds a world full of possibilities, so we need to know ourselves and take things forward in the same vein. It is with this first step that we open our eyes and learn to suffer.

CHAPTER 2 – The Human Condition: Suffering

I firmly believe we are all born a little broken and spend the rest of our lives healing.

Why?

We are born into a set of circumstances that are not our own—we have no say in the matter, or the cards dealt. Yet we, ultimately alone, have to deal with these circumstances, so we scour the earth looking for answers and meaning. A purpose. A direction. Significance. Relevance.

Suffering is different from adversity. Merriam-Webster defines suffering in the following ways (not an all-inclusive list):

- The state or experience of one that suffers.
- Pain.
- To submit to or be forced to endure.
- To sustain loss or damage.
- To put up with the inevitable.
- To endure death, pain, or distress.

Which one of these do you identify with the most? I can pinpoint a time and place when I've experienced all of them, and I'm betting you can too. If we're all born broken and spend our lives healing to find purpose and relevance, then the human condition is suffering. We know it, live it, and now we must admit to it and, most of all, own it.

A friend recently reminded me that the one thing we all have in common is the yearning for unconditional positive regard, whether romantic, professional, or platonic, among other things. In this search, I've found my way to create the circumstances to quell that yearning. These lessons, I hope, will help you find yours.

We must endure or quit when we suffer since there is no other option. Suffering refers to the experience of pain, distress, or discomfort. It can be physical or emotional and is often associated with negative experiences such as illness, loss, or trauma. Incidentally, suffering can be intense and overwhelming, and it can be challenging to cope with it.

When we suffer, we must endure. Adversity, on the other hand, refers to a challenging situation or circumstance. It can be a personal setback, a difficult task or goal, or an external challenge such as a natural disaster or economic downturn. Adversity can cause stress, but it does not necessarily involve the same degree of pain or distress as suffering.

While suffering and adversity are not the same, they are closely related. Adversity can lead to suffering, mainly if the situation is particularly challenging or if the individual is not equipped with the necessary coping skills or resources to deal with the situation. However, it is possible to experience adversity without suffering, mainly if the individual can maintain a positive attitude and find ways to cope with the challenge. Suffering we endure, but in adversity, we can pull our bootstraps up and work to overcome.

Disclaimer: These first pages will primarily be a rambling of my childhood. In my experience, suffering is the greatest of all teachers, whether from external circumstances or due to your choices. I like the old saying,

"Rock bottoms will teach you lessons mountain tops never can."

To this day, I hear people say that one cannot truly understand suffering until they themselves have been brought to their knees, begging to come in from the cold, starving for survival. I learned the most about the realities of the human condition while growing up in Chicago. However, I didn't translate those lessons into an actionable path until many years later.

This is what it feels like to be at the absolute bottom. I had an innate drive to do and be better than those around me for as long as I could remember. So, I took the punches and carried on toward an unknown opportunity. Business as usual for my siblings and me—evictions, homelessness, and hunger, among other things. My father spent much of our young life in prison, and my mother, a drug addict, crack cocaine if you want to know. Both my parents are Class X felons which, short of first-degree murder, is the most severe felony offense on the books in Illinois.

I always knew my mother tried. She really did. She didn't want this life for us, but it was the hand life dealt her. After my mother passed, we found this old letter she wrote to her family, begging them to come and get her out of Chicago. I had just turned four years old, and my father was still in prison.

My Mother's Desperate Cry for Help

Like many other Chicagoans, we came to know life through the streets, hard times, and genuine suffering. Earlier, when I said that I'd heard people say that one cannot truly understand suffering until they have been brought to their knees, I sometimes asked them, "What about those of us who were born of it?"

For those of us born of it, we have but one option: Survive.

Visiting My Father in Prison

I was a product of the Illinois DCFS (Department of Children and Family Services). Like me, my sister and all my brothers were born with cocaine in their systems.

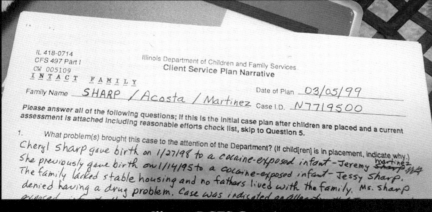

Illinois DCFS Case Assessment

DCFS was a roller coaster experience for us as we fought to stay out of the system. They had detailed reunification plans, but none of it mattered. We just did what we did and went on surviving.

| CFS 497 Part II | Illinois Department of Children and Family Services |
| Rev. 6/92 | Client Service Plan |

CFS 497 Part II — Illinois Department of Children and Family Services
Rev. 6/92 — Client Service Plan
Problem/Objective/Task Statement # __1__

Family Case Name __SHARP__   Date of Plan __3/5/99__

Minimum Parenting Standard, Problem or Condition to be Addressed __Ms. Sharp has a history of cocaine abuse that goes back 7 years__

1.   OBJECTIVE: Outcome needed to resolve problem __Ms. Sharp will demonstrate her ability to maintain a drug-free lifestyle__
   Date Established __3 / 5 / 99__   Planned Achievement Date __9 / 30 / 99__

Client and Service Tasks
Identify: 1) Who will do the task; 2) What the task is; 3) Time-frame (when task is to be done); 4) Evaluate the progress using Achieved, Satisfactory, Unsatisfactory, Discontinued

Illinois DCFS Case Plan

I learned at a young age this very lesson. To live, we must first survive. My parents did their best with the hand this life dealt them, and I know that to my core. Addiction is a destructive S.O.B., and it drives our daily lives like a fucked up busted ass rollercoaster. Today, I ask myself if there is value in addiction. Does it teach us anything real at all? I would argue that it has incredible value, albeit not the kind we may want, but it does carry value.

For instance, it showed my sister and me what not to do. It taught me first-hand the powerful, deadly grip it has, and once its teeth were sunk in, good luck prying that locked jaw open.

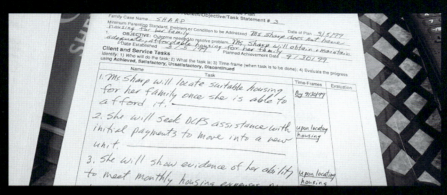

Illinois DCFS Reunification Plan

Illinois DCFS Reunification Plan

Sadly, one of the many lessons of my young life was not to trust anyone or anything. While I can remember quite a bit of my childhood going back to kindergarten, I couldn't make much sense of it. I remember a gang shoot-out in our playground, and our teachers rounded us all up and said, "Run home!" Right in the middle of the fucking shoot-out. Yes, you heard that right. No active shooter drills to lean on here. Just a bunch of kids running through gunfire.

I was around seven years old during my first memorable life lesson. Living in Humboldt Park at the time, my father brought home a nice BMX-style bicycle gleaming with chrome rims!

It was simply amazing.

Who knows where he got it, and at the time, I could care less. Nowadays, I know better, and he definitely received it for payment or collateral for a service provided. I fell asleep that night staring at it, dreaming of all the fun times I'd have the next day, rocking my new bike up and down Belden Street near Sacramento. It turns out it was all exactly that, a dream. A short-lived fantasy of something so good it couldn't possibly have been true. I woke to find my mom laid up and cracked out.

"Where was my bike?" I thought to myself.

I went to ask her, and she could barely utter a coherent syllable. My older sister turned to me and said, "Mom took it out last night, Jason, and she didn't come back with it."

I cried. I was angry and heartbroken. At this moment, I learned not to rely on people, not to trust that something which may have been true when I fell asleep would be true in the morning when I woke. At this moment, I sealed my understanding of the world around me: those of us born into suffering tend to gain less than we lose. It was a constant battle between these feelings. Do I trust and carry on, rationalize, and fight harder? Much of the world around me lived in a willful naïveté to this life.

Here's the rub: I was as lucky as a pigeon who finds a meal under a Chicago viaduct that a local bum hasn't already claimed. Charles was his name. He was my secret weapon of sorts, but not in the way you might think. To this day, he is my blessing and awkward trouble now and again. My father threw him from a second-story window in upper Jefferson Park because he decided to chew on my stepbrother's ear while ironically high on a drug my father sold him.

Ain't that some shit? Unknowingly, Charles' actions one fateful day would decide the course of my life. We'll get to that. Given my father spent much time in prison, Charles wasn't his only bad decision. Meanwhile, it was business as usual for us, and our mother remained a severe drug addict.

During my first residency at the Bloch School of Management in Kansas City, I confided in a close teammate, Eric, who, on his own spiritual journey, provided a sounding board for me to bounce my thoughts. He shared his grandmother's recent passing and the pain associated with that. This sparked a feeling within me, so I thought, "Would I mourn my parents when they passed away?"

I asked Eric this same question, and we engaged in a serious conversation in which I realized my appreciation for my parents all along. My parents did the best they could with the hand life dealt them. We often ate after midnight from a dumpster behind Dominick's, but we ate. We slept, most often in a shelter or crack house, but we slept. We bathed, usually in the bathroom at Clark gas station, but we bathed. We learned, mostly, how to beg, borrow, and steal, but we learned.

Their lesson: survival. So we did exactly that, and I know deeply that they did their best with what the world offered us at the time. It may be easy to say they could have done better, but who am I to honestly know the situations and circumstances surrounding our lives during this time? I consider myself a resilient, mentally tough man, and I credit my parents for laying that foundation.

We spent years like this. There were occasional breaks in between, living with family here or there and juggling one or two of my mom's boyfriends (my parents were never married). Looking back at my Chicago childhood, my brother's father always comes to mind—Sergio was his name. We haven't seen our brother in over ten years, but that's another story for a different time. Sergio was a real son of a bitch, and to this day, I have no idea what Mom saw in him.

My father was locked up, so as far as I can figure, it was about stability since there was constant yelling and fighting. While most of it is hazy, I remember the fighting as vividly as you are reading the words in this book before you. As with everything we encounter, one moment usually defines a memory forever.

My sister Jodi, "Jo" as we called her, always liked to eat her rice with ketchup. It was silly to some of us, but it made her smile. Sergio never liked this for whatever reason and always ensured we knew it. What kind of dumbass pet peeve is that? Especially for a child's choice of food. So, one unusually heated evening, Sergio was hot on the trail of that ketchup and rice my sister asked for. My mom handed her the ketchup, and she squirted a sizeable helping on her plate just next to the rice. We sat at the table, and all he could say was, "Really? You and that fucking ketchup!"

When mom was well, she always made the best chicken and rice. Hands down the absolute best, and it's one of my favorite memories. This night though, wouldn't end up being a happy memory. As dinner came to a close and we finished our meals, there was nothing on our plates to be found except for a little ketchup on Jo's plate.

She hadn't quite fully finished the ketchup with her rice. This was the trigger, and I knew we were in for it, especially Jodi. He raised his voice the first time, saying to her, "You better finish your dinner." She replied, "I did," with literally nothing left on her plate but a little ketchup.

I remember chuckling as if it were a joke but not this night. No one was laughing after what happened next.

Sergio stood up and said, "You better finish your fucking dinner!".

My sister ignored this comment and, as any child would, glanced at him with a confused look, then began to rise from her seat to take her plate to the sink. This was when he snapped. He was a broken man; he would take it out on her tonight. He grabbed that ceramic plate, wiped the ketchup off violently, and with the full force of a grown man, he crushed that plate on her face.

All I remember after that was our mother instinctually charging at him, tackling this six and half-foot man to the floor so my sister could break away from what would surely be another blow. Mom didn't have the upper hand for long, and that night she took the beating, so we didn't have to. My brother Jeremy, who Sergio fathered, would be born soon after all this.

As I look back at my childhood, only a few memories genuinely give me nightmares, and what I am about to share with you is one of those memories. As I mentioned, we moved around a lot. If we weren't evicted, we were on the run for any other number of reasons. In this case, we ended up in a basement apartment on Kimball near Foster Avenue. My sister and I had to grow up quickly in this home. Incidentally, in this home, my mom brought home a guy who stayed with us for weeks on end and spent real time with us—he taught us how to pick locks. He taught us how to steal, too. Just down the street from us was a community living center, and he would take us there, break into the basement and meticulously make our way through the random storage units. We'd come out with bikes, power tools, and the works and sell all of that to make a buck. Because of this place, I watched my mom get arrested right in front of our building.

Police roll up, and she screams at us, "Run upstairs and ask the neighbors to let you in." We grabbed Jessy, a toddler in a shitty diaper, and bolted. We ran out the backdoor and right up to the neighbors as directed. We knew exactly why we had to run. If we didn't, we'd be in the system. And no one wanted that of all things.

They immediately took us in, and we were safe for the moment. Safe from a third-story window to watch her get cuffed and hauled away as our baby brother kicked and screamed. What the hell were we going to do? We had no idea, but after the dust had settled, we returned to our basement apartment and took inventory. Many questions crossed our minds.

"Was there food?"

"How would we care for Jessy?"

"How long before we were kicked to the street?"

"When would DCFS come?

That night, I walked down to the gas station and stole my first loaf of bread. Jessy needed to eat. Shit, we needed to eat. The next night was a half-gallon of milk. I was caught and scolded by the owner. Those days they told you to cut the shit and go home. Nowadays, it's a much bigger tragedy. Eventually, I stood outside the A.T.M. on Foster and Kimball, asking for money. It was fucking terrible.

However, there was still no sign of mom. In the coming weeks, Chicago Public Schools would also knock at our door. DCFS too. We would just run out that back door and make it work. My sister and I took Jessy out for a long walk, and we talked.

"There's no way mom was still in jail. Someone would have found us by now. And where's Sandy?" Sandy was my mom's sister, who, arguably, was the one who got her addicted to drugs in the first place.

Sadly, Sandy's kids, our cousins, were already taken by the state at this point.

We're a month in without mom home. Just me and my sister and baby Jessy. Sergio always took Jeremy. It was around this time we started to see Jeremy less and less. We were out of food and, of course, had no money. It was only a matter of time before our troubles really boiled over.

We finally made it home after our walk, but something was wrong. The door was smashed in, and everything was ripped apart. We thought someone had broken in. And even worse, they might still be inside. I made my way in slowly as Jodi kept Jessy safe. My heart was throttled, and I had no idea what to do if someone was in there.

Thankfully, it was just us. Jodi brought Jessy inside, and we worked our way through the house, thanking God it was a burglar. To our surprise, it wasn't just a burglar. Instead, we found what looked like a murder scene. We entered our mom's bedroom and found multiple knives stuck in the plaster with some red substance that appeared to be blood all over the walls.

"Who the hell could have done this?" I said.

I looked at Jodi and had her take Jessy out of the room. I walked up to the wall, and I found two things. The first was an apparent handwritten note stabbed into the wall. What I discovered next was unreal and something I had thought long forgotten. It wasn't blood on the wall. It was fucking ketchup. And that damn handwritten note was from the one and only piece of shit, Sergio.

My sister came back into the room, and everything fell silent. It was deafening. I could hear the fear in her eyes. His note read, "Tell your mom I want my money." At this point, we at least knew mom was out of jail and alive. But what the hell, why wasn't she home? It's been four weeks. We had to find her.

As we cleaned up and settled Jessy, we debated who should be responsible for going to find her. I was 11, and she was 12. No less, I thought it should be me. No way Jodi should be out there alone. Besides, what the hell was I going to do with Jessy by myself?

Jodi left and went to Logan Square—it should have been me. She found mom. She found her in an alley, half naked and cracked out, next to a dumpster. This shattered her soul, and I will forever regret not going myself.

We tried to recover as best possible in the coming weeks, but it was much the same. Mom would come and go, and we would make do with or without her. We knew things were kind of ok when mom cooked. She always made the best chicken and rice. We absolutely loved it, and she loved making it. When things weren't ok, powdered milk and cereal with a hint of cockroach was our daily menu.

Occasionally, we'd make it across town to food pantries and the coveted Meals on Wheels. Those were great nights; everyone was happy and went to sleep wherever we were. The massive cans of pork from the pantries were the best. I remember it being my favorite, for sure. Things weren't always this way, and it was during this time I started to really beg, borrow and steal.

I continued to stand outside of A.T.M.s, and I continued to steal. It was easier that way since I didn't really have another solution. We lived once with a man in a corner apartment on Kimball and Irving. He had one arm, but for the life of me, I can't remember how we came to be there except that my mother found a way to keep us alive.

"I caught a train," he said to us kids, with a probable meaning that he was either hit or run over by a damn train. It was probably the drugs talking, but it was a good story. As far as I could remember, he wasn't mean to us, and we were warm. Mom kept us safe as usual. We spent many nights digging through the dumpsters at the old Dominick's on Kimble near Belmont. It was damn good chow.

So, as with all things, it ended. At least this time, it wasn't a disappearing act. Things were different though I never really understood why. My mom finally convinced my dad to take me in as she struggled to find places for us all to stay together. She never would allow Jodi or Jessy to be apart from her, no matter what DCFS had to say.

The year was 1999 now.

Jessy was four, Jeremy was one, and I went to live with my dad. At the time, he lived in a basement apartment on Humboldt Blvd and Armitage. He had a snake named Mr. Bojangles. He said he got it cause the landlord used to enter the apartment when he was gone without permission. Mr. Bojangles easily curbed that shit. Life was difficult as I fought a lot with my dad. Meanwhile, I tried to keep up with school and spent many nights cleaning up after him and his friends.

During this time, I began having trouble at school with bullies. It was different, though; I wasn't being bullied. I was the kid who targeted bullies. We had one rule on our playground, and it was simple. Someone does you a 1, you do them a 10, and they will leave you alone forever. This rule applied to friends and family too. I got arrested a couple of times. District 023 lock-up is where either my dad or mom would have to come to get me. I will shed some light on that later.

On one occasion, I was arrested for carrying dangerous weapons, and my dad had to come to get me, of course. It was a snowball effect from there. Not only did he have to interrupt his day to come to get me, but he got a ticket while doing it. We got in the car, and he was mad as hell. The kind of mad that shook your soul.

He used to have these old, somewhat well-kept Cadillacs. As we pulled away, he hit a decent pothole (I mean, c'mon, it's Chicago), and his fucking windshield splintered from one side to the other. All I could say to myself was, "fuck". He looked at me, and I knew I was in for it. We got into a raging fight that night, and I honestly don't even remember the real root of it except that he had to take time to come and get me from the police, and his windshield was now busted. I remember he demanded I clean up after his party, but I did not. No way.

Now we're talking about a massive 6'3" man with hands that would scare anyone—he was both scary and dangerous. Incidentally, my dad's bark came with a bite. I remember picking up what seemed like a brick and hurling it at him. He was drunk, so his response time was slow, so I managed to bolt. I ran like a motherfucker and was unconcerned about where I would end up. We didn't have any money, and we didn't have cell phones available during this time, so it was just me. I ended up at the old Belmont blue line train station, also a CTA bus hub. Here I would pitch tent—not literally, but if I wasn't riding the train from end to end, I would huddle up at the bus stop shelters with working heaters.

Like any other night, I was just sitting there, watching the sad, happy, and plain old batshit crazy people walk by. Then a white Chevy Suburban pulled up, and the windows rolled down. I thought to myself, "Well fuck, here we go." To my surprise, it was a Mexican lady, unfamiliar to me at the time.

She said, "You're Matthew's friend from Batemen, right?"

I responded, "Who?" trying not to be an ass. After some thought and seeing Matthew's face, my memory jogged instantly like a lightning bolt just hit the parking lot next to me. I nervously cackled like everything was fine and said, "Ha ha, yea, it's me, Jason. What's up?"

Matt and I went to elementary school together briefly, and while we weren't best friends, we sure as shit stirred up some trouble. We used to steal super soakers, piss in them or even fill them with Nair. We'd target every bully we could find.

"Fuck 'em," we said.

We had fun doing it, and it was so fun to watch those assholes squirm.

She pulled over and asked, "What are you doing here?"

I responded, "Just catching the bus."

It was almost midnight, and Matthew's mom saw right through my bullshit. She looked at me and said, "Get in the car."

And there was no way in hell I would do that.

I said, "I'm okay, really."

She got out, smacked the shit out of me, and said again, "Get in the fucking car!" She was yelling in Spanish, and Matthew's brother, Hugo, whom I didn't really know yet, was laughing hysterically. Looking back at that day, I know he was laughing because someone else was finally getting his mom's wrath.

Of course, I got in the car—I certainly didn't want to catch her left hook. They took me to their home off Central Park near Milwaukee Avenue, and I settled into the back room with Matthew and Hugo. I slept on the three extra couch cushions. Hugo had the others. Over the coming year, I would grow closer and closer to Hugo and the family. The girls were so young when I joined the family that it wasn't until they were in high school that they finally accepted that I wasn't their blood brother. Anytime we tried to tell them that I wasn't their brother, they laughed it off like I was trying to prank them.

We often joked that Hugo and I were brothers and Matthew was a friend off the street. I spent a lot of time with the Baca clan, and they did everything they could to provide for me as much as they could. We spent many days and nights running the streets together, looking for our next hustle. We made out pretty well, actually. Hard work was never an issue for us, so we weren't afraid. We would stand outside laundry mats and ask who needed help or carry laundry home for the elderly for five bucks.

Now and again, we'd find a ride out to Six Flags and make a killing. So, we only had to buy a couple of Six Flag hats and find ticket stubs from the same day. Tickets were costly then, just as they are today. All we had to do was approach a younger couple and ask if they wanted to get in for half the price. They'd pay us half the ticket price, we'd give them the same day stub and a Six Flags hat, and all they had to do was walk up to customer service and say, "Sorry, we ran out of the park and forgot to get our hands stamped." Nine times out of ten, the rep would stamp their hand, and they were in. We'd split the profits from these stints.

Matthew wasn't always willing to toe the line with Hugo and me, but he occasionally jumped in for fun. One afternoon, we didn't feel like hustling much and decided to dig for coins instead. We had some old cereal in the house but no milk. However, there was a lot of powdered milk in the house, but it was lumpy, and you had to filter the roaches and rat shit out of it.

God!

How nice would a fresh glass of milk be and, even better, a real bowl of cereal? Those of you born in the cereal generation know what I'm talking about. We searched every crevice of the house for every penny we could find. We needed $2.50 to buy a gallon of milk at the corner store, and we will find it. After a few hours, we hit our mark and set off for the corner store as planned. As usual, we joked and laughed along the way. Hugo was always a funny fucker, and we couldn't help but laugh. To this day, we laugh primarily because of this man. Milton Berle once said, "Laughter is an instant vacation," and we sure as shit needed it today.

We made our purchase, and here we are, a couple of kids staring at a gallon of milk as if it's the holy grail of beverages. We huddled over the gallon of milk, our eyes sparkling with excitement. We whispered to each other, "This is it, man. We have hit the fucking jackpot. The milk gods have smiled upon us."

We examined the label and let out a collective gasp. "Only $2.50. We're living the high life now!" Hugo, of course, says, "And it's vitamin D fortified!"

We grabbed that gallon and hauled ass back to the apartment, giggling like we just made the teacher say, "Your anus." Little did we know, the milk would be gone sooner than we thought. Our dreams of living like milk royalty would come crashing down as Matthew thought he was an all-star athlete throwing it into the air and catching it like he was Curtis Conway of the Chicago Bears.

That last catch didn't go so well, and it crashed into the concrete like a pile of bricks exploding into what could soon be categorized as powdered milk. But during that brief moment, we relished in the glory of this excellent, cheap, vitamin-fortified milk of the gods.

Time would come to pass, and over the year, I managed to stay in school, get arrested only once, and make valid attempts to reconnect with my mom and dad. I started riding my bike everywhere, too, just like my dad—I was once hit by a car that cut in front of a bus. I flew, hit the pavement, and finally, the curb. I was breathing so hard that it felt like my lungs rolled down the road in a patch of shattered glass. However, that is a story for another time.

My mom would eventually move in again and find her way to a new guy named Niko. This was 2000, and we came through the Y2K hype with no issues. He was a nice guy and did care for us. Niko was definitely my favorite—he genuinely cared, and I am sure he never really trusted anyone except me. They lived near Hamlin and Montrose in a 2nd-floor apartment with an entrance off the middle gangway. Cat lady Holly used to help watch Jessy and Jeremy. I remember thinking he was rich because he once let me watch 'The Matrix (1990)' on cable television—it was like I was in heaven. As time passed, we had great meals and bad nights all the same. Mom was trying to get clean and even got a job as a C.N.A. We were proud of her but always concerned about what was next.

As 2000 raged on, we had many fights, ups, and downs. I was still spending lots of time with Hugo and the fam, and we continued to hustle. I remained at Le Moyne Elementary School, where I would eventually be expelled that year. As I indicated earlier, I was the bully's bully. I never put up with anyone trying to pick on my friends, and to that end, I did what I had to in order to protect them.

I wasn't a bad student. I did my homework and was always in school on time unless I was home caring for my brother. I just didn't put up with anyone's shit, especially when it came to my friends. Interestingly, our old playground is now a Chicago Police Department if that tells you anything about my childhood.

We fought a lot, and one day the playground rumors spread that a particular bully was going to have a bunch of his friends jump me. I brought weapons to school, brass knuckles, and such, to fight this fight. We fought, we got busted, and that was that. We were both arrested and sent to district 023 lock up.

CPD Arrest & Referral

CPS Referral to Alternative School

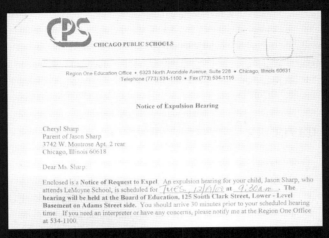

Notice of Expulsion Hearing

At the hearing, the school board recommended that for the remainder of my 8th-grade year, I would attend the Chicago Foundations Alternative Safe School.

Funny how things work out, though. I'd end up becoming good friends with the kid who got me expelled. He was a bully, so as you can imagine, I wasn't having any of it. The circumstances were different now, and neither of us knew anyone at this safe school, so we teamed up.

While all of this was going on, I still had to deal with the Juvenile Court. On top of my requirement to attend the alternative school, the juvenile court accepted CPD's recommendation, which resulted in my referral to the West Side Youth Network (WSYN), where I would go to counseling and do community service.

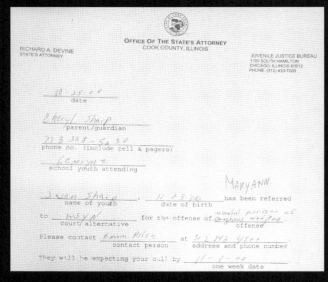

Juvenile Court Hearing

Juvenile Court Adjudication

I was a damn good student at the alternative school, just as I was at LeMoyne. I usually received high remarks both academically and behaviorally. My issue—I wasn't good at taking shit from bullies, and I was punished for it. I recognize that I made some poor decisions, and I needed to own it. So when I got to Chicago Foundations, it was a no-fail event, and I needed to do well. If not, the school board would overturn the referral and graduate me to a full expulsion. I worked my ass off day and night to prove myself, and when the time came for the school board to re-visit my case, I made sure everyone in the alternative school was on my side.

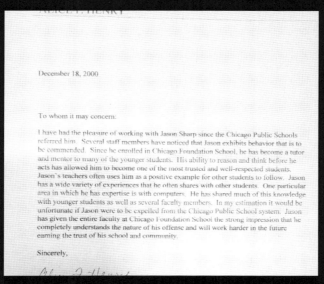

Letter of Recommendation from Chicago Foundations Alternative Safe School before my 12/19/2000 Expulsion hearing.

Thankfully all was successful, and I was able to continue my 8th-grade year at the safe school. As things began to settle, I began to spend more time with my dad. He had this janky loft apartment up on Elston and Lawrence, but it was warm. He would re-introduce me to Charles Allen, eventually leading me to where I am today. However, it was not Charles per se but his wife at the time and my soon-to-be surrogate mother, Yael.

It was from this janky apartment that Charles would be tossed out of the window after, high on whatever he was on at the time; he bit Noel's ear. My dad's girlfriend, Christine, at the time, snapped, and of course, my

Sadly, Sandy's kids, our cousins, were already taken by the state at this point.

We're a month in without mom home. Just me and my sister and baby Jessy. Sergio always took Jeremy. It was around this time we started to see Jeremy less and less. We were out of food and, of course, had no money. It was only a matter of time before our troubles really boiled over.

We finally made it home after our walk, but something was wrong. The door was smashed in, and everything was ripped apart. We thought someone had broken in. And even worse, they might still be inside. I made my way in slowly as Jodi kept Jessy safe. My heart was throttled, and I had no idea what to do if someone was in there.

Thankfully, it was just us. Jodi brought Jessy inside, and we worked our way through the house, thanking God it was a burglar. To our surprise, it wasn't just a burglar. Instead, we found what looked like a murder scene. We entered our mom's bedroom and found multiple knives stuck in the plaster with some red substance that appeared to be blood all over the walls.

"Who the hell could have done this?" I said.

I looked at Jodi and had her take Jessy out of the room. I walked up to the wall, and I found two things. The first was an apparent handwritten note stabbed into the wall. What I discovered next was unreal and something I had thought long forgotten. It wasn't blood on the wall. It was fucking ketchup. And that damn handwritten note was from the one and only piece of shit, Sergio.

My sister came back into the room, and everything fell silent. It was deafening. I could hear the fear in her eyes. His note read, "Tell your mom I want my money." At this point, we at least knew mom was out of putting weight back on, but sure as shit, she was pregnant with my now-brother, Justin. It was time to raise the black flag and start slicing throats.

Jodi raced over to Niko's apartment, and we took off with the first weapon of mass destruction I could find. I stormed out of the car carrying this golf club—I kicked the door with all my power and with a thunderous boom! I was inside. I swung at the first person I saw and cracked his face right open. He hit the floor, and I kept moving forward. Let's use an analogy here—I was a bull in their China shop, and nothing would stop me from destroying that house and the people in it.

I was angry and sad—I felt every emotion all at once. I was violent, and Jodi was the only person who could stop me. We found mom in the back, and I started screaming, "Get the fuck out of this house...what the fuck is wrong with you?" "How could you leave Jessy?" I screamed again, "Let's go!" but she refused. However, at that moment, I knew with certainty that nothing would ever change. This was how mom wanted to live her life.

Jodi was able to break me away, and we left. Jodi was crying uncontrollably, and my heart was pounding. It felt like a ten-thousand-drum army was inside my chest. I remained furious but needed to calm down and help Jodi with Jessy. Mom and Niko split, and my sister and I would hold Christmas in the alley with Justin for many years to come. Niko would never let him be with our family alone after this.

The Clinic

Desperation led me to reconsider my options. Eventually, I convinced myself to call Charles and told him I'd be interested in his offer. I quickly found myself in a pair of blue scrubs and cleaning the floor at PetVets Animal Hospital in Oak Park. Of course, I wasn't of legal working age, so Yael was taking a major risk. At the time, I don't think she had any idea what she was going to do with this 13-year-old boy from the city.

We're now well into the winter of 2000, and I spent nearly every day at the clinic with Yael. I was hyper-focused on doing everything I could to maximize this opportunity. I was the only male on the staff, so I did my best not to be dumb. All the women in this facility were way above my level of intelligence, and I was trying to keep up and avoid termination.

I remained in school, working toward graduating in the 8th grade. I would take the Blue Line train daily from the city to the Austin exit in Oak Park. Eventually, I would ride my bike everywhere, including Oak Park. Come rain, shine, snow, or otherwise—I was never late except whenever I got hit by a car, which happened more often than I liked. Fortunately, Yael would always fix me up.

Yael Removing Road Debris from My Hand

As spring 2001 rolled in, I would spend more and more time at the clinic or with Hugo and Matthew. I took every job I could get my hands on, from tile work to painting half the clinic. I was there to do the jobs no one else wanted, and I loved it! I was meticulous in every detail, and I worked my ass off until 8 or 9 pm some nights, followed by an hour-long bike ride back to Hugo's. I was dedicated to making it work and showing what I could bring to the table.

Eventually, Yael asked me if I'd like to try something new. They brought me to the pharmacy area, so my new role was locating and getting meds ready for the animals in our care. This was easy, but no less had to be perfect. Mistakes were not acceptable here or anywhere, especially with the animals. Otherwise, it could cost a life.

I moved again rather quickly, except this time assisting in lab work, drawing blood, x-rays, dental, and even surgery prep on occasion—it was a blast. Yael gave me a key and the security code. She trusted me, and I was in. But not for long. Lessons from the school of hard knocks I came from kicked in pretty hard. To this day, I don't know why I did it except that I could, and that's what my mom would do.

I was alone one night closing up shop, walked right over to the register, and took a $20 bill. I closed, set the alarm, and went on my way. I can't believe I thought for one second this would get past Yael. The woman was a precision instrument of unbound skill and intelligence, and here my dumbass was trying to steal.

The next day, she pulled me into her office and confronted me. My heart sank, and I felt awful. I had let down the one person who truly believed in me, and for what? Twenty Bucks! She didn't scold me —it was much worse. She was disappointed and sad.

I fell in love with Yael that day, however. She taught me a lesson that has become one of my top leadership principles today— that people can fail without becoming a failure. Yael looked at me and said, "Jason, if you needed money, you should have just come to me and asked."

I would pay her back with my devotion and dedication to being better and working day and night at the clinic. During this time, I started to heal everything that was broken about me.

The Lesson

So, what did my suffering teach me at this point? What is it about the absolute truth of the human condition that we can learn from? The following is a brief list I've developed over the years. Furthermore, each detail is elaborated upon at various times throughout this work.

Trust

Until this point, my early life experiences laid a weak foundation for trusting others. I learned not to trust well. This translated into almost everything I did: work, school, or recreation. I learned to trust but verify, which, loosely translated, is a lack of trust. Does it work? Yes. People must earn your trust. They must earn the right for you to be vulnerable with them. This happens through consistent, demonstrated performance, whether personal or professional. That is, people keep their word and do what they said they would do.

Who I Was. A True Sense of Self

It was during this time that I really started to figure out who I was and, more importantly, who I wasn't. This goes back to Chapter 1's point that we all must have a gut check. Most of us either refuse or don't have anyone in our lives who will give us "no bull shit" feedback. I was fortunate to have Yael, G, and many others. It is imperative that you define who you are and what you believe. Write it down. Knowing who you are is vital to all future outcomes, but as discussed in Chapter 1, it is inherently difficult to achieve.

Who Others Are. Who They Truly Are

When it comes to relying on others, it often comes down to one or two people out of the hundreds of potential contacts or even thousands on Facebook, LinkedIn, and other platforms. That is, first and foremost, learn to rely on yourself first. Then, at best, you might be able to rely on someone else who isn't your parent.

Finally, I learned that suffering means we're still alive and that my number one priority was figuring out what to do with it. I learned to use my suffering as a catalyst for getting better every day. When we experience setbacks and failure, some of us blame and point fingers. When do you turn inward and start looking in the mirror and asking why? What did you do to contribute to these setbacks and failures?

Given where I was at this point in my life, there was no possible way I could point a single finger at anyone. If it was going wrong, it was definitely my fault. In all things, no matter the outcome, I had to own it.

On the other side of owning our outcome, we must also recognize and acknowledge that sometimes, life makes choices for us. Be comfortable with that and do something to generate different circumstances. It will all be ok if you focus on what you can control. As Bruce Lee's teachings taught me, "I've always been buffeted by circumstances because I thought of myself as a human being affected by outside conditioning. Now I realize that I am the power that commands the feeling of the mind and from which circumstances grow."

CHAPTER 3 — St. John's Northwestern: The Halls of Discipline

In Chapter 2, we explored the deep realities of my childhood suffering from the perspective of a broken human existence as lived from the moment we take our first breath. Because of this, we spend the rest of our lives healing in search of meaning, purpose, and relevance.

In the forgotten corners of Chicago, where the winds whispered tales of my struggle, I was just another lost soul navigating the shadows. But fate, in its mysterious design, led me to Yael. She became my guiding light, reaching out her hand to pull me from the cold streets, nourishing my hungry body, and clothing my tattered spirit. Yael not only provided me with the basic necessities of life, but she also bestowed upon me something far greater—a chance at redemption.

It was through her unwavering compassion and tireless dedication that I found myself standing at the threshold of St. John's Northwestern Military Academy, where the fragmented pieces of my existence began their journey toward healing. In a world where I once felt invisible, this institution granted me purpose, meaning, and a newfound relevance, igniting a flicker of hope within a heart that once believed it was nothing to no one.

St. John's Northwestern Military Academy

Most significant life events are unannounced and usually unfold at 3 pm on a random Tuesday. This is one of those events. I will try to keep this short: Yael and Charles sat me down and said, "Jason, we have a school we think you might like to attend. It's called St. John's Northwestern Military Academy, and it's in Wisconsin."

I immediately replied, "I don't have money for that," to which they responded, "We'll figure that out."

Like kicking that crack house door down, I felt every emotion, except this time in reverse. I was happy and sad all at the same time. I was nervous and didn't know what to say or how to say it, even if I did. I thought, how could I leave my sister and brothers? I didn't know anything except the Chicago streets and this clinic. I looked at them and said, "I'll have to ask my mom, but I don't think she will sign the papers."

Charles was an apparent 1985 graduate of St. John's, and this was the connection. He convinced Yael that I would be a great candidate to thrive and grow in that place. This is probably the one thing Charles did that I am truly grateful for. I continued school through the Spring and graduated 8th grade on time from the Chicago Alternative Safe School. Yael and my clinic family threw me an awesome surprise graduation party there, too.

8th Grade Graduation at PetVets with Yael

8th Grade Graduation at PetVets with Michele

I talked with my sister and worked with my mom for signatures. Selfishly, I wanted to leave. Talking with Jodi, I said, "One of us has to leave so that we can pull everyone else out." A lot happened that summer of 2001. Justin was born in June. I continued my court-mandated counseling with the West Side Youth Network, and I set eyes on the Academy for the first time.

The place was so wide open and massive that I couldn't wrap my head around it. I immediately felt lost and overcome with fear. A thousand questions ran through my mind.

"Do I belong here?"

"Should I leave Chicago?"

"What about Jodi and my brothers?"

I knew I had to do something dramatic, and St. John's was it. Yael promised me everything would be great and that I could probably get a scholarship. She assured me I would thrive in a space like that and come out the other side capable of greatness and caring for my family.

I started at the academy that falls with Lancers Football Camp, followed by my plebe year as a "New Boy." Soon after, I met my greatest mentor, SFC (R) Brian Galarza. When I met him, I knew Yael was right all along. At this place, with this man, I would develop my moral compass and start to understand myself and what I could do.

"G," as we affectionately called him, essentially became my surrogate father. He was a man's man, a Soldier, and a truly genuine human being who cared about us. He was my TAC Officer (Trainer, Advisor, Counselor), and he was the best the Academy had to offer.

G and I at The Academy, Fall of 2001.

G taught me everything I know about being a man in this world and owning my responsibilities. If it wasn't for Yael, I would have never met him. If it wasn't for G, I would not be the man I am today. Period.

Without fail, I look back at my time at the Academy on a daily basis. Sometimes twice a day and sometimes all day in a nostalgic haze of the many memories lived. I will try and do the Academy justice within this short chapter, but it truly deserves its own book.

I spent four years as a military boarding student walking the one-hundred-and-twenty-year-old campus. Many came before me, and many would come after, including my own brother Jessy. My "New Boy" year was chock full of experiences forever burned into my memories, from "hell week," where we earned our cross rifles, to experiencing the excruciating pain of death as my roommate learned of his father's passing from a world away.

Hell Week, Fall of 2001

I said before that with everything we encounter; one moment usually defines a memory forever. Only one of my St. John's memories genuinely gives me nightmares, and what I am about to share with you is that memory.

Foxtrot Company was stationed on the first floor of Scott Johnston Hall in 2001. I distinctly remember the night G came into our dorm room just after we crested the midnight hour. The memory is so vivid I remember the smell of sweaty football socks in the corner of the room. He

71

asked me to wait quietly in the hallway, to which I responded, "Is everything ok?". His reply was classic in that he looked at me with his eyebrow but never said a word. I knew to shut my mouth and stand there. I had never before seen the look on a man's face like I saw that night on G's. He entered our dorm room, handshaking and with a shattered sense of hope.

In the quiet stillness of the night, as my Academy brothers slumbered, my roommate's world shattered into a thousand piercing shards of anguish. It was a scream born from the deepest chambers of his soul, a raw and primal wail that tore through the darkness, echoing the torment that consumed him.

The sound reverberated with haunting desperation as if the very essence of his being was ripped open. It was a scream that spoke volumes of the immense pain and sorrow that now enveloped his heart. Every fiber of his being convulsed, each anguished note carrying the weight of an unbearable truth. That his father was gone.

In that solitary moment, he stood alone, worlds apart from the only family he had ever known. Separated by an unfathomable distance, thousands of miles between them, mocking the impossibility of physical comfort except for that of his Foxtrot brothers. His cries of anguish ricocheted off the old Scotty J walls, filling the hollow emptiness of his surroundings as he yearned for the solace of familiar arms and the comforting embrace of loved ones.

The realization and sheer helplessness of his situation, the impossibility of bridging the chasm that separated him from his shattered family, added an indescribable layer of tragedy to his mournful scream.

His only solace lay in the presence of his fellow boarding students and mentor. We gathered around him, our own hearts heavy with shared grief. In our eyes, he found a glimmer of understanding, a flicker of empathy that offered a sliver of comfort amidst the desolation.

Humberto's horrific scream that early morning encapsulated a profound loss that words alone could never fully express. It was a scream etched in the depths of memory at our old school, a haunting melody of sorrow that would forever resonate within the hearts of those who bore witness. It served as a haunting reminder of the fragility of life and the unyielding power of love that binds us, even in the face of unimaginable pain.

In the wake of that heart-wrenching scream, a shattered boy was left to navigate a world forever altered. So many of us at the Academy were already wandering aimlessly, it seemed, and this moment added layers of pain not previously known.

My friendship with Humberto was solidified in concrete that night, and so too, was my faith in St. John's Northwestern. In those hallowed halls, I embarked upon a transformative journey that shaped the very core of my being. It was within these storied walls that I learned the true essence of manhood, forged unbreakable bonds, and experienced adventures that surpassed the bounds of the imagination.

My roommates, those fantastical and sometimes troubled souls who shared in both the triumphs and trials of our cadet lives, were not mere companions but brothers. They would become my fellow Old Boys in the years to come. Together, we embarked on daring escapades, filling the pages of our youthful stories with tales of camaraderie and bravery. I watched cadets save lives, play amazing concerts, and become masters in their own right on and off the field. Through laughter and tears, we discovered the strength of friendship and the indomitable spirit that arises when hearts beat as one as they certainly did in Foxtrot Company.

Foxtrot Company, Fall of 2001

Guiding us on this remarkable journey were our TACs and teachers, who personified dedication, molding us into more than just students. From SFC Galarza to 1SG Brown, LTC Kebisek, and SSG Andrasic. Teachers like Perry Siebers, Jon Bennett, Tim Vice, Tim Shramek, Joe Niemczyk, and a great many others. They were mentors, imparting wisdom with unwavering passion and instilling within us the values of discipline, honor, and integrity. They pushed us to our limits, recognizing that true growth emerges from the crucible of challenge, where comfort zones cease to exist.

In a world where participation trophies were commonplace, our old school stood as an emblem of grit and resilience. Here, we were taught that success is earned through hard work, perseverance, and an unwavering commitment to excellence. We strived not for empty accolades but for the satisfaction of knowing we had given our all and pushed ourselves beyond what we believed possible.

But it was not just in the pursuit of academic and physical prowess that we found fulfillment. Our old school understood the importance of nurturing our souls and fostering a connection to something greater. We prayed hard, seeking solace and guidance in moments of doubt and despair. Through devotion and reverence, we discovered the power of faith and the unbreakable bond between the individual and the divine.

Yet, amidst the discipline, the rigors, the guard path, the parades, and the hell weeks, we also reveled in the joyous moments of youthful abandon. We played hard, embracing the fleeting moments of respite and revelry that balanced the weight of our responsibilities. In those moments, laughter echoed through the corridors, and the spirit of camaraderie ignited like a spark, reminding us of the beauty in celebrating life's simple pleasures. We enjoyed every possible moment of we could, and we made sure of it.

Foxtrot Company Camping on St. John's Island

Next to Yael, St. John's Northwestern, steeped in tradition and reverence, laid the foundation for my moral compass. It sculpted the very essence of my character, engraving within me the values that guide my choices and actions. The lessons learned within those hallowed walls continue to resonate, reminding me of the power of honor, the importance of perseverance, and the everlasting bonds of our brotherhood.

My alma mater deserves my deepest gratitude. It shaped me into the person I am today, instilling within me the courage to face the challenges of the world and the humility to recognize that true strength lies not in individual triumphs but in the collective spirit that thrives when honorable hearts unite.

In the story of my life, St. John's Northwestern will forever hold a cherished place—a beacon of inspiration, a sanctuary of growth, and a testament to the power of an education that reaches far beyond the classroom.

I remained under SFC Galarza's mentorship as I grew up in Foxtrot Company—the Superior Company! As I closed my new boy year, I earned the Alice Smyth Mouso Medal for the Most Outstanding New Boy Soldier in the Corps, and I was invited back for Cadre Leadership Training. This would be the first time in my life that I was truly recognized for my efforts. Yael sacrificed so much to allow me this opportunity, so I put the work in.

I worked my way up the ranks in Foxtrot Company and spent my summers in Chicago, working for Yael at PetVets, of course. I was at constant odds about what to do with my family and how to do it. At the end of the day, the no-fail event was to return to the Academy and thrive. Summers in Chicago remained difficult despite my time at PetVets. The usual challenges with my mother and drugs layered by my father and his issues at the time.

Hugo and I lived in the basement of an apartment building owned by his uncle. We were 15 years old and didn't want to be troubled by anyone's bullshit, so we chose the basement. Together, we remained focused on working, saving money, and staying out of trouble. Yael and I grew closer each passing summer, and I continued to do my best to prove that she did not waste a second of time or an ounce of energy on me.

I returned to the Academy that Fall of 2002 in high spirits. I continued to play football, and I did well at Cadre. I wasn't a particularly good football player, but I enjoyed playing for Jay Wayland, Tim Shramek, and Tim Vice. They made sure we had fun, and they praised our efforts as opposed to focusing only on the outcomes.

Junior Varsity Lancer Football, Fall of 2002

I spent my sophomore year at the Academy as a Platoon Sergeant in Foxtrot Company. My relationship with G grew stronger, and I became a more vital member of the company. I felt empowered, and he enabled all of us in leadership roles to own the outcomes of our company. He held our feet to the fire and made sure we were on top of our game every day.

As I grew in rank, responsibility, and character, I took after G more and more with each passing day. I wasn't making too many friends as I took my responsibilities seriously, and let's just say that some didn't, or they wanted me to use my positional authority to their benefit. I maintained high academic marks and ensured my Cadets did the same as best possible. In the winter, I would usually lift weights in the "General's Gym," followed by track and field or rugby in the spring.

Funny story—it was in the "General's Gym" that I was choked out for the first time in my life. I've been in many fights over the years but never choked out. I thought it'd be funny to hide 1SG Zimmer's Beret as a joke. I thought wrong. Very wrong. For those of you who know 1SG Zimmer, you know he grabbed me without twitching an eye or moving a muscle on his face. It was lights out for me. I'll never forget it. We remain friends today, and his contributions to the Academy and the Raider Program were second to none.

1SG Paul Zimmer with Brenan Harris, Fall of 2014

I stayed the course with G, and Foxtrot had a successful year full of storied memories, hard-won awards, and a solid crew ready to take over during Junior year. As the summer came, I would again spend a lot of time at PetVets, where I would graduate to assist the exam rooms, X-Rays, dental, and much more. I'm pretty sure this was the summer I painted the clinic with Hugo too.

It was during this summer I began to experience more issues with my mother. Of course, our "home front" was still very rocky, with my sister spending most of her time caring for Jessy. Any money I received from PetVets or other hustles would go directly to Jodi to care for Jessy. Justin remained in Niko's care with an off-and-on relationship with my mom.

I entered my junior year at the Academy motivated, ready to fight the good fight. G had me fired up. I was ready to kick ass and take names, as he would say. This year was a little different as I was "Top," the Cadet First Sergeant responsible for 65 other Cadets in Foxtrot Company. I was responsible for everything we accomplished or failed to do alongside the Company Commander, Chris Wheatly. Chris was a stud. He still is, for that matter, having spent most of his life in some military unit or operation. We made a great team in those days, and we remain friends today.

Junior year was the most difficult I had experienced to date, especially in the first part of the year. Joe Niemczyk did not help my cause. His famous wall of red pens spent correcting our papers will go down in history with all those who had his classes. I am thinking of a specific one right now, though, American Studies. Arguably, it was the most challenging course the Academy offered to Juniors and certainly not one to be taken lightly. Now, let's add some layers to this for perspective. If you were a Junior taking the American Studies Course, even as a new boy, you struggled beyond your wildest dreams. But, if, while taking American Studies, you were also a Company First Sergeant and played Lancer Football, you were a true glutton for punishment. The school/workday was a regular and grueling 20 hours. It was times like these that I began to really understand what I was capable of, and it was thanks to teachers like Joe Niemczyk.

As Cadet First Sergeant for Foxtrot Company, again, I wasn't making any friends, and I was ok with that. In fact, if you recall my Chicago years, I was the bully's bully, which got me in trouble from time to time. The same held true here at the Academy, and if I came across one personally, they knew it. If I came across one messing with one of my Cadets, they felt it. In those years, a company consisted of a mixture of all grade levels, from 12-18 years old, so we were responsible for protecting the "preps."

As we drew closer to commencement weekend, I came across one bully who thought he was on top of the world. G taught me a valuable lesson this year, and it manifested at this moment. The only time we start on top is when we're digging ourselves a hole. This bully was one of a kind and found himself in a pretty big hole with me. In his eyes, not only did his shit not stink, but it smelled good. He was a senior, getting ready for graduation in just a short couple of weeks.

I caught him on my floor selling chewing tobacco to 12-year-olds, my preps. Despite that it was against the rules of the Academy, it was a personal no go for me, especially when targeting peps. Foxtrot Company had moved from the first floor to the second floor of Scott Johnston, which allowed us to better control traffic and unwanted visitors. I caught him red-handed, and I asked him point blank to get off my floor and not to come back. We were standing in the middle of the hallway where the old bathrooms were. We were directly in front of a stairway that fed the middle of the building.

He looked at me and said, "What are you going to do? Make me leave." I demanded again, "Get off my floor and don't come back." I had no intention of reporting this violation; we handle our own problems in Foxtrot Company. He stepped toward me and again said, "Make me," and then what he did next was unforgivable in my eyes. He spits directly at me, with most of his disgusting saliva landing on my face, my shirt, and even my freshly shined shoes.

I looked at one of my Platoon Sergeants and said, "Well, now he's not leaving." I grabbed him with all the power I could muster, and I slammed him violently into the wall. He hit the floor with a thud that still makes me smile to this day. I admit I lost control that day, but he was a bully, and I didn't play nice with bullies. I was quickly swept up by my old Chicago days where the rules were simple: if someone does you a 1, you do them a 10, and they leave you alone forever.

I saddled this bully, and I unleashed a barrage of unfiltered strikes on his face. I held nothing back. When I got tired of punching, I started to monkey-fist his face. It was as if I was back in that crack house looking for my mom. Thankfully, Bobby Jarvis was there to pull me off. This "boy" was sent to the infirmary to be looked at by the nurse. He was ok but spent the next few weeks, including graduation, looking like Frankenstein.

Bobby Jarvis and I became good friends over the years. We grew together, took care of everyone around us, and maintained the spirit of Foxtrot Company day in and day out. Bobby and I remain friends to this day, and for that, I am forever grateful.

Marching With Bobby Jarvis, Spring 2004

G found me and said, "Jason, we have to report to the Admiral's office." Admiral Ronald J. Kurth was president of the Academy at the time, and I was shitting my pants walking over to his office. G told me that the "boy," who was one year my senior, was messed up pretty bad and refused to walk the stage at graduation based on how his face looked. I wish I could say I cared about him at that moment, but instead, I was more worried about letting Yael down.

As G explained the situation further, this bully's parents were on their way to the Academy, and they were not happy. They would be arriving two weeks before graduation to be with their son. I approached Admiral Kurth's office on the Main Drag. I stood at attention in his doorway and decisively knocked twice, "Sir, Cadet First Sergeant Sharp reporting as ordered, sir!"

"You may enter," the Admiral directed.

G Stood outside the doorway, and the Admiral waved him in. I was relieved someone who really knew me was in the room, at the very least.

The Admiral proceeded, "First Sergeant Sharp, did he deserve what you did to him?"

"Sir, I was protecting my youngest Cadets. He was selling chewing tobacco on my floor, and I asked him to leave multiple times."

"Did he leave?"

"No, sir. He spit on me."

"So, he deserved it?"

"Yes, sir."

"Carry on. You are dismissed."

I promptly saluted, did an about-face, and marched my ass right out of the Main Drag, thanking the universe that I just might survive this. Thankfully, things were different back then. People got what they deserved, to say the least. Two weeks later, I was promoted to First Captain of the 121st Corps of Cadets. Getting promoted to First Captain almost immediately following this incident split the staff and the cadets in terms of support. They either loved me or hated me. Those who hated me knew that I would call their bullshit and confront them directly, no matter the circumstance.

First Captain Promotion Certificate, June 6th, 2004

The First Captain is the only Cadet promoted at the end of the academic year to demonstrate an official change of command from the outgoing commander to the incoming commander. The First Captain serves as the Battalion Commander, the highest-ranking Cadet in the Corps responsible for every Cadet and every outcome. I went from eating out of dumpsters to being responsible for over 450 Cadets, thanks to Yael and SFC Galarza.

Despite all of the excitement, change was on the horizon, and I wasn't sure if I was ready. Admiral Kurth would retire this year, and President Albert would be Head of School. I would also come to lose SFC Galarza as my mentor.

Change of Command, June 6th, 2004

I went home that summer and once again clung onto PetVets as my heart was heavy in anxiety over the changes that were coming to the Academy. I was legitimately scared about not having G around for what would be my final year at the Academy. No less, I had to face the fact that my time was coming to an end there, and I needed to do everything in my power to make it the most successful year of all.

It was a typical summer for me in Chicago, and I wished I was back at the Academy. I finally broke and called LTC Kebisek to ask if I could come home early. Home being the Academy, of course. LTC K said that I'd have to ask 1SG Brown, the Commandant, for permission to come back early and move into the First Captain room. It was located in the coveted DeKoven Hall, and its luxuries included a private shower and bathroom.

The Academy dorm rooms were truly my first stable living environment in terms of a place to lay my head, and to have a private bath and shower was a complete luxury. Generally speaking, Cadets shared community bathrooms and showers, but my bed was mine, and it wasn't going to be missing whenever I came back to it. When I was promoted to First Captain and told I would have my own private bathroom and shower, I was on top of my world. My days of sleeping outside or sleeping on couch cushions were forever gone. I didn't start on top, so I wasn't digging any holes. I struggled and fought for many years both within the Academy walls and outside of them. I crawled out of the hole I was born into. I worked tirelessly to honor Yael and to prove to the world that I wasn't just another Chicago statistic. Along my journey, I stood on the many shoulders mentioned above, and simply put, I worked my ass off.

It would be my First Captain year when I became very close with LTC Kebisek. He would become one of my greatest confidants and teachers. He had endless vision, no room for laziness or failure, and accepted nothing less than a 20-hour day! I knew all of this, and still, I asked to come back to the Academy early to help prepare for Cadre Leadership Training. I arrived on campus in early August of 2004, several weeks before the rest of the Corps leadership would arrive and six weeks before the main body would report for the school year.

I decided not to play football this year, which ended up being a very controversial decision. Even President Albert attempted to convince me to play. In their eyes, if the First Captain decided not to play after dedicating the three previous years in a row, then the message to the main body was that something was wrong. The bottom line was I did not have an agreeable relationship with the new coach, Gary R., despite what goals he had in mind.

I missed the days of Tim Shramek and Tim Vice. I missed the days of focusing on the game and the effort we put in. The days when the player mattered more than the win. The days when every player mattered and not one or two who were now untouchable because they could throw a ball. This book is certainly not about the Lancer Football team, but those who know, know. For everyone else, I chose to move on a path that was better aligned with my values and goals. We came through Cadre training, promoted the Corps Leadership, and kicked off the year with our Corps Motto, "Return to the Standard."

Things got a little interesting for me this year as communication with my mother was very limited. The Academy required my biological mother's signature to let me take leave. No matter what kind of adventures I planned with other Cadets and their families, I still needed to have her signature.

I befriended the ladies at the Cadet Store over the years, and they knew my situation exactly. They knew so well they offered to help all the time. Eventually, they would even let me fax my own leave requests to the Commandant's Office. This simple fax allowed me to take breaks, see my sisters and brothers, and spend time with new friends from the Academy.

I began taking the Hiawatha Train from Milwaukee to Chicago, which at the time, was only $16. The Commandant's Office was run by Mrs. Elissa Spencer, whose funeral I would later officiate. We were close. She would never charge me the $25 transportation fee to get from Delafield to Milwaukee and back. She, too, knew my story, and I worked every angle I could to minimize expenses on Yael. I began to truly enjoy riding trains because of this experience, and this eventuality brought me to Johnnie Blue Hands and this book.

My experiences as First Captain began to change my perspective on leadership. Thanks to LTC Kebisek, I was introduced to the three levels of leadership in years past but serving as First Captain really solidified the concept. Leaving Foxtrot Company to assume battalion command meant I would be largely disconnected from what was happening at the lowest levels of leadership. It meant that I would not be as close to the New Boy Cadets or any of the nitty-gritty work happening in the halls each morning and night. It was a hard pill to swallow for me as I spent so many years at that level, and I very much enjoyed helping the young ones grow and succeed.

As the year went on, I became more and more hyper-focused on successful outcomes for the Corps. I worked day and night for the LTC Kebisek, developing the strategies and plans for the many requirements we had, from the Veteran's Day Parade in Milwaukee to Drill Competitions and the Chicago St. Patrick's Day Parade. Despite all of that, I spent a very real and very serious time focusing on my connection with the lowest level. I always made myself available to everyone for whatever support and guidance they needed. It was in this way that I discovered how much I enjoyed mentoring and helping others grow. It kept me grounded, and it motivated me to stay the course, too, with everything I was doing, which primarily involved honoring Yael and changing the course of my family's trajectory forever.

I have many amazing memories from this year, but one that truly stands out is Mid-Winter Ball. Yvonne Donaldson was our Senior Class Advisor, and she was simply amazing. She, too, knew my story and allowed me to participate in night and weekend events nearly free of charge. Yve cared deeply about all of us, she was our hero, and we loved her. She led the way for our Mid-Winter Ball, which was a reggae-themed military ball. It was our version of a high school prom.

I asked Kayla M. to be my date and guest of honor. She and I were childhood friends growing up in Chicago, and I couldn't have imagined anyone more beautiful to be my date for this magnificent event. It took some major convincing, especially her mom!

Our military balls were very special back then, and they remain that way today at the Academy. It was a fantastical weekend event full of surprises, enchantment, laughter, and love. The weekend was chock full of dinners, outings, chapel services, and of course, the ball itself. There was even an after-party for Juniors and Seniors.

Kayla arrived, and we had an amazing time from the very beginning. From the comedy show to the dinner, we laughed and smiled all the way to the receiving line. Yve was a talented planner, and she injected love into everything she did. She had flowers and notes waiting on the pillows of every girl who attended the ball. It was such a loving touch on her behalf. It made each of us feel special. Unfortunately, the evening got interesting pretty quickly, and to this day, I feel horrible about what was about to happen next.

The evening was nearly over. Kayla and I were on the dance floor having a nice time. She was, at least, I have always been a terrible dancer! 1SG Brown walked in, hollering, "Where is the First Cap at?" They tracked me down, and I reported over with my Command Sergeant Major (CSM), Alex P. He proceeded to explain that I needed to be in Chicago Sunday morning with the CSM to accept an award on behalf of the Academy. My heart sank immediately, it the floor, and I could feel it shattering as I imagined walking over and explaining this to Kayla.

Of course, I briefly argued with the Commandant for a moment, but this was a direct order from the President, and it was my duty. I felt the wind get sucked out of me as I explained the circumstances to Kayla. She was a trooper, of course, but I am certain none of this experience would be a happy memory. The Academy arranged transportation for Pollema and me to head to Chicago immediately and grab a hotel. This is another example of how much things have changed with the world today and the level of trust bestowed upon high schoolers.

1SG Brown sent us on our way, by ourselves, to downtown Chicago. He gave us an Academy credit card and a couple of hundred dollars in petty cash to get through the next couple of days. We said goodbye to our respective dates, and we moved out. Every year, as the City of Chicago gets ready for the current year's parade, they select and hand out awards from the last. The next day, at the Chicago Plumbers Hall, we would accept the award for 1st Place, Top Marching Unit, in the 2004 Chicago St. Patrick's Day Parade.

Award Acceptance in Chicago, Morning After Mid-Winter Ball

Following Mid-Winter Ball and the oddity that was my exit to represent the Academy in Chicago, the Corps found its way out of our winter funk, and we were motivated to keep moving toward commencement weekend. We got through the 2005 St. Patrick's Day Parade, Spring Parent's Weekend, many General Inspections, which were white glove room inspections, and many other requirements before we made our final approach to Commencement Weekend.

One event this year stood out above all for me. St. John's Northwestern was invited to march in the Cinco de Mayo Parade in Puebla, Mexico, and I would lead them. We arrived in Mexico, and to my surprise, my face was on the side of the hotel! It was a very humbling experience, and I was proud to be there. It also meant that everyone was counting on me to be the face of the Academy, and in that vein, I had zero room for error—zero. The pressure was very real, and I felt every bit of it each day I served as First Captain and especially in leading a contingent of Cadets during a highly publicized event in another country.

Mexico Cinco de Mayo Parade, Spring 2005
Victor Trevino (Left) and President Jack Albert (Right)

Thursday, May 5th, 2005, came quickly, and we did what we were there to do. The Corps marched with pride, and we represented the Academy and the great United States of America with precision. As we traveled home from this unforgettable opportunity, I began to reflect deeply on this chapter in my life and all of the people who loved and cared about me. Who reached out with an open hand and said, "Come with me. Let me show you something."

We returned home and began cranking out final exams and inspections. My time at the Academy was coming to a close, and again, I reflected on my circumstances and how grateful I was to be standing here. It was just a few short years ago I was eating from dumpsters and running from the Department of Children and Family Services. Each passing day I would think about how hard my sister had it in Chicago while I was here marching in parades. She was there taking care of Jessy and Justin, trying to keep my mom from knowing where she lived. Anytime my mom figured out where Jodi's apartment was, she would either rob it with her crackhead friends or she would sit outside the door all night begging to let her in. The pressure remained very real, and I knew it would be time soon to pass the baton. It would be time for me to run the race. It would be on me to take care of Jessy, who was coming up on 11 years old, the age I was when I started to have problems in Chicago Public Schools. My heart beat to a near explosion, and my fists clenched with sweat every time I thought about this. Everything I was doing was a no-fail event. My meaning, my existence, and my purpose was to go home and relieve the burden from Jodi. To bear the weight of our family again. I had to finish this so that I could get home and do something about our family's future.

As we approached the end, we spent all week preparing to exit the Academy. We turned in computers, books, uniforms, etc. We closed accounts, signed forms, and did everything it took to close the last 4-6 years of our lives. For those of you who served or are serving in the military, think of clearing post and PCS'ing to your next duty assignment. We conducted parade rehearsals and barracks inspections and even took a day for ourselves to enjoy a "skip day" at Six Flags near Chicago. The mood was infectious. Everyone was ready to close this chapter and open the next, but at the same time, sad and nostalgic as we looked back at the last four years of living, eating, and breathing together in the halls of St. John's Northwestern.

Commencement weekend was upon us, only a week away, and it was more glorious than I could ever have imagined. Commencement weekend at St. John's Northwestern was not a run-of-the-mill high school graduation—Commencement here meant the most robust and grandiose pomp and circumstance. The events and ceremonies were each brilliantly coordinated and executed with the greatest of detail, all to honor those of us who just spent the last third of our lives at the Academy. Even more, it was meant to honor all those teachers, TACs, mentors, and staff whose shoulders we stood on to get there.

Parade Honoring Old Boys, Commencement
Weekend, June 2005

Four years had just passed since I walked through the gates of St. John's Northwestern. Reflecting on my journey, I can't help but feel an overwhelming sense of gratitude. I survived the unforgiving streets of Chicago, where hope was a scarce commodity. Now, I stood at the Flagpole, transformed, shaped by the lessons learned and the opportunities embraced. This school became my sanctuary, a place that nurtured my soul and propelled me toward a brighter future. I am grateful for the chance to rewrite my story, break free from the shackles of my past, and emerge as a resilient and capable individual. The doors that opened before me, leading me here, have forever changed my trajectory. And as I march forward, I carry within me the gratitude of a survivor, eternally grateful for the chance to rise above my circumstances and forge my own path.

St. John's Northwestern was the most pivotal time in my life, and I cannot ever fully express how much I love my old school. As I said before, this chapter truly deserves its own book. Hopefully, that will come someday, very soon. By way of Yael, through the mentorship of G, St. John's Northwestern saved my life. To this day, I stay involved as best I can, and I am now a sitting member of the Board of Trustees.

Leaving Chicago, Aug 2001   Commencement, June 2005

Lessons From the Halls of Discipline

Life Is a Sliding Door Event.

Life is a remarkable journey, often shaped by unexpected encounters and unpredictable events. It is like a series of sliding doors, each leading to a different path, presenting us with opportunities and challenges. My journey, from the streets of Chicago to becoming the First Captain at St. John's Northwestern, exemplifies the transformative power of sliding door events.

Imagine for a moment that your life is a long corridor with numerous sliding doors lining its walls. As you traverse this corridor, some doors slide open before you while others remain closed. Behind each door lies a potential future, a chance to change your trajectory, and a new chapter waiting to be written.

In the beginning, the only door opened to me was that of hardship and struggle. Growing up on the streets of Chicago, fighting for survival, and enduring the desperation of homelessness and dumpster-diving, I witnessed the harsh realities of life. It would have been easy to succumb to despair, to believe that this was the only door available to me.

But life is full of surprises, and sometimes, when we least expect it, a new door sliding door opens. Perhaps it was the chance encounter with Yael, the helping hand extended by G, or the spark of determination that led me to discover new opportunities. Regardless, I recognized the door was opening, and I didn't just walk through it. I jumped through it with Chicago grit and motivation. I saw my sliding door, and despite the pain that was leaving my sister to fend for herself and Jessy, I chose to enter a realm of possibility. I did so knowing that I might be better equipped to return home and pull them from the pain of those streets forever.

St. John's Northwestern became my sanctuary, a place where discipline, perseverance, and resilience became my guiding principles. The sliding door of opportunity opened wide, presenting me with the knowledge and skills needed to transcend my past. I embraced the challenges, committed to my personal growth, and dedicated myself to becoming the best version of myself in this life.

Reflecting on my journey, I again stand at a crossroads, surrounded by numerous sliding doors, each representing a future yet to be explored. The lesson in this metaphorical corridor of life is that every door we encounter holds the potential to change our lives. Some doors may be more challenging to walk through than others, requiring perseverance, courage, and determination. But remember, it is often the most difficult of sliding doors that lead to the most profound transformations.

My journey from the streets of Chicago to St. John's Northwestern is a testament to the resilience of the human spirit and the power of sliding door events. It teaches us that no matter where we start or what circumstances we face, we have the ability to shape our own lives. That we can, in fact, own our outcomes.

So, as you stand in the corridor of life, never forget the sliding doors that have brought you this far. Embrace the uncertainty, be open to new possibilities, and trust in your own strength. Remember that each sliding door represents a potential future waiting to be discovered. Step forward with courage and curiosity, for you never know what lies beyond the next sliding door.

Find Mentors Who Will Call Your Bullshit

Amidst the intricate weave of our existence, finding dedicated mentors who genuinely care and provide honest feedback is an invaluable gift. You must be intentional about finding these mentors and asking them to help you grow. Their guidance can illuminate your path, accelerate your growth, and transform your journey. Yet, it is not enough to stumble upon these mentors; you must actively nurture these relationships for maximum benefit and ultimate success.

True mentors are more than just advisors; they become our advocates, confidants, and sources of inspiration. They possess the wisdom and experience to guide us through the trials and tribulations of life, helping us avoid pitfalls and seize opportunities. However, finding such mentors requires intention and discernment.

When we encounter potential mentors, we must observe not only their expertise but also their empathy and genuine concern for our well-being. Solid mentors invest their time and energy in understanding our aspirations, challenges, and dreams. They see our potential and believe in our capabilities, even when we doubt ourselves. These are the Dr. Yael Cidon's and the SFC Brian Galarza's of the world. The once-in-a-lifetime LTC Jim Kebisek's. These are the Jon Bennett's and the Tim Shramek's. The Tim Vice's and Perry Siebers'. These are the 1SG James Brown's, the SGM Poe's, the MAJ Mayers, the Chief Schweiss', and the now CSM Derek Andrasic's. These are the kind of mentors who will tell you exactly what they think and will never hold a punch.

The responsibility does not solely rest on their shoulders. Once we identify these rare gems, we must actively cultivate and nourish these relationships. We must be open and receptive to their guidance, even when it challenges us or makes us uncomfortable. Honest feedback is not always easy to hear, but it is essential for growth.

To nurture these mentor relationships, we must show gratitude, respect, and reciprocity. We should seek opportunities to learn from them, whether through conversations, shadowing, or collaborative projects. Additionally, we should strive to be receptive and implement their advice, demonstrating that we value their wisdom and trust their judgment.

By embracing the power of true, meaningful mentorship and nurturing these relationships, we unlock a world of possibilities. We have to be unafraid to embrace these people. We must be fearless in our pursuit to learn from them and to ask for their help. The guidance, support, and honest feedback they provide will catapult you toward your goals and accelerate your personal and professional growth. So, I challenge you to seek out these mentors, cherish their wisdom, and cultivate relationships that become a catalyst for our ultimate success while building lifelong relationships.

Honor Those Whose Shoulders We Stand On

In our journey toward success, it is imperative that we never forget to honor those on whose shoulders we stand. Teachers, mentors, friends, and confidants—these extraordinary individuals have imparted nuggets of wisdom and provided the gentle nudges that propelled us to achieve amazing things.

Every achievement I celebrate today is built upon the foundation of their guidance, support, and belief in my potential. They selflessly shared their knowledge, time, and experiences, illuminating my path and instilling in me the confidence to pursue greatness.

Let us remember those who saw our potential before we did, who encouraged us when we doubted ourselves, and who celebrated our victories as their own. It is through their contributions that we have become the successful individuals we are today.

Honoring them is not merely expressing gratitude but actively paying it forward. We can pass on their invaluable teachings to others, becoming mentors and confidants for those who seek guidance on their own journey. By doing so, we become a part of the beautiful cycle of inspiration and empowerment that perpetuates growth and achievement.

As we rise, let us never forget the hands that lifted us. Let us acknowledge the profound impact they have had on our lives and extend our heartfelt appreciation. For it is through their influence that we have been able to reach new heights, and by honoring them, we ensure that their legacy lives on in our actions and the lives we touch.

Within the fabric of our achievements, let us weave threads of gratitude and remembrance for those who have shaped us. Their imprints on our journey will forever be cherished, serving as a reminder of the power of human connection, mentorship, and the unwavering support that propels us toward greatness. I hope, truly, that this book is seen as the most powerful symbol of gratitude I can show toward all those who helped weave the tapestry of my life. This is my thank you to each of you. I love you all.

CHAPTER 4—Ranger School: Leadership in the Face of Suffering

This book is all things leadership—I must emphasize this.

I hold it extremely important to understand the fundamentals explained through the lenses of what I think is the most capable body of growing leaders—The United States Army. Most skills of this caliber are essentially non-cognitive skills, however taboo the term has become. They are demanded among quality leaders—the thing about non-cognitive skills is that they're best learned through experience, mentorship, and example.

Certain qualities among solid leaders must be mastered completely. It's simple—you can get all "As" in school and still flunk life if you don't master non-cognitive skills, or as I call them, executive function skills. I will go into great detail in Chapter 8, explaining the history, research, and need for non-cognitive skill development. However, here, we talk about leadership.

First, we will pick up where we left off in Chapter 1 on self-awareness, which I think is central to leadership. Self-awareness can be defined as the ability to focus on ourselves, our actions, thoughts, and emotions and steer clear of internal standards. Self-aware people can gauge themselves in several areas like emotional management, self-evaluate and understand how others see them from their lens.

Simply put, highly aware people can expertly manage their actions, feelings, and thoughts rationally and objectively. This skill is rare since many people descend into emotionally charged interpretations and rationalizations of their circumstances. I know because I am one of those people. We have to be intentional about countering this natural tendency. Self-awareness is essential even for leaders who must do a course correction and help gauge their growth and effectiveness in whatever they do.

Interestingly, self-awareness is a journey in itself. The most self-aware people view themselves on a course toward mastery instead of arriving at a particular destination. As we accomplish more and more, we should remain focused on pursuing our personal best every day.

Self-Awareness is a Life Skill

Self-awareness is an essential tool that must be developed and inculcated. Previously, a stark absence of self-awareness may have been deemed a benign human trait. However, our world has become increasingly complex, so daily reflection has become more necessary if you haven't figured it out by now.

It (self-awareness) is a key driver in ensuring a more fulfilled life—and for good reason. We become more aware of our emotions, find it easier to manage them, and know how to operate better with friends, family, and work colleagues.

A Lack of Self-Awareness

An absence of self-awareness is nothing short of disastrous and counterproductive. It keeps people, leaders, and organizations on the ropes from exploring our full potential. We could be victims of tunnel vision and may not see much beyond our thoughts. There are cues of people who lack awareness and how they see things generally.

I was one of them.

A lack of awareness is one of many areas that hold us back, and I know damn well it held me back.

We don't know what we don't know—simply put, we cannot fix what we don't know is broken in the first place. The presence of self-awareness allows us to see our natural shortcomings and how they impact us and those around us. When we don't reflect and aren't intentional about knowing who we truly are, we will most likely overestimate our strengths and underestimate incoming challenges.

Leadership In Theory

Let's start with two simple definitions taught by the United States Army—what is leadership, and who is a leader? These two aren't necessarily the same, but they're closely aligned. Simply put, leadership is the action of leading a group of people or an organization toward achieving a common goal. A leader is anyone who, under an assumed role or assigned responsibility, inspires and influences people to accomplish organizational goals. Leaders motivate people inside and outside the chain of command to pursue actions, focus on thinking, and shape decisions for the organization's greater good. Sound leaders influence, operate, and improve; they influence others by providing purpose, direction, and motivation while working to achieve common goals and improve the organization.

Influencing: Getting people to do what is necessary through words and actions. This consists of three aspects—Purpose & Vision, Direction, and Motivation.

- Purpose and direction are relatively simple if you have a well-defined strategic and operational objective.

- Motivation, now that, is truly the essential thing in life. Without it, no dream, goal, or vision can ever come to fruition. Motivation is encapsulated by "The Why." Why are we doing this, and what does it mean for me? Understanding the why and tying it to some moral component within your peers and followers is critical to success.

Operating: These are our actions to influence others to accomplish our goals and set the stage for future endeavors. Operating is planning, preparing, executing, and assessing. If you will, this is the meat and potatoes, the bread and butter, the cat's meow, whatever you want to call it, you get me.

Improving: This is an invaluable investment made by capturing and acting on important lessons learned from ongoing and completed projects and goals. Some tools used to achieve this include after-action reviews (AARs), individual and group developmental counseling, and continuous improvement models.

Leadership Attributes and Competencies:

The United States Army has a fantastic model, as shown below, outlining a leader's various attributes and competencies. It's slightly out of date, but the fundamentals remain the same. A leader of character, presence, and intellectual capacity coupled with leading, developing, and achieving core competency is a potent recipe for repeated success in guiding cross-functional teams.

Leadership Requirements Model

Attributes
What an Army Leader Is

Core Leader Competencies
What an Army Leader Does

A Leader of Character
Army Values
Empathy
Warrior Ethos

A Leader with Presence
Military bearing
Physically fit
Composed, confident
Resilient

A Leader with Intellectual Capacity
Mental agility
Sound judgment
Innovation
Interpersonal tact
Domain knowledge

Leads
Leads others
Extends influence beyond chain of command
Leads by Example
Communicates

Develops
Creates a positive environment
Prepares self
Develops leaders

Achieves
Gets results

Leadership Styles:

Effective leaders stay flexible enough to adjust their leadership style and techniques to the people they lead.

I call this staying liquid. Pour water into a bowl and takes the shape of the bowl. Pour it into a glass, and it takes the shape of the glass. I firmly believe that every one of us has a different productivity method, so as leaders, we must pinpoint that method and capitalize on it. If you lead a team of ten, you have ten different personalities and ten different methods of productivity. Thus, it would be best if you adapted your style and approach for each unique individual until the team bonds under common values and goals. I'll take a brief moment to expand on the most common styles deployed by today's military.

Directing

☒ This style is leader-centered.

☒ One way street.

☒ Needs action now

☒ All outcomes must be correct.

Participating

☒ Centers on leader and team.

☒ Gets subordinate input.

☒ Leaders who have time or are dealing with experienced subordinates, their subordinates can opinionate and comment until a command decision is made.

☒ Then your response is, "Roger, that!" and you execute.

Delegating

☒ Here, leaders give subordinates authority.

☒ Leaders with highly trained and experienced subordinates foster a learning environment.

☒ The leader is ultimately responsible, but he still holds the subordinate responsible.

☒ They can delegate authority but not responsibility.

Transformational

☒ It allows you to take advantage of the skills and knowledge of experienced subordinates who may better understand how to accomplish the mission.

☒ Additionally, some level of exchange is taking place to positively transform (ideally) the leader, the subordinate, and the organization.

Transactional

☒ Motivation through rewards and punishments.

☒ Prescribes tasks in writing.

☒ Outlines all conditions for given tasks, benefits of success, and consequences.

Many factors heavily influence leadership styles. Some of those include training & education, experience & personality, situation & mission, subordinates, and flexibility.

*****

I've met and worked under some genuinely outstanding leaders and others not so much throughout my career. So, I've listed some of the top qualities of influential leaders I've noted over the years.

☒ **Listen to Understand:** This is among the essential qualities. Most often, we tend to listen to respond. We hear people speak words, and we immediately begin formulating a response before truly understanding the guts of their message. So, listen to understand to better help those who need you.

☒ **Tactical Empathy**: This one is a bit tricky as there are a couple of schools of thought here. I've heard arguments that you aren't empathetic if you have to deploy tactical empathy intentionally. On the other hand, tactical empathy as an intentional quality can be a tool to adapt to each unique person you are leading. I will expand on this more in Chapter 9.

☒ **Understand how to repurpose yourself & others:** By this, you can see problems and shift mentally and physically to address those issues easily. The same with others you work with or who may work for you—if you are close enough to your people, you know their strengths, weaknesses, and overall capabilities. You can repurpose people to either help them grow or to help finish a project more rapidly. I use a simple framework to make decisions about repurposing myself and others:

- ✓ Time available to solve the problem
- ✓ The complexity of the problem
- ✓ Capabilities of my team

If I have a new, highly complex problem and am short on time, I know which team member I will delegate to, or I may have to do it myself. If I have a new, highly complex problem and I have a considerable amount of time, I will ask someone who needs to develop in that area and give them a mentor.

Next to Yael, SFC Brian Galarza, a 20-year US Army Infantry Veteran, was and still is, in many ways, my greatest mentor. Just as Yael did, he made sure I understood the value of hard work and held me to very high and exhaustingly tough standards. It was G who first taught me to do it right the first time or do it again.

Of course, I will painfully revisit this philosophy in Ranger School.

As you read in Chapter 3, G was like a father to me and didn't hold any punches. His leadership style stood above all his peers and carried our team to multiple year-over-year successes. He knew how to care for us and exactly when and where we needed development. He was also one to light you up real quick if you chose not to carry your name well or the name of our unit, Foxtrot Company.

There are many ways to define leadership, *so don't take my descriptions as gospel.* We all come from different walks of life and see leaders differently. Some are very good, and some very bad. They all add to our toolbags, and it's your duty to decipher which tools to deploy or hold in strategic reserve.

Everything I have learned about leadership has come from only a few sources. Of course, I like to read many books, but that's just reinforcement. My foundation was laid at the Academy, but the house was built at The United States Army Ranger School. We can know all the rules about boxing, but that doesn't mean we're ready to get in the ring. That's how I think of the difference between leadership in theory and leadership in action —this is where I truly learned to embrace the human condition and navigate suffering. Ranger School was meant to prepare you to take the blows and successfully deliver your counter strategy.

Ranger School – Not for The Weak or Fainthearted.

After my time at the Academy, I started college at the University of Wisconsin – Milwaukee and simultaneously joined the Wisconsin Army National Guard. After some brief enlisted time as an Infantryman, I was convinced by my Commander at the time to go to Officer Candidate School (OCS). I was commissioned a Second Lieutenant and Branched Infantry. I was assigned to C Co., 1-128th, IN, and it was a blast. As I trained for Infantry Basic Officer Leader Course (IBOLC), I decided I needed to do something dramatic to set myself apart and confidently stand in front of my soldiers as their leader. I knew what I had to do.

These kinds of thoughts, when they hit you, give you goosebumps and make the hair stand up on the back of your neck. You know right then that it would be hard but extremely worthwhile. A few months before leaving for IBOLC, I went to my Company Commander and Battalion Commander (BC) and requested their support in sending me to Ranger School. My BC had me take the Ranger Physical Fitness Test (RPFT) on the spot, and I thought to myself, "Too easy," although I had never completed one before (this goes back to my discussion on having a gut check and knowing what you're capable of). Sure as shit, not only did I fail, but I tripped coming back from the 5-mile run—let's just say I had a bit of a run-in with the concrete, and it wasn't pretty. My face decided to introduce itself to the sidewalk in a not-so-graceful manner while my BC stood and watched it all unfold. Needless to say, I wouldn't be auditioning for any face-first acrobatics anytime soon, and I definitely hadn't convinced the Colonel I was ready. I had work to do. I needed a gut check and a concrete plan (pun intended) to achieve my goals.

Let me explain why.

The US Army Ranger School is considered one of the world's most demanding military training programs. It is designed to push soldiers to their physical and mental limits and prepare them for the rigors of combat. Historically, the graduation rate has been around 50%, but this does fluctuate. According to the Ranger Training Brigade, the graduation rate has dropped below 50% in recent years: 49% in 2008, 46% in 2009, 43% in 2010, and 42% in 2011. It was 48% in 2012 when I was there and has hovered at 49% recently.

Ranger School is divided into three phases—each phase lasts several weeks and focuses on different skills and terrain, as described below.

The Benning Phase is the first week of Ranger School, also known as RAP or Ranger Assessment Phase. This phase historically accounts for 60% of Ranger School failures. RAP comprises the RPFT, a 5-mile run over rolling terrain, a combat water survival assessment (CWSA), night/day land navigation, and a 2.1-mile buddy run. This is followed by the infamous Malvesti Obstacle Course and worm pit, demolitions and airborne refresher training, Army Combative, and a 12-mile forced march with a full combat load. The rest of the Benning Phase is conducted at Camp Darby, emphasizing the instruction and execution of Squad Combat

Operations. The Mountain Phase takes place at Camp Merrill near Dahlonega, Georgia. Its instructional focus is on military mountaineering tasks, mobility training, and techniques for employing a platoon for continuous combat patrol operations in a mountainous environment. Finally, the Florida Phase, sometimes dubbed Swamp Phase, is conducted at Camp Rudder, Eglin Air Force Base, Florida.

Swamp Phase focuses on the continued development of the Ranger student's combat arms functional skills. Upon arrival, students receive instruction on waterborne operations, small boat movements, and stream crossings. Practical exercises in extended platoon-level operations executed in a coastal swamp environment test the student's ability to operate effectively under extreme mental and physical stress conditions.

What sets Ranger School apart from other military training programs is the high-stress levels and sleep deprivation that soldiers experience throughout the course. The instructors are tough and demanding, and soldiers are constantly under pressure to perform—they must learn to work as a team and make split-second decisions in difficult and dangerous situations.

The attrition rate for Ranger School is high, with many soldiers dropping out due to injury, exhaustion, or failure to meet the rigorous standards. Those who do complete the program are considered some of the best soldiers in the Army and are highly respected for their skill, discipline, and mental toughness. Ranger School Graduates are considered to be the 1%.

The door prize was the coveted Black & Gold Ranger Tab. Less than 1% of the US Population is serving in the Military, and less than 1% of those serving are Ranger Qualified.

I knew it was the toughest school in the Army due to its intense physical and mental demands, high stress and sleep deprivation, and rigorous standards I'd have to meet to graduate. So, clearly, I needed to be ready—I needed to be more than ready. I was hyper-focused and dead set on being successful. No way could I come home to my soldiers and stand in front of them without that Black and Gold Ranger Tab.

I read books and sought mentorship and coaching. Everything I read or gleaned was to train for the cumulative effect. That is, wake up at 430 AM and do an RPFT. Eat breakfast, then play a soccer game. After that, eat lunch, then swim a couple of miles. Eat dinner, then do an 8-mile foot march. And lastly, do your homework. The technical and tactical components of Ranger School are also highly complex—from operation orders, weapon systems, combat capabilities, and so on. We had to show up as experts, or you would be dropped. This was no place for beginners or anyone who didn't put the work in beforehand.

I dropped everything in my life and trained for months leading up to IBOLC—I secured my BC's trust and confidence and got my orders for Ranger School. When I got to Ft. Benning, I immediately continued training. We had many weekends off during IBOLC, and I trained each one while others were hitting the bars and getting reprimands. I made it fun too. It was a lifestyle. I grabbed a buddy, and we drove to Mount Currahee, where the 506th Parachute Infantry Regiment, 101st Airborne, would train leading up to World War II.

Interestingly, "3 Miles Up and 3 Miles Down" was made famous by the highly acclaimed Band of Brothers book and series. We ran that mountain, one of the most challenging runs I've experienced. The impact on my knees coming down was painful, but I knew I would need this experience for the Mountain Phase. I did well at IBOLC, but another setback occurred as we were wrapping up our final Field Training Exercise (FTX)—I blew out my ankle. It was a night operation, and I was carrying a buddy on my back when my foot collapsed into some kind of sinkhole. "Fuck!" "I'm screwed. No way I will be ready in time for Ranger School." They had to cut my boot off to access my new softball of an ankle. "What a fucking mess," I thought.

Thankfully, I had met all of my physical and academic requirements for IBOLC and could graduate successfully on December 15th, 2011. Even more fortunate was that I had the holiday shut down in front of me. My report date was January 12th, 2012, so I had less than a month to recover before reporting to the Ranger School.

```
ORDERS 252-025                                    07 November 2011

SHARP JASON L          ▬▬▬▬▬      CO C 1ST BN 128TH INF
(PLEC0-249) 1350 E WILSON AVE          ARCADIA WI            54612

You are ordered to active duty for training (ADT) for the period shown plus
allowable travel time. Upon completion of the period of ADT unless sooner
released or extended by proper authority, you will return to the place where
you entered ADT and be released from such duty.

Period (TDY) : 12 January 2012   - 30 March 2012
Report to: Fort Benning, GA 31905
Reporting time/date: 1600 / 12 January 2012
Purpose: Ranger
```

Whom do you think I went to see when I got off the aircraft? You got it, the one and only who would always fix me up at a moment's notice—Yael! She put me back together and used an innovative infrared laser therapy to expedite the healing of my ankle. I couldn't start running again until the week before I reported, but I kept moving no less. I swam, biked, and focused on healing and building my technical knowledge. In all my life, I probably took care of myself the best during those 28 days—no way I would fail.

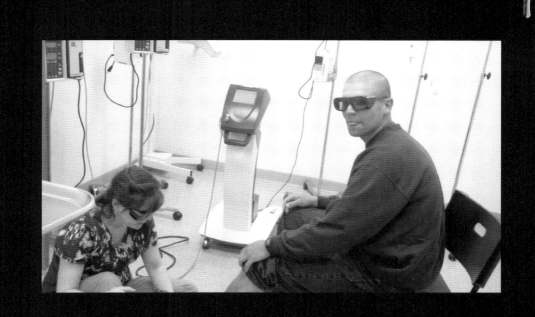

I reported for Ranger School on time and ready to rock. To set expectations, I have no intention of walking you through the daily struggles of Ranger School here but know this, it sucked. Whole books have been dedicated to the Ranger School experience alone. Next to having my first son, Xavier, Ranger School was the most worthwhile experience I had to date. I will walk you through the 30,000-foot view in order to shed light on the leadership and life lessons I picked up along the way. We were winter Rangers, given our start date, and winter Rangers suffered the most.

Benning Phase Week 1 – RAP was a beast. This was my first real experience of imposed stress which I think is truly one of the top takeaways of Ranger School. I arrived, and everything was calm. We got to our bunks but didn't stay there for long. There were lots of logistics and introductions etc. They held a shakedown pretty quickly, where we laid out all our gear to ensure we had no contraband—that would be an honor violation and an immediate drop. However, I didn't have any contraband, although they did take my deodorant! Still, we continued with preparation and orientation.

These Ranger Instructors smoked us every chance they got. Training for the cumulative effect was the right answer.

By the end of day 1, we were doing iron mikes around the training area until almost 01:00. Day 2 started at 04:30 with the RPFT. Incidentally, I crashed hard. My legs were thoroughly smoked (Noodles already). I woke up to a mostly empty bay. "Shit, I'm fucking late!" I hauled ass to toe the line in the training area only to realize I wasn't late at all. In fact, I was early. Most of the bay had packed up and quit overnight.

Here we go.

RPFT went well despite being wrought with anxiety. I ran a little over a 32-minute 5 mile and crushed the pull-ups. We were off to Ranger Stakes and CWSA next. Ranger Stakes is where they test your expert knowledge of weapons and communications equipment. I put in the work beforehand, so this requirement was reasonably easy for me. The CWSA nearly got me. It busted up my nose pretty good as I dropped from the zip line at a high rate of speed—this reminded me of when I made contact with pavement in front of my BC. "Well, shit, I signed up for this." I watched as Ranger Students nearly drowned and dropped out of the course. We lost another 25 or so at this event.

We lost several more as we moved through the day with land navigation and other requirements. At least we were still eating in the chow hall. At the end of Day 2, we were doing combative in the pit through the early morning hours. Day 3 kicked off with the 5-mile individual run, of which I was considerably slower. I came in at 36 minutes. I lost 4 minutes overnight, it seemed. We continued through RAP with more Ranger Stakes and demolition training. We also spent some time getting ready for the forced march, adding as much water and weight to your load as possible. By early evening we kicked off the buddy run, which takes you right into that son of a bitch Malvesti. It was during RAP that I first learned of the 40% rule.

The 40% Rule

The 40% rule is a concept that is often associated with Army Rangers and the Special Operations community. It states that when your mind and body are telling you that you're done, that you have reached your limit and cannot go any further, you have actually only reached 40% of your potential. We use it as a mental strategy to push through extreme physical and mental challenges.

The idea behind the 40% Rule is that humans are capable of much more than we think. Our minds and bodies have built-in mechanisms telling us to stop when we are tired or in pain to protect us from injury or harm. When we feel like we have reached our limits, we are actually experiencing a mental barrier rather than a physical one. However, in situations such as Ranger training or other high-stress, high-performance situations, pushing past that initial urge to stop will be necessary to succeed. We can tap into the remaining 60% of our potential by pushing through this barrier and continuing to push ourselves.

While the 40% rule is not scientifically proven, it can be a useful mental tool for those looking to push themselves beyond their perceived limits. It can help build mental toughness and resilience and be applied in various areas of life, including fitness, work, and personal relationships. It encourages people to push past their perceived limits and tap into the additional 60% of their potential that they may not even realize they have.

Even though the 40% Rule is often associated with the Special Operations community, it can apply to anyone trying to achieve a goal or overcome a challenge. We can achieve things we never thought possible by pushing ourselves beyond what we think we are capable of.

Darby Phase

So, we completed our forced march and made it to Camp Darby. Immediate medical evaluation and foot checks before we had any chow. I remember being directed from the med bay to the back of the LMTV for chow. I was so exhausted as I walked with my Ranger buddy to find chow. "You pumped for some calories!?" I asked. Calories were the new currency in life, by the way (I'll get to that soon). We arrive at the back of the LMTV. To our surprise, the RIs dumped the mermite into the dirt right there in front of us in all its glory. It was a slosh of Spaghetti and red sauce mixed with that forever memorable Georgia clay. We flocked to the dirt like everyone else, all of our humanity was out the window now. It didn't take long before they made us stop and move out.

I will never forget what happened next. On our way back to the bleachers, double timing, of course, I had imagined that I was holding my Ranger Buddy's hand and we were doing "Skip-to-my-Lou" like a couple of kids. "Shit, I'm hallucinating already…get it together, Jason!". As we arrive at the bleachers, I wake from the hallucination, and I'm chewing on sand. It was damn good too. Eventually, we came to call this mental effect "droning." That day, we would painfully navigate the legendary Darby Queen Obstacle Course—it was a gut-punching 2-mile long course that would break you off many times over.

The Darby Queen Obstacle Course is a challenging and physically demanding course designed to test the strength, endurance, and agility of United States Army Rangers. The course includes various obstacles such as walls, ropes, monkey bars, balance beams, and other challenges that require mental and physical toughness. The course is used to assess the readiness of Army Rangers and develop and maintain their physical and mental conditioning. It is named after Colonel William Darby, the founder of the Army Rangers, and is considered one of the toughest obstacle courses in the world. In my opinion, the weaver is one of the toughest obstacles on this course. We must navigate the obstacle by "weaving" over-and-under bars set at an incline on the way up to the peak. And then, we have to do it on a decline on the way down.

Trust me when I say this—it will break you.

Following the Darby Queen, we initiated squad-level operations orders and in or planning shacks, and we're off on patrol shortly after. Unfortunately, day after day and night after night was the same. We'd wake up around 0500 to start our 15-minute foot checks. They'd give us our breakfast MRE, which we had to finish by the time foot checks were over. They always made us give back the candy. If you were caught with candy, it was an honor violation, and you were out. So, good luck getting a brigade-level commander to recommend you back to the course.

Right away, you learn the hard lesson that you must pay attention to all things simultaneously, whether in charge or not. You listen to understand (always). There is no room or luxury in just following the leader. At a moment's notice, you could be selected to take over the mission, and you better know what's going on, or you were a "NO-GO." You can only afford a single "NO-GO," no matter how many times you got selected to lead a patrol. In other words, the 'fuckening' is real, and you need to be on your "A" game every minute of every hour of the day.

We wrap up foot checks, chuck our MRE trash, execute priorities of work, and await our briefing, which usually happens around 0615. From there, we start planning and rehearsals. On a good day, our patrol would SP around 1300 and spend most of the afternoon and early evening conducting movement. If things went well, which they rarely did, we'd initiate patrol base operations around 2000 and initiate reconnaissance of the objective. Usually, the RIs would change over leadership a couple of times to keep us on our toes. Depending on the mission and the results of our recon efforts, actions on the objective would kick off around 2200. When the mission was complete, we'd make our way back to the patrol base and initiate security plans and priorities of work. Once everything was accounted for, weapons clean, and work priorities had been completed, we'd get our dinner chow around 0100. If things go well, we we'd rack out with a sleep and security plan by 0200. So if you do the math, we get our breakfast and dinner chow within a few hours of each other.

I was finally selected to lead a patrol. Of course, I was in the back of the pack carrying the M240B but still monitoring my map and compass. I knew where we were and where we were going. RI approaches a fellow Ranger Buddy, Z, next to me and demands, "Show me where we are on the map. 30 seconds.". That was a "NO-GO" for him. He turns to me and demands the same. I responded, and he ever so softly said, "You're in charge now. Direct a halt and re-group. You have 15 minutes to move out." I assumed I was right about our location, but that wasn't necessarily a "GO." Not only was I right about where we were, but I had to earn my "GO" by leading from the front. I was simultaneously terrified and excited—though I was tired, hungry, wet, and dirty. But I was motivated and hungry—the kind of hungry that matters. Hungry to prove myself. Proving that I could stay in the fight and accomplish the mission.

I was successful that day, and so too was my Ranger Buddy, Z, in the coming weeks. We returned to Camp Rogers and prepared to move out to Mountain Phase in Dahlonega. We couldn't call home, but it was satisfying enough to take our first shower in almost three weeks.

At Darby, I began to lock in my understanding of what resilience meant. During the RAP/Darby Phase, you had no choice but to bounce back, or you were out—it was that simple. I defined resilience back in Chapter 1 in detail, but here you can see how important it is if you want to achieve your goals. The ability to recover quickly from setbacks, shock, injuries, adversity, and stress while maintaining the mission and organizational focus is paramount in military operations and to successful outcomes in your personal and professional life.

Mountain Phase

We arrived at Camp Merrill at midday, and the barracks were shit. "It was nicer than being in the elements," I thought. I later discovered that we would only sleep one night in those barracks. This would be the day we came off the Chattahoochee Mountains. Planning shacks, Mount Yonah, and patrol bases were home for us. We initiated mountaineering training, and I remember the smell of delicious blueberry pancakes wafting through the air each morning. We'd eagerly make our way to the chow hall, ready to indulge in the scrumptious breakfast we could smell so perfectly. Do you know how they say dogs smell like humans see? Yea, that was us at Ranger School. Everyone could smell a ketchup packet being opened across the parking lot.

We did our pull-ups, recited the Ranger Creed, and made our bellies ready to take that first bite. As should have been expected, the RIs wouldn't let us touch a single fucking blueberry pancake. It was crushing! Eventually, we realized that the blueberry pancakes were not meant to be eaten—they were a test, a rite of passage, designed to weed out the weak and the faint of heart.

While Mountain Phase started with blueberry pancakes, my one true memory from the first week will stick with me forever. My Ranger buddies still laugh at me to this day. We made our way off the wet rock and back to the bleachers for instruction. The wet rock is where they simulated the harshest of military mountaineering conditions, and it was a hell of a day.

It was midday, cold as shit, and I could barely feel my fingers. I was in the top left seat of the bleachers, and there were no guard rails of any kind. I felt myself fading, but I knew I couldn't fall asleep. You get caught racking out mid-day, and it was a major minus. Three minors accounted for a major, so three major minuses meant you were out of the course.

My Ranger buddy kept kicking me, and I was thankful. I made sure he knew it too. It didn't matter that much, though, cause gravity is a bitch, and it got me this day. No shit, I fell asleep, rolled right off those bleachers, and smacked the mix of dirt and rock. They say, "God made dirt, and dirt doesn't hurt," but this dirt will bust your ass! It was epic, and everyone erupted in laughter—even the RI. The thing about laughter is that it just may get you off the hook.

I watched 'The Simpsons' growing up, and at that moment, I remember Homer saying to Marge, "Hehe, made you laugh. I'm off the hook!" I made it out clean that day and was one lucky SOB. I thanked my Ranger buddies for having my back.

Mountain Phase was tough on everyone. Many of my Ranger Buddies didn't make it. I saw boot soles being ripped off and feet that looked like ground beef. The absolute worst was when someone dropped their ruck, and we would watch it roll down hundreds of feet in epic slow motion. It was demoralizing, but the lesson was; to take care of your equipment and always maintain focus.

We went through Yonah and probably over a hundred miles in the Chattahoochee mountains. The terrain destroyed us all—more some than others. One of my Ranger buddies hit a bad branch and went down. He fell probably 50 feet, and that was it for him. Incidentally, Yonah took a couple of us with him along the way. We learned to sidestep and pinpoint every foot movement we made. It was pivotal to survival in mountain operations.

The cold was unbearable. It really beat the shit out of us. We carried all our cold-weather gear but were never allowed to use it. During Mountain Phase, I learned what a "man-ferno" is. You tend to learn all the tricks of the trade to keep warm in what seems like a single night. We fought winds like you couldn't imagine too. All the while, we were soaking wet with no real way to dry off. So, the wet socks you started with were those you finished with. It was a shit show, and all you could do was endure and stay in the fight or risk a "NO GO." As each patrol passed, I remember getting colder and colder—the cold you never really returned from. Some guys were huddled in sleeping bags while the rest of us kept the man-ferno going.

As we suffered the challenges of the mountains, we had to remain focused on the mission set. Movement was the key to staying warm, and reaching our objectives was critical to getting through this phase and one step closer to graduating. Cross-country movement in the Tennessee Valley Divide was the usual path, but in this phase, we'd also parachute into small drop zones or air assault into mountain-side landing zones. The key to success here was commitment and physical-mental stamina. It took everything I had to get through this phase, and I was fortunate to pass each of my patrols to get there.

Our last night in the mountains was the worst, but we knew it was almost over. It was freezing cold to the point where our bones hurt. We stopped caring eventually and looked forward to the next foot check cause we knew we were done.

It was 2300.

"Holy fucking shit!"

We made it to our patrol base grid and initiated priorities of work and the security plan. Everyone was smoked, and I could tell no one was actually paying attention to our surroundings, including me. It was almost midnight now. We were tired and ready to shower. Most of us were looking forward to the phone call we expected to make when we returned to the barracks the next night.

Sure as shit, a fucking truck comes hurling toward us.

"Ambush, ambush, ambush!" we screamed. "Take cover!" "Heavy weapons on me, 1st squad flank to the north", commanded the platoon leader. This fucking truck spearheaded our formation, and we opened fire like you couldn't imagine. We were preparing to approach and take the driver down. What happened next is a memory I will cherish forever.

We approached the truck, "What the fuck is that?" I said as my Ranger buddy screamed at the driver, "Get the fuck out! Get the fuck out now!" The driver puts his hands out the window, "I'm unarmed!" Our platoon leader approached the truck and confirmed what I had seen just moments before. The fucking truck bed was stacked with MRE boxes, wood, and no shit, a fucking burn barrel.

We fucking stumbled upon a Golden Walk. I thought this was a thing of the past, but we're no shit in the middle. It was amazing. On his last mission as a Ranger Instructor, the RI chose us. We couldn't have been luckier. He tossed each squad a box of MREs, we built the most amazing fire you could ever imagine, and he shared his wisdom with us for the next hour. It was truly an epic night. He released us from pulling security and directed us to get a good night's rest. You couldn't possibly imagine how important this was to our spirits.

The following day was operations as usual, but we were rested, well fed, and all had shit-eating grins. I remember having a little extra time to sit for a minute and shave while looking over the mountain—it was bliss. We got our last brief, initiated planning, and moved out to conduct our final mountain phase operation. This time when we exfil, we'd be heading to the barracks.

We arrived back at Camp Merrill around 1800 and initiated priorities of work. We accounted for all sensitive items, cleaned our weapons, licked our wounds, and prepared for what can arguably be the worst and best thing about Ranger School. Peer Evaluations. As with each phase, we would spend a couple of hours on the last night rating each other. Generally, the bottom man was either recycled (forced to repeat the phase) or dropped from Ranger School altogether.

Fortunately for us, none of this would start until after we finally got some hot dinner chow. We were so fucking excited. Like a bunch of school kids giggling on the playground. We lined up, did our pull-ups, and recited the Ranger Creed.

"No. Fucking. Way!"

The food of the Gods was before us. We inhaled those blueberry pancakes. It was like a magical act of breakfast sorcery—we had Blueberry pancakes for dinner. With each breath, the stack of pancakes disappeared before our eyes as if they were never there. It's like we had a superpower that turned pancakes into a delicious cloud of happiness, filling your lungs with the Breakfast Gods' warm, buttery, blueberry aroma. One moment you're staring at a mountain of pancakes, and the next moment you're left wondering if you actually ate them or if they just vanished into thin air. It's a beautiful and mysterious phenomenon that most will probably never truly understand. Now I look back on the blueberry pancakes with a mix of horror and nostalgia but knowing I had survived one of the toughest challenges of my life. The real quest now was, "Would I survive peer evals?

We spent the next couple of hours cranking through briefings and peer evaluations. It was painful. How do you rate your team, and how can you rank someone last? Sometimes it was easy. Some teams had real sandbaggers or "Spotlight Rangers," as we called them. Those were too easy. But most of the time, it was excruciatingly painful to get through and always a bad night. Thankfully, I made it through. A couple of my close Ranger buddies didn't. They were on the list to repeat Mountain Phase.

Mental Toughness: Leading with Grit

What does it mean to be mentally tough? To be mentally tough is to resist the urge to give up in the face of failure, to maintain focus and determination in pursuit of one's goals, and to emerge from adversity even stronger than before. In Chapter 1, I laid a brief foundation on mental toughness so you'd have a framework to reference when reading this chapter. Wrapping up Mountain Phase and moving on to Swamp Phase seems like the right time to talk through the lessons learned at this point.

Mental toughness begins when a person takes notice of specific and unique thoughts going through their mind. However, we don't personally identify with those thoughts and feelings, so each thought is new and scary. A person is not born with mental toughness. It is an acquired skill learned over time and comes through conditioning the mind in a certain way. For me and those of us born into suffering, we're at an advantage. We're ahead of the game in that respect. If you want to survive, you have to be mentally tough. Chicago instilled in me the initial resilience I needed, but it was during Mountain Phase that I truly fortified my mental fortitude.

The principle for shaping and strengthening mental toughness and mental strength requires commitment and self-awareness. Generally, mentally tough individuals have a higher track record of accomplishment than those who are mentally sensitive. This is why the former will also enjoy a higher sense of contentment. I learned much about Mental Toughness from the Army and Ranger School, but I like to cite a well-known model developed by Professor Peter Clough of the University of Huddersfield in the UK.

The 4 Cs of Mental Toughness

<u>Control</u>: This implies the degree of control you think you have over life, including emotions and a key sense of purpose. The control component could be self-esteem. So, when self-esteem is high, a person is comfortable in their own skin and has a sound sense of whomever they are like.

Furthermore, the person is well in control of their emotions and less likely to reveal their emotional state to others. Incidentally, such a person is less distracted by other people's emotions. So, if people exert less control on this scale, they feel like things happen to them and exert less control over their life's circumstances.

<u>Commitment</u>: This implies a degree of personal focus and reliability. If a person ranks high on the commitment scale, then such a person sets goals consistently and accomplishes them without any distractions. A high level of commitment shows that a person is sound in a familiar setting, and the habits accompanying it results in success.

If a person is low on the commitment scale, then such people have issues setting and prioritizing goals. And that is not all. Such individuals will also have trouble adapting to routines and cultivating habits indicative of success. Thirdly, such a person will also be distracted by other or competing priorities.

When combined, commitment and control comprise the resilience portion of the mental toughness premise. However, it makes sense, considering overcoming setbacks requires a certain life control and knowing oneself. Secondly, this requires focus and a sound ability to cultivate habits and hard targets to return on track and soldier along the chosen path.

Challenge: This implies the degree to which a person is driven and adaptable. If a person is on a large scale of a challenge, they are driven to achieve their best and accommodate challenges as they come, adapting as things shape up. They also take adversity as an opportunity instead of a threat. So such people are agile and flexible for the most part. Conversely, if a person has a low ability for challenges, they see any development as a threat and avoid challenging or novel situations from fear of failure.

Confidence: This signifies the degree to which a person believes in their ability to be capable and productive. People with high confidence will have a high self-belief and believe they can influence others.

If a person scores high in confidence, they can complete tasks successfully and view issues as temporary hurdles. Any hurdles along the way do not deter them since it strengthens their resolve and helps maintain their routine like before. Conversely, if a person has a low confidence scale, they can be put off easily by setbacks and fail to follow through on their goals and challenges. Secondly, they will also have less influence over others due to low confidence.

This showcases a person's ability to pinpoint and seize an opportunity and look at situations as opportunities for self-growth and self-development. It opens the horizons and prospects of a person by adopting this approach. It will make sense only when a person is confident, has faith in their abilities, and finds engagement easier with others. So it should be no surprise that such people will translate their challenges and setbacks into successful and beneficial outcomes.

The United States Army's performance model summarizes all of this rather concisely. We use this process to build and strengthen mental toughness within our formations. It revolves around five themes. I relied heavily on each of these to get through Mountain Phase and Ranger School as a whole.

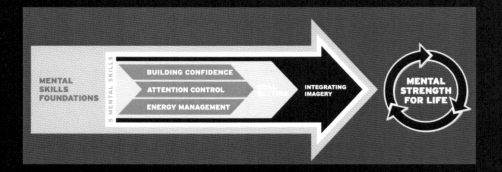

- *Building Confidence*
- *Attention Control*
- *Energy Management*
- *Goal Setting*
- *Integrating Imagery*

Mental toughness was paramount to getting through Mountain Phase, especially for those who didn't make it. If anyone says it differently, they're full of shit. We wrapped up peer evals and spent time consoling our Ranger Buddies, who were dropped or recycled. And yes, getting dropped or recycled is soul-shattering. These Rangers were deeply and profoundly impacted emotionally, mentally, and even spiritually. They felt lost, overwhelmed, and utterly broken. The grief and pain that followed were all-consuming, leaving them feeling like they had lost a part of themselves. The sense of loss and emptiness was so profound that the rest of us could feel it in our bones. Yet we were the ones who peered them out. They felt totally helpless, with a biblical sense of fear and uncertainty about the future.

Their sense of identity, purpose, and place in the world was under question. These moments leave us questioning our beliefs, values, and the meaning of our existence. The process of healing from such an experience is long and arduous, but we never had that kind of luxury around here. It was brutal, but now was the time to be mentally tough. Now was the time to resist the urge to give up—to maintain focus and determination. To emerge from this experience even stronger. They knew their job and what had to be done next.

We knew ours.

When we returned to the barracks and lined up for our first phone call home, it was 0130 in the morning. Most of the guys who didn't make it never got in line to make a call home, and I don't blame them. No one answered for me, but that was all right. I just needed to stay focused and make it through Swamp Phase now. Those of us Airborne qualified would travel by bus to a nearby airfield and conduct an airborne operation, parachuting into Swamp Phase. The rest of us, non-airborne, were bused to Eglin Air Force Base to kick off this final phase.

Swamp Phase

We arrived at Eglin and went to the barracks for a re-fit and load out. Many of us talked of our brothers left behind to suffer through Mountain Phase again. It was a gut punch every time I thought of B and T—they were good buddies, and T really suffered. From the beginning, I remember him struggling with a busted Achilles and working twice as hard as the rest of us to accomplish the mission. That man was one tough son of bitch and pretty hard to forget.

As with the start of Mountains, we'd only spend a couple of nights in the barracks. Nothing mattered at this point because we were about to hit an Air Force Dining Facility (DFAC). Air Force DFACs were top of the line—a real Taj Mahal. We kicked off Swamp Phase training necessary skills the first couple of days. Skills that would keep us alive. We began technique training for small boat operations and expedient stream crossing techniques. Before moving out on patrols, we trained the skills to survive and operate in a rainforest/swamp environment. We learned how to deal with reptiles and how to determine the difference between venomous and non-venomous snakes. As can be expected, RIs here were specially trained experts who taught us not to fear wildlife.

We set out on our first patrol, and it was so flat that we were lost immediately. No terrain association opportunities here, so we had to be hyper-focused. We sometimes had to navigate with the sun, moon, and stars. I could tell this phase was about how sharp your mind could operate given the stress and challenging circumstances. In this phase, if you messed up, you suffered for it. RIs would just switch out every 6-8 hours while we kept going around the clock. If you got your grid wrong, they'd let you walk mile after mile in the wrong direction until you figured it out and had to course correct. In other words, if you were in charge, there was no room for failure if you didn't want to be peered out. It was that serious.

Getting to the fight is one thing. We often forget that we still have to fight when we get there. We learned this in the most painful ways on our first patrol. We entered to clear a compound, and there they were. Opposition forces (OPFOR) are standing by to attack and fight you literally. We were in all-out fights day after day in Swamp Phase. Better stay sharp, or you were an immediate "NO GO."

Many think Swamp Phase is the most physically and mentally demanding portion of Ranger School. It was definitely Mountain Phase for me, but we all suffered differently. Training in the swamplands tests the endurance, teamwork, and leadership abilities of each of us—every minute of every day. We navigated through thick vegetation, muddy waters, and swarms of insects. Each patrol was more intense than the previous, often carrying heavier and heavier packs while trudging through waist-deep water and thick mud. The extreme weather conditions, including oppressive heat and sudden rainstorms, were icing on the cake. I could always handle the heat and rain better than blistering cold and a blanket of wind.

Despite these challenges, we're always expected to maintain composure or risk everything. We did exactly that—we risked life, limb, and eyesight daily for our families, the Army, and fellow Ranger Buddies—some of us more than others. One of our Ranger Buddies was getting sick, which worsened daily.

If you recall, back in Darby Phase, I said that calories became the currency of life. It got real in Swamp Phase—we traded calories constantly for the craziest shit. Guys would give three hundred calories to carry ammo or heavy weapons. You name it, and it was for sale. Calories accepted. It was like an auction floor whenever we got to break open our MREs. It was hilarious, fun, and a total shit show all at the same time. Little did we know that our calories would become the most important asset for our team.

"What the hell is wrong with you? You ok, man? Get up!". This guy was fucked. He was sick as hell and could barely walk. We hid it from the RIs as we tried to figure out what to do. We carried all his equipment, shielding him from as much work as possible. He begged us not to let the

RIs see him. He had already exhausted all his sick time. We're allotted about 6 hours, as far as I can remember.

We knew what had to be done.

At the patrol base that night, we pulled the squad together and decided to take the bullet to save him. We were all ok with suffering a little bit more so that he didn't have to. We had to help our Ranger buddy heal and make it through graduation. Each squad member would donate half their allotted calories daily to our Ranger buddy. This was a no-fail event. We did this for the next three days until he was at least ambulatory. Those three days were unbelievably difficult for our team but equally necessary, and we all knew it. We were not leaving a man behind.

We made it through patrol and after patrol successfully. Our minds remained sharp despite the chaos, lack of food, and sleep deprivation. The droning was real but wasn't enough to keep us from earning our tab. We were given a new mission toward the end of the Swamp Phase—a downed helicopter. Our mission was to rescue the crew and recover its cargo. I was the platoon leader.

We planned our approach route, recon, actions on the objective, and exfil. Everything mainly went to plan, if you get me. Those of you who know, know. No plan survives first contact, and this was exactly that. We hit the objective, rescued the downed pilots, and began to exfil. We were hit by another unknown force who took us by surprise. We re-grouped, established defensive positions, and countered the attack. We successfully drove back to the opposition (OPFOR) and thought we were ready to return to base. As we swept the area to recover intel, we came across a couple of enemy vehicles I had the team thoroughly search.

All was good and well until an RI screamed, "ENDEX!". This means "end exercise" for whatever the training event was. He gathered us all around and immediately barked, "Front leaning rest position, move!" which is the push-up position. I had no idea what the fuck was going on, "we completed the mission," I thought to myself. "What the fuck are they doing?".

"One of you is a piece of a shit liar! One of you stole from me!" the RI yelled. I jumped to the position of attention, and I screamed right back, "No fucking way, sir! My team would never!" After all we have been through, there was no way any of our guys would risk it now.

The RI countered and said, "One of you stole my fucking Snickers, and half my hotdogs are gone! You're all fucked!" he screamed, "This will be an honor violation for you all!"

While I didn't believe his words, I still had to get the crew together rapidly for a shakedown. I lined them all up, and we checked pockets, packs, etc. Remember when I compared a Ranger student's nose to that of a dog? It was time this skill came in handy for us. We checked each other, smelling each other's breath and checking teeth. We would have immediately been able to identify who the culpable one was.

"Nothing, sir! It wasn't us," I said.

He didn't care and went on to smoke the shit out of us. OPFOR was sometimes a recycled Ranger student. "It had to be them," we all mumbled. Didn't matter because we'd be the ones to pay the price. We called them the "Fucking Hot Dog Bandits." Whomever the hell they were, they fucked us real good.

The rest of our time in Swamp Phase was total shit—RIs didn't trust our team, so it was awful. However, the inevitable happened. It turned out we were all recycled, and it was a total gut punch. They don't tell you a specific reason when you're recycled, just that, "You didn't meet the standard." We all knew, however. It was a total disaster, but we had no choice. It was one of the most painful phone calls to my Battalion Commander.

"How do I tell him that I failed?" I thought.

When I look back on it all now, recycling Swamp Phase was one of the best things that happened to me. First of all, both my Ranger Buddies who recycled Mountain Phase were going to catch up with me. It was a comforting thought as each day passed, given that everyone felt like shit around the clock. We trained and got ready to receive the next Mountain Phase crew.

You'd be indispensable to your team if you played your cards right. We've all been through the wringer once (twice for some), and our experience was gold. Everyone relied on us to lead the way—period. Even better, we knew how to manage our calories, which we no longer cared about. We gave away every calorie to those who needed it most. We wanted all our brothers to make it this time.

We had to tighten up real quick. The Mountain Phase crew would arrive soon. I was looking forward to seeing my Ranger buddies. Honestly, I missed the hell out of 'em. Sure as shit, there they were, so I couldn't have been happier then. B & T were recycled in Mountain Phase, and I recycled Swamp Phase. It's almost like it was meant to be. As a Swamp Phase recycle, I was in the best position to carry everyone through, and I devoted myself to giving and being there for others. So did every one of my recycle buddies.

Sure, those who gave up our calories and sleep suffered more, but our return on investment was priceless. I look back now and realize that this experience truly reinforced the concept of learning to suffer with eyes wide open. First, we'd lock in every lesson from Swamp Phase as true experts. I remember it didn't matter how tired or hungry I was. The RIs could throw any problem at me, and I felt like I could handle it, "Can do easy, sir!" It was indeed a fantastic feeling. We suffered, but we became experts in our craft. It was both muscle memory and liquid, enabling us to make decisions and support the mission.

Second, we learned what many of us now call tactical patience. The concept is relatively simple, however. It is the struggle between decisiveness and knowing when to take a knee. Yes, it is vital to be decisive and act at times, but not every situation requires this. Learning to suffer with your eyes wide open will help you to understand the difference. Know when you play your hand and when you are to fold. Know when to take the tactical

As I worked my way through Swamp Phase for the second time, I took every lesson I could. It is hard to remember exactly where we were, but I remember my final patrol. It was 0700, shitting rain, and we'd barely finished foot checks. RI walks up to me and says, "Ranger Sharp, you're the platoon leader. Get your shit together, gather your team, and report for briefing in 10 minutes".

I needed this "GO."

I remember taking a few steps into the brush. I sat on a sopping wet log, and I cried. I was ferociously ready to get my final "GO." More importantly, I missed my family deeply but was ready to prove I could do it. I was ready to go to work. My eyes were wide fucking open, and nothing would stop me from accomplishing the mission.

Our mission involved movement to contact, patrol base operations, and initial reconnaissance for our final mission. We drudged through challenging, swampy terrain, fought off minor OPFOR assaults, and finally reached our patrol base near the beach. Our recon mission was critical to planning our follow-on mission that evening.

This would be our capstone mission for both Swamp Phase and Ranger School. It would be a predawn amphibious assault across the Gulf of Mexico onto Santa Rosa Island. We began recon and assault preparations around 1600 hours. Our intelligence collection would give us the necessary information about the island while our briefing identified the mission's objectives. We knew what to do and how to do it. Every unit began planning and rehearsing for a major coordinated assault.

We embarked later that evening on what would be the most challenging mission of Ranger School. The assault on Santa Rosa Island was a complex operation involving multiple stages. We had to move across the open ocean in our zodiac boats navigating through waves and swells to reach the island. This required every ounce of skill and energy we had left. Grit, mental toughness, and resilience were critical to maintaining our focus and stamina in these challenging conditions.

We finally hit the beach around 0400 and were immediately met by defenders. To reach the objective, we had to fight ashore and go through dense vegetation and swampy terrain. We moved quietly and quickly through hostile territory to get into position for the assault itself.

We engaged in close-quarters combat with enemy forces for over an hour to locate and secure our high-value target, a known drug lord.

To date, one distinct memory that stands out to me is running along the gulf coast beach around 0100 toward our zodiac boats. Teams were emplacing heavy weapons in support by fire positions along the beach while also preparing to receive the main effort back from actions on the objective. I remember looking up at how vividly bright and crystal clear the moon was in the night sky—it was so beautiful and quiet that I could hear myself think.

We were successful that morning. Completing this mission brought with it an incredibly satisfying feeling. We're done, barring any stupid fuck ups. The feeling of accomplishment was unparalleled compared to anything I'd done in the past. It was the moment when all our hard work, dedication, and perseverance culminated in a tangible result. The sense of pride and accomplishment remains truly unforgettable and serves as a source of daily motivation for me to tackle new challenges with the same level of enthusiasm and dedication.

And that's what Ranger School is about.

We made it back to the barracks and couldn't believe our eyes. No shit, there were stacks of Oreo cookie pies everywhere. We destroyed pie after fucking pie, and it was epic. Peer evals kicked off later that day— you know how the story goes. Some of us made it. Some of us didn't. We got our shit together, cleaned our gear, and returned to Ft. Benning for graduation. I'll tell you what, though, oreo cookie pie remains on my menu of available offerings at home.

Our Tab Pinning took place during an elaborate ceremony at Victory Pond. We'd pin the coveted black-and-gold Ranger Tab on our left shoulder and henceforth permanently worn above our unit patch.

T and I After Pinning Our Tabs

In full transparency, I left Ft. Benning that afternoon and went to a local Waffle House, where I devoured probably ten peanut butter waffles. I vomited for almost an hour after that. It was awful and amazing all at the same time. I hope you get a chance to experience that someday too!

When I started this chapter, I said this book is about leadership. The lessons I took from Ranger School are forever and continue to guide me to this day. Any chance I had to reflect, I did exactly that and wrote. It was during Ranger School that I truly began to journal. I wanted to remember all of it and make sure I could pass on my lessons to my Soldiers, my children, and anyone who would listen.

I developed my leadership philosophy from these lessons using my journal notes to remind me of "the why" and to fortify the need. I will briefly describe them here but expand in great detail later in the book.

My Leadership Philosophy

✓ Leaders who reach the end of their rope have no choice but to make more rope.

✓ Leaders must have a vision: Where are we going, who's coming along, what are we doing, and for what purpose?

✓ Leaders must know how to fail. More importantly, leaders must allow their people to fail without necessarily becoming a failure.

✓ Leaders will never know as much as their people on the ground; empower them to make decisions.

Part Two – The Path Forward

The Path Forward continues to look at the nature of the human condition — suffering and how we can learn from it. In the book's first part, we talked about our experiences with pain and the role it plays in our personal growth and development. In Part Two, we will focus on practical ways to move forward and find meaning in the midst of difficult experiences.

Through a combination of personal stories, insights from experts, and actionable tips and exercises, we will explore how to build resilience, develop a growth mindset, and cultivate a sense of purpose and meaning in life, even in the face of adversity. Whether you are currently experiencing suffering or simply seeking to understand its role in your life better, "The Path Forward" offers a roadmap to help you navigate the challenges of life with greater strength, wisdom, and grace.

CHAPTER 5 – A Cancer Diagnosis: Learning to Suffer

"Bask in the glory and challenge of overcoming difficulties that would crush ordinary people." - Mark Twight

I came home from Ranger School and continued my career in the military and at the Academy. I would go on to take C Co., 1-128th through an amazingly memorable Annual Training. It was the Summer of 2012, and I was only a few months downstream from pinning my tab.

I was most certainly hungry to pass on every lesson to my Soldiers. I was the 1st Platoon Leader, and I made every Soldier in my platoon earn their pay that summer. They used to poke fun at me and say that I was making them achieve the stitching to their own Ranger Tab.

We had many great laughs that summer, but more importantly, I learned something deeply meaningful about leadership and Soldiering during this time. When soldiers are confident to crack jokes and take the time and energy to share those laughs, it isn't because they don't respect you. It is because they love you and have enough confidence in your love for them that they know you are a leader who can handle the mantle of responsibility it takes to keep them alive.

They can feel it in their bones. They carry maximum trust and confidence in you that some silly joke isn't going to cause retaliation or hatred against them.

When it came time for the annual roasts, if you were untouched, it signified that you were unloved by your Soldiers. That's the bottom line. They simply didn't give enough shit about you to want to stand up in front of a hundred Soldiers and roast you. They knew you couldn't handle it, and hence they feared retribution or retaliation.

Now think, what kind of leader does that make you?

My picture hangs on the wall to this day at that unit, and I was proud to know and lead each one of them.

The Picture of Me Hanging In The Armory

I would carry on through the year, spending as much time as possible with my son and discovering ways to grow. I began supporting the Raider Program at St. John's while caring for Jessy, who would graduate from the Academy in the Spring of 2013. It was Ranger School where I first learned to suffer with my eyes wide open. Ranger School laid the foundation, but what happened in June of 2013 would build a mansion in this case.

The Fuckening

I distinctly remember LTC K telling me, "You should go that checked out."

To which my reply was, "Nah, I'm OK. I've had stress knots in the past." As time passed, it only got worse, and eventually, he convinced me to get checked out. On June 12th, 2013, I went to see an oncologist. It came as shocking news to me that I had Cancer. Yes, sure as shit, it was Cancer, Advanced Stage III Hodgkin's Lymphoma.

I looked at the doctor and said, "Well fuck, how long will I be out of the fight?"

He responded with a stern look and an even harsher tone, "You should probably worry about this fight right now."

What was running through my head was that I had Annual Training with C Co. the very next week, and I had no intention of missing it.

Starting of Treatment

I needed surgery and chemotherapy that very day. I went under the knife, and they took multiple masses out of my neck and chest. Looking back, I vividly remember that the first sign of my Cancer was shoulder pain. I did everything I could to figure out what I did to cause that pain. I went to see doctors and therapists' months before I was diagnosed. Nothing. No answers. Who the hell knew it was Cancer? When the docs removed those masses, my shoulder pain was gone.

Funny how things that seem so impossible tend to be the most impactful.

I kept everything a secret. I told no one. I was so afraid of losing everything and scared that people would look at me like I was weak and needed their pity. I wanted none of it. I would deal with this on my own. I drove myself back and forth to treatment to avoid having to tell anyone.

My treatment plan was ABVD. It included the drugs Adriamycin, bleomycin, vinblastine, and dacarbazine. I dare to tell you; Adriamycin was most certainly not a walk in the park. I'd have to consume ice cubes while getting this infusion because it caused instant mouth sores.

Of course, all of the other side effects that come with it, too, like nausea, vomiting, hair loss, & fatigue.

Some years later, I was told it was also cardiotoxic. I found this out as my oncologist suspected enlargement of my left ventricular, which was later confirmed by my cardiologist. Adriamycin damages the heart muscle, which can eventually lead to heart failure.

One of my most vivid memories is the immediate impact on my urine. Adriamycin literally turns your urine red immediately, and I remember having to make my way to the bathroom soon after my infusion started. It's nauseating just to write about it.

Within a week of my first treatment, I found myself in the field with C Co for XCTC. eXportable Combat Training Capability is a training program that enables brigade combat teams to achieve the trained Platoon readiness necessary to deploy, fight, and win battles throughout the world.

I wasn't necessarily struggling, but I was certainly not a peak performer. I found it hard to make my way up small hills and was always tired. My anxiety was through the roof, too, because I knew this could either kill me or my career.

I was constantly distracted by these thoughts but kept telling myself to Ranger Up and drive on. I didn't spend any real-time coping but instead, trying to figure out what I could do to prevent losing ground in my life.

I would eventually confide in my Commander at that time, and he convinced me to open up to my family and friends.

I said yes at the moment, but when I got home, I changed my mind and went on driving myself back and forth to chemotherapy. It was easy at first. I'd leave chemo and head right to the gym. Everything I read led me to believe that chemo does its job quickly, so the longer it was in my system, the more damage it would do to the rest of my body. I maintained my resolve and focused on recovery daily, especially on chemo days.

The Life-Altering Accident

Then one day, it happened. Like any other chemo day, I woke up and took myself to the Vince Lombardi Cancer Clinic. I meandered a bit and made my way to the chemo wing. I was probably two or three months in at this point, and the cumulative effect was bearing down on me. The nurses made their way through my infusions. My veins were shit at this point, and it always took forever to plug my drip line in. I didn't have a port yet at this point. I figured this would be over quickly.

I felt normal as we got through the first couple of chemo drugs. Well, at least the new normal for now. They hit me with the third drip, and all I could remember was waking up a couple of hours later. I had no idea what had happened, but it knocked me out. I was not the same when I woke up. I was beaten to shit, and I knew it. It felt like it took an eternity to pack my gear up and make my way to the car. I was in a trance, almost like I was back in Ranger School, hallucinating and droning.

I sat in my car and started the ignition. I felt like I was drunk. It was 11:00 when I left the chemo treatment, and I thought to myself, "Shit, I could get a DUI like this!"

I started making my way home, and as I turned onto 94 East, I started fading really hard. "Keep it together; this shit is too easy," I told myself, trying to comfort and keep myself together. However, that was of no use. Not even two minutes later, these words came out of my mouth, "Fuck, I'm losing consciousness." I drifted right the fuck off the highway and into the ditch. I was lucky no one was even close to me. Thank God no one was hurt.

Thankfully, I was fine, and so was the car. Now that the adrenaline was pumping, I had enough juice to make it home. When I arrived, I sat down and had a real gut check. "Jesus, I need to tell someone," "I can't keep doing this alone." I was stupid to think I could go it alone, and now, many years later, I look back and know how silly it really was. I guess my instincts kicked in, and I figured I could only rely on myself. I WAS WRONG!

I finally gathered the guts and told everyone. The first person I told was DJ, my best friend. We put a plan together to manage the next few months. DJ started a great tradition too. We started throwing "chemo parties," and he brought friends from all around any time I was on the drip line. DJ always drove me to chemo, and if he couldn't make it by conflict, he ensured someone else did.

I was still working at the Academy, and they remained faithful to me — every one of them, from MAJ M to President A. I worked day in and day out for our Cadets. I loved them, and they loved me. While I certainly took time for my health, I spent as much time as I could keeping everyone around me motivated and moving forward.

Flight School VS Cancer

I was supposed to be Cancer free that October. What I was not expecting was a call from the Aviation Branch that my flight packet had been accepted. I said to myself, "Well shit, what the hell do I do with this opportunity? I'm fucking sick". I decided to risk it. I never really

148

mentioned it, but I took the SIFT and applied to flight school back in June, right before I was diagnosed. That's a whole other story, but I always wanted to fly.

```
SHARP JASON L                                  CO A 1ST BN 147TH AVN
(TQZA0-763) 1954 PEARSON ST                    MADISON WI                53704

You are ordered to active duty for training (ADT) for the period shown plus
allowable travel time. Upon completion of the period of ADT unless sooner
released or extended by proper authority, you will return to the place where
you entered ADT and be released from such duty.

Period (PCS) : 05 August 2013    - 18 October 2014
Report to: Fort Rucker, AL 36362
Reporting time/date: 1600 / 08 August 2013
Purpose: Aviation BOLC / IERW
```

Life at Flight School

I finished my treatments, and without hearing any results, I went straight to flight school, thinking I was good to go. "I can handle this. I'm fine," I told myself. "I'm a Soldier." I did my first Physical Fitness test, and while I didn't perform at my best, I smoked those aviators! I went to rotary wing classes and passed everything. I got to dunker training, officially known as HOST (Helicopter Overwater Survival Training), and I was dying.

It is an intense and grueling process that simulates a water crash scenario, teaching us how to survive and escape from a submerged aircraft. It involves multiple simulations in a dunk tank, where we're trained to remain calm and follow the proper protocol for escaping the submerged aircraft.

Similar to Ranger School, it is physically and mentally demanding, and the goal is to overcome the fear of drowning while maintaining focus in a high-pressure situation.

I was literally sucking at life. I struggled to breathe like you couldn't imagine. However, It didn't stop me, though. I would take hour-long showers with my face in the shower head, mouth open, learning to breathe in the chaotic splashing water that was drowning me every minute. I needed to figure this out, and that's exactly what I did. Every morning and night before class, I would go to the pool and hold my breath. I'd swim for hours. Each time I motivated myself and boosted my confidence by saying, "I am going to pass this damn course."

The day of reckoning was here, and I would either be a "GO" or a "NO GO." Here we are again, and the damn go / no go stage of my life. I gave myself a gut check, saying, "No fucking in-betweens here. You are either good enough, or you are not."

I jumped in the pool and swam like I never swam before. At this moment, I remembered the famous Eric Thomas quote, "When you want to succeed as bad as you want to breathe, then you'll be successful." The story has been told many times and in many different versions. When I first heard of it, I was practicing Brazilian Jui Jitsu (MACP – Modern Army Combative Program).

There was a young man who wanted to make a lot of money, and so he went to the guru and said, "I want to be on the same level as you are."

To which the guru said, "If you want to be on the same level I'm on, meet me tomorrow at the beach at 5 a.m."

So, the young man arrived at the beach on time at 5 a.m., ready to do as the guru would direct. The old man grabbed his hand and said, "How badly do you want to be successful?"

The boy replied, "Real bad."

The guru told the boy to walk on out in the water, which he did. When he first walked out into the water, the boy went waist-deep and said to himself, "This guy is nuts." He heckled the old man saying, "Hey, I want to be successful and make money, but you have me out here in waist-deep water."

To which the old man said nothing except, "Come a little further."

The boy was now about shoulder-deep in the water and thought to himself again, "This guy is crazy!" but the old man had him continue.

"Come on out a little further," the old man said.

The boy was now up to his mouth in the water. Scared and timid, the boy said, "I am going back to shore," as he convinced himself that the old man was out of his mind.

"I thought you said you wanted to be successful?"

"I do."

"Then walk a little further."

The boy gave in and walked a little further. At that moment, the old man grabbed the boy and shoved his head underwater, and held him down. The boy kicked and screamed for his life. He was scratching at the surface of the water to come up. Flailing about for air as if he was going to die.

Just before the boy was about to pass out, the old man raised him up above the water. "I have a question for you, boy: what did you want the most when you were under that water?"

"Air!" the boy said. "I wanted to breathe."

"When you want to succeed as bad as you wanted air to breathe at this moment, you will become successful."

I kept that story in my head the whole excruciating day. Every time they dunked me under the water, I asked myself, "How bad do you want this?" I wanted it really bad. Cancer wasn't going to defeat me. Not today and not ever. I struggled the rest of the day, having to retry some of the tests, but ultimately, I was successful. My lungs were on fire, and my body was limp, but I did it. I was on my fucking way, "Too easy."

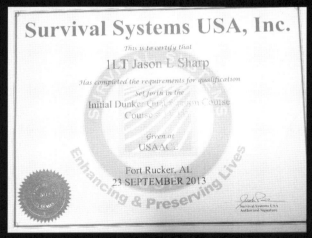

Dunker Cert

The next couple of weeks were business as usual. Pulling into December, I was worn out and more exhausted than usual, but things were OK. That was until I went for my next flight physical. I ran through the gamut of tests all damn day, per usual. You know if you know. I finally made it to 1600 and got pulled in.

Doc looked at me and said, "You good?" He was an old black man, Soldier type, chock full of grit, and no one to bullshit by any means.

"Yes, sir, I'm good."

"Are you sure? Because I'm pretty sure you have cancer".

"Fuck."

I looked at him and had no choice but to give my backstory. He looked at me and said, "Well, damn, Soldier, you sure gave these aviators a run for their money."

I made it pretty far before being sent home on medical to be reunited with my old and faithful oncologist at the Vince Lombardi Cancer Clinic. It was gut-wrenching, heartbreaking, and an all-around failure. I had to swallow a fat ass piece of humble pie.

To me, failure is a failure. I couldn't blame it on the Cancer. Despite what some may think, I was still a fucking failure in my heart. I had to return home as a failure. After this, I didn't have a restful night for months. I made some poor decisions and probably should have focused on my illness. Not probably. I just plain old should have.

Back in the Fight – A Cancer Rollercoaster.

I returned home, and I went to visit the doc immediately. He ran the usual tests and also put me through another PET Scan. I am realizing now that I never actually described what that is.

PET (Positron Emission Tomography)

I was diagnosed and monitored with these insanely expensive scans during my initial cancer diagnosis. A PET (Positron Emission Tomography) scan is a medical imaging technique that uses a small amount of radioactive material to produce detailed images of the body's internal organs and tissues. PET scans diagnose and monitor various medical conditions, but in my case, Cancer.

During the scan, I am given a small amount of radioactive material, called a radiotracer, through injection. The radiotracer is then absorbed by my body's tissues and organs and emits a type of energy called positrons. These positrons collide with electrons in the body, producing gamma rays that can be detected by a special camera.

The camera captures the gamma rays and produces images that show how the radiotracer is distributed throughout my body. The images reveal abnormal metabolic activity in the organs and tissues, which was used as an indicator of my residual disease.

The challenge of having a PET scan is mainly because of the preparation that is required beforehand and the discomfort it causes during the procedure. Before the scan, I would have to fast for several hours and avoid "strenuous physical activity" to ensure accurate results. The injection of the radioactive material made me vomit and break out in hives every time. They had to begin pre-medicating me with steroids and Benadryl to prevent episodes during the scan.

During the scan, I had to remain still for almost an hour, which got pretty tough at times with my hives and itching and whatnot.

I completed my PET Scan and went to my exam room to talk with the doctor. I swear I waited in that exam room for 2 hours before he came in. When he did finally arrive, he had no answers. "Jason, the results aren't in yet. There isn't anyone available to review your PET Scan" I went home, poured a stiff three-finger rum, and waited for a call.

It was late afternoon when the call came in, "Jason, I have your results." "It appears the first round of treatment didn't do anything for you, and the tumor is still there." It was the size of two of my fists smashed together. "Well, that's not fucking good," I said.

I thanked the doctor and callously responded, "Well, I fucking suppose we'll be in touch." I hung up abruptly, sat at the end of my bed, and cried. It was unusual for me, but I was fucking pissed off. Honestly, I was heartbroken that this shit would continue to beat me.

I look back now, and I remember a quote from Paul Kalanithi's book *When Breath Becomes* Air, "I know suffering builds character, but who the fuck needs this much character." I can't quite remember how I came about this book, but I remember reading it front to back on the train ride from Chicago to Kansas City.

Sure as shit, my first round of ABVD didn't do a damn thing. I was running against the best of them in flight school with tumors and a damaged lung all the same. None of it stopped me from wanting it as bad as that boy wanted to breathe. I always said to myself, "If it weren't for those damn medical regulations, I would have fucking killed it." Still, it wasn't enough to beat the system, and that system sent me packing.

After my soul settled a bit, I called the doc the next day and apologized for hanging up on him. I then asked clear as day, "What the fuck happened? I'm supposed to be Cancer free!" His response was nothing more than cliché, "Just happens sometimes, Jason." Not only was my cancer still trying to kill me, but it was back with a vengeance. Doc said we needed to start another round of ABVD treatment before we could even consider other options.

Chemo parties started all over again, except this time, I had a much larger crowd. I was learning to welcome people into my suffering, and I'll be honest, it was a much happier time despite the chaos that was in my life. The shit show of ABVD remained, and this time it was worsened by my shit veins. They were flat, and the nurses found it increasingly difficult to plug my lines. They had to use my hands at this point.

I finally caved and decided to get a port. Getting a port for chemotherapy isn't a walk in the park, as some might think. It's an invasive and painful procedure that can be described as nothing less than brutal. First, a surgeon will make an incision in the chest to create a pocket for the port. Then, a catheter is inserted into a vein, typically in the neck, and threaded down into the chest pocket. The catheter is attached to the port, which is implanted just under the skin, leaving a protruding bump on the chest. This bump is always painful and uncomfortable, and the catheter causes bruising and soreness around the insertion site. Getting a port is a grueling experience in and of itself.

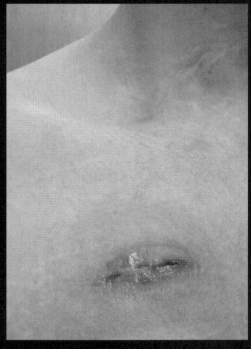

Power Port Post Surgery

It was just one more thing that would limit my mobility and shit. I could barely take a shower at will without having to remember to tape it up. All that said, it did make it much easier to tap and get my infusions. It didn't last long, though, and I would soon need a Tri-Star. We'll get to that later.

I left my first treatment and went straight to Revere's with DJ. I asked for Levi, the bartender and friend to many. I needed a fucking drink, and Levi wouldn't turn me away. He always kept a special bottle for me behind the bar; I am thankful for it to this day. He poured my classic rum, and I took my first sip. It was perfect.

This was my first drink of rum in a very long time. It was a deeply emotional and liberating experience. For many of us cancer patients, the disease and its treatment take a toll on our physical and emotional well-being, leaving us feeling drained, anxious, and depressed. In this case, with my recent news, the simple act of enjoying a drink symbolized a return to normalcy and a celebration of life, no less. I wanted to enjoy something finally.

This first sip was bittersweet, as the taste of the alcohol was a reminder of the struggles and challenges I faced during my initial round of treatments and what was to come. For me, it was a brief moment of joy and relief, a way to mark the end of a difficult chapter and the beginning of the next. Next to my best friend, DJ, this drink was warming and comforting in ways I can't explain. It reminded me of the joys of life that had been temporarily lost.

It wasn't long before we laughed about the craziest shit. The drink was just as amazing as I described, but what happened next may seem a bit too much. I started to break out in hives, "What the fuck?" "I can't be allergic to rum now. How much more shit can this garbage deal me?"

Levi and DJ laughed at me, and I couldn't help but laugh with them. Levi cooked up a whole experiment to see if I was, in fact, allergic to rum. It was funny as hell. He lined up shots of every type of rum he had in the bar, and I was to take a shot every 15 minutes.

The logic, of course, was that 15 minutes in between shots was enough to see an allergic reaction. "You're fucking stupid, man. I love you. Pour the next shot!" I said. Thankfully, I wasn't allergic to rum. I was just having reactions from the multiple chemo drugs I took that day.

My treatment continued throughout the winter of 2013 and into the early spring of 2014. As much as I enjoyed my time with Levi and DJ, it was short-lived, and things were only getting worse. The treatment wasn't working, "The doc said this could happen," I said to myself. I was sure as shit tired of it, though.

The doc had me continue ABVD throughout the spring as planned, but in March, he finally came to me with a potential solution. A solution that might actually end this chapter of my life. The problem was that this solution could very well end me too.

Fighting On All Fronts

I would soon agree to undergo a stem cell transplant, but my doctor first had to find a way to shrink my tumor size. The plan was a brentuximab treatment cycle that, if effective, would carry me to my stem cell transplant. At the time, brentuximab was not FDA-approved, and I was to be one of the lab rats for its efficacy.

Of course, I did my research. As a chemotherapy drug, brentuximab was known to have some truly horrifying side effects. We'd experience a known range of unpleasant symptoms, including nausea and vomiting, extreme fatigue, and hair loss, but I was used to that at this point.

While these side effects can be challenging to cope with on their own, some of us would also suffer from more severe complications. For example, nerve damage caused by the drug led to intense pain, tingling, and numbness in my limbs, which I struggle with to this day.

Lung problems were another potential side effect, with some patients experiencing shortness of breath, coughing, or wheezing. Thankfully, my lungs were not impacted by the treatment. The radiation would take care of that later.

To start the transplant process, I would need to get what was called a NeoStar Port, sometimes called a Tri-Star port. This would be the opposite of my power port and serve the primary purpose of harvesting my stem cells and other infusions or specimen draws. This port was not implanted but rather in between and needed constant care. It was, of course, internal but also had three external access points.

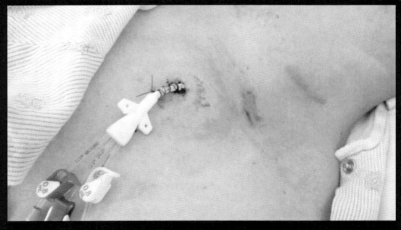

NeoStar Port Post Surgical Insertion

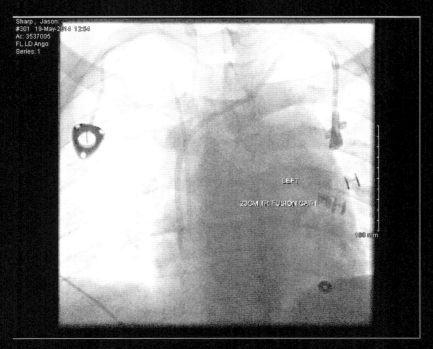

X-Ray Depicting both my Power Port & NeoStar Port

Leading up to the transplant, I underwent multiple iterations of stem cell harvesting and bone marrow biopsies. The term is Leukapheresis, and it was certainly a first for me.

Leukapheresis is a medical procedure in which the blood is circulated through a machine separating white blood cells from the other components. This procedure was used to collect a large number of my white blood cells, which were then used as part of my stem cell transplantation.

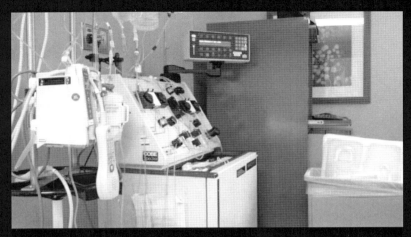

Leukapheresis Machine Hooked To My NeoStar Port

Bone marrow biopsies involve removing a small amount of bone marrow tissue for examination. Most procedures are typically performed under local anesthesia to minimize pain and discomfort, but mine never were.

To adequately evaluate the quality, health, and power of my existing stem cells, I was not allowed any drugs whatsoever. No numbing agents were permitted, and the long and short of it is simple. It hurt like hell.

During the biopsy, a needle is inserted through the skin and into the bone to extract a sample of bone marrow. Without numbing medication, let me tell you, the pain was intense, especially as the needle penetrated the bone and tissue. It was an awful burning sensation with a very sharp pain as the needle twisted and turned to collect the sample. It felt like a corkscrew going right through my hip.

As mid-winter came to pass, I made my way through all the harvesting, the bone marrow biopsies, and the brentuximab treatments. I was showing promise by April when I was finally approved for a transcript. It was go time. It felt to me like I was reporting for Ranger School, and it was a no-fail event.

A little context for those unfamiliar, a stem cell transplant is a highly complex and risky medical procedure used to treat various types of advanced Cancer, including my advanced stage III Hodgkin's Lymphoma. The procedure involves the use of high-dose chemotherapy to destroy cancer cells and the immune system. After this, the patient receives healthy stem cells to help rebuild their immune system. I remember reading every document and initialing every line. The image that remains in my head to this day is how casually the language said something like, "If this doesn't work, you will die." There was no in-between.

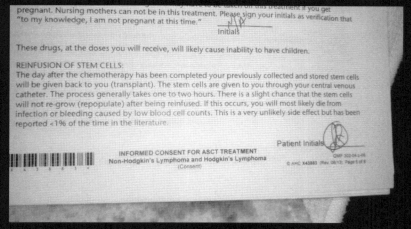

Informed Consent for a Stem Cell Transplant

The complexities of the transplant arise from the risks associated with the procedure, such as infection, bleeding, and graft versus host disease (GVHD). GVHD occurs when the new stem cells recognize my cells as foreign and attack them. This causes various complications, from rashes and diarrhea to liver damage and death.

High Dose Chemo

The high-dose chemo rounds hit me hard. The sessions were an all-day and all-night battle for days. I was on a constant high-dose chemo drip. During my ABVD chemo, I didn't really lose all my hair. It just thinned out quite a bit. The high-dose chemo took care of that, though.

High Dose Chemo Hair Loss Manifesting

The doctors looked at me with funny gazes when I asked if I could have an exercise bike in my room during the high-dose chemo. I never stopped exercising during my illness, and I would hold true to it even now in my hospital isolation room, just as I did during my ABVD treatment cycles.

I took my high-dose chemo drips every day, and I maintained my strength for the most part. A couple of days before the stem cell transplant, it hit me like a brick wall, and all of a sudden, I was totally bedridden. It felt like my insides were being torn out. Like someone was standing there gutting me with a dull knife, and I had to watch them do it. Doctors said it was normal, so I had no choice but to stay in the fight.

"What the hell is normal these days anyway?"

Enduring high-dose chemotherapy prior to my stem cell transplant was in itself an incredibly difficult and grueling experience. The chemo drugs used in this treatment, like other chemotherapy drugs, are designed to kill cancer cells, and of course, they also damage healthy cells and tissues in the body, just as they did during my ABVD cycles. This was different, though.

For starters, this high-dose regimen caused much more intense nausea and vomiting, which was really difficult to control even with medication. None of the anti-nausea meds they gave me worked. I had to deal with the side effects. I never experienced diarrhea with ABVD, but this was a whole different shitstorm, pun intended. The abdominal pain was excruciating, and the cramping was even worse, which made it very difficult to eat or drink. Surprisingly, I was on an ice cube diet, which was a two-fold win. I avoided, for the most part, intensely painful mouth sores, and it helped me to stay hydrated. No doubt, though, the mouth sores took their toll, too, making it very difficult and painful to swallow or speak.

Doctors called this phase "the conditioning."

All of this was unfolding while I was alone. In addition to the physical symptoms I mentioned, high-dose chemotherapy significantly affected my mental and emotional health. The isolation required during this time, due to my weakened immune system, led to intense feelings of loneliness, anxiety, and depression. I was totally isolated and cut off from everyone I cared about, and all I could do was remember that, at one point, I did try to do this alone, so I knew this could be done, and I needed to own the fucking outcome. I could either be a victim, or I could have a gut check. I told myself to Ranger up and do the damn thing.

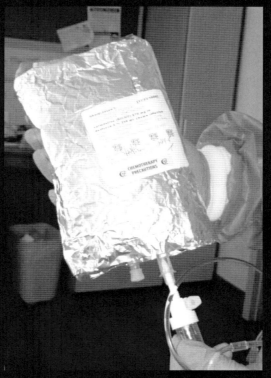

High-Dose Chemo Bag

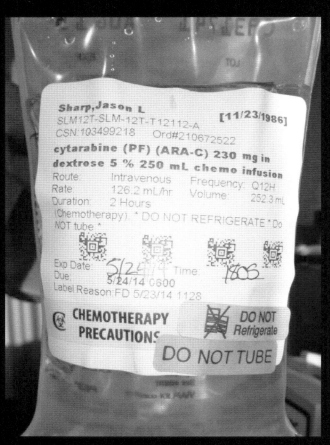

High-Dose Chemo Bag

The Transplant

Once the high-dose chemo-conditioning regimen was complete, the stem cell transplant itself began. The doctors infused healthy stem cells into my body to replace the damaged and diseased cells. I am just going to say it. The whole fucking experience was painful and numbing. Secretly, I prayed and hoped that the "informed consent" I initialed a few weeks earlier didn't manifest into reality.

"There is a slight chance that the stem cells will not re-grow (repopulate) after being infused. If this occurs, you will most likely die from infection or bleeding caused by low blood cell counts."

Stem Transplant Infusion Preparation

Do you see the "GET WELL SOON" sign in the background of the last image? Alyssa, daughter of Sandy Rosch, who I will introduce in-depth shortly, asked her class to write letters of motivation to me, and they came through! To this day, that sign hangs in my home as a reminder of how many people helped me through this difficult time.

Alyssa's Class of Superheroes

The First 24 Hours

The first 24 hours after the transplant were pure hell. The new stem cells were like poison to my body, and I was writhing in pain as they took hold. My skin was on fire, hot to the touch, and my body shook uncontrollably. I remember screaming in agony as the pain tore through every inch of my being.

My heart raced, and I struggled to breathe as my body fought to reject the new cells. It felt like my organs were shutting down, one by one, as the stem cells ravaged my system.

The nausea was overwhelming, and I vomited bile repeatedly, unable to keep any food or water down. My throat was raw from the effort, but I could not stop retching.

The pain was beyond anything I had ever experienced, even in Ranger School. I begged for relief, but there was little the doctors could do other than administer strong painkillers, which only provided a temporary lull.

Earlier, I mentioned that one of the most common side effects of a stem cell transplant is graft-versus-host disease (GVHD), which occurs when the transplanted cells attack my own tissues and organs. It sure as shit unfolded that way, and I faced the worst effects, from skin rashes, diarrhea, and abdominal pain to liver and lung damage. It ran the gamut on me over the next week and was both painful and debilitating. It was like my whole body was a blister with open sores. My skin became thick and leathery, making movement painful and difficult. All I could do was lay there and take it. The fucking exercise bike was useless at this point, and amidst my delirious reality, I vaguely remember them coming to take it away.

It was brutal, and the challenge was very real. It reminded me of sitting on that sopping wet log in Swamp Hhase crying in the rain. It required all my strength and every bit of resilience left in me. Just as it was in Ranger School, I only made it through because of the significant support from the team around me.

My medical team, family, and friends helped me cope with the physical and emotional toll of the shit show I was dealing with, and I am forever grateful. As I write this, I think about how impossible it would have been to go through that procedure alone.

My pride got to me back when I was diagnosed, but today, I know better. A small piece of humble pie on occasion is a damn good thing.

Stem Cells Coming Out of the Cryo Freezer

Eventually, if all was successful, I would also require strict isolation to prevent any infections that could be life-threatening. I will get to that shortly.

From the moment healthy stem cells hit my system, it took two excruciating weeks for my body to recover. My white cell count needed to be at a certain "safe" level in order to manage any bacteria or viruses in the short term. I say the short term because the transplant wiped out my immune system. That is, every anti-body or vaccination I ever received was totally wiped clean until I was made whole again. I would eventually need to receive every immunization I received over my lifetime again but in grown-man doses.

I was finally able to see my son. They made me wear all the protective gear they could find, from gloves to masks, to gowns, so he most certainly didn't recognize me at first. He was afraid of me, of course, but he eventually realized I was Daddy. We had a lot of fun that afternoon until they made me return to my hospital bed.

My Son Finally Able to Visit Me

It's interesting to think about what I just wrote about living a post-pandemic life. Then, it was completely foreign to me, my family, and everyone I knew. Now, we are all very accustomed to regular and constant PPE (Personal Protective Equipment).

Thankfully, I was able to receive other visitors, including Sharon from my former team at Lake Country Fire & Rescue (LCFR), who I will introduce shortly, and many friends from the Academy, including LTC K.

Sharon Visiting During Post-Hospital Isolation

Recovery

The recovery time for my stem cell transplant was long. I had to spend three weeks in the hospital following my transplant, followed by close monitoring and medical follow-ups to manage any complications and side effects that arose during my recovery period. It was during this time, my recovery period, that people really showed their true colors.

Doctors told me that I would need a space to recover that was exceptionally clean, free of children and pets, and offered limited access so that I wasn't disturbed, and neither was my little ecosystem as my immune system was re-building.

My Gear at LCFR

I had an amazing relationship with Lake Country Fire and Rescue (LCFR), formerly the Delafield Fire Department, and they came out to support me in droves. I spent some time with LCFR as a volunteer firefighter, where I worked with some of the most amazing firefighters and paramedics in the country.

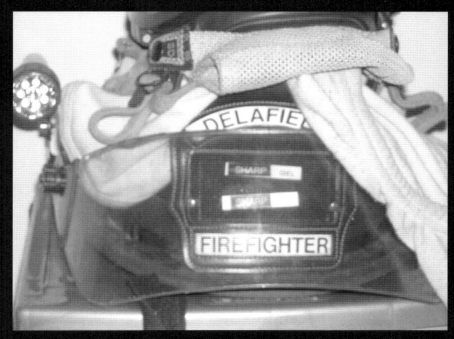

My Firefighter Helmet

I learned a lot about life and death during my time with them, and if I am being honest, my Lieutenant, Sharon Dyer, is the one who helped me to see how important it is to really care and empathize with others. I never told her that, so hopefully, she will read this someday. Thanks, Sharon.

Sharon and I after I signed the Pink Heals Fire Truck in 2014.

Led by Sharon Dyer and Sandy Rosch, LCFR figured out a way to take care of me. I needed a space to recover, free from distraction and free from pets and children. While I would have liked to, I could not go back to St. John's. The Academy was bustling constantly, and there would be little room for recovery.

LCFR was expanding and had a vacant "station 2". This is where I would spend the next six weeks in isolation. It was here that, as I said previously, people really started to show their true colors. When things are going wrong or people in your life are suffering, the most important thing we can do is show up for them. My people and friends showed up for me, and I will never forget it.

To start, Sharon and the rest of the crew from LCFR sterilized station 2 for me. I stayed in one of the crew bunk rooms while there. Sharon and the team cleaned every crevice from top to bottom, including bathrooms and kitchens. It was truly amazing to watch all of that unfolding. I was then, and I am now forever grateful.

A very dear friend of mine, Deborah F., was in my corner from day one, and she made sure that I had everything I needed to recover properly. She even set up a GoFundme to help cover my ongoing medical costs. Her support helped remind me of how fortunate I was to have people in my life who showed up.

Like Deborah, the Marshall Family was also in my corner from day one. They took care of me better than I took care of myself. They brought me food, clothing, supplies; you name it. I was never really able to thank them fully, so again, hoping they, too, are reading this and recognize how much I appreciate them.

There were so many people who came out to support me; it was unbelievable. To think a year before, I was operating in a silo: total secrecy and darkness. I was pushing a boulder up a hill in the mud, and, like Sisyphus, who cheated death, every time I thought I made it to the top, I'd lose my grip, and that boulder would go crashing down. While they couldn't carry it for me, people like LCFR, Deborah, and the Marshalls helped to pick me up and re-position me behind my boulder.

Lori S. and Michele R. were also on my team. Over time, I would come to get to know each of their sons, who would both end up in some capacity being involved with St. John's. They were great kids, and I enjoyed mentoring them. Lori was always there to bring me good food and entertainment. I think, at one point, she brought a whole stack of DVDs to binge through. Between her and Michele, I never went hungry.

One of the coolest things that happened while I was held up at station 2 was from an old St. John's friend, John G. This man literally brought me a treadmill so I could focus on getting healthy again. I was a total addict to running and lifting, and John helped me get through this chapter.

Post Recovery

I came out of recovery in late June 2014. I had either been in the hospital or in isolation for the last six weeks. You know me, I went right back into the fight and started working again at the Academy. Even though my military career at this point was over, I immediately began focusing on my physical fitness. I wanted to rebuild and regain all of my strength and stamina back. I went right back to 4:30 am workouts which included running, swimming, Olympic-style lifting, and everything in between.

It wasn't too long before LTC K approached me and asked if I could come up with a concept for a new summer program to prepare our Raiders for the upcoming 2014 Fall Season.

For context, The US Army JROTC Raider Program is a high-intensity athletic and leadership development program designed for young people who are interested in military and outdoor activities.

It includes a range of physically challenging activities, such as obstacle courses, rope bridge construction, cross-country runs, and team-building exercises. These activities help students develop physical fitness, mental toughness, and leadership skills.

The Raider Program became my life, and I loved every minute of it. In collaboration with several other instructors, SFC T and I built a really awesome program, and we called it "Raider School." It was based on imposed stress and optimal deprivation in order to push the students past their perceived limits. Like Ranger School, Raider School was meant to violently break apart the winners and the losers so we could build a strong competition team. The program we built in 2014 survives to this day as a "go-to" summer program for the Academy and the Raiders.

I was doing monthly checkups with my oncologist after my isolation period, and everything was fine. So, I thought, at least. Soon after our first successful Raider School in August of 2014, I went in for a PET Scan, and the results were much the same as when I left the hospital post-transplant. I was OK and supposedly in remission. Nonetheless, my doctor said there was a high risk of residual disease and that I would need to undergo radiation treatment to "nail the coffin shut," as he put it.

"Here we fucking go again."

I wanted this to be over. I was ready, and I felt strong, but my doctors knew otherwise, and given they had brought me this far, I maintained my faith and trust in them.

The doctors explained to me that radiation therapy following my transplant was needed to totally destroy any remaining cancer cells that might have been present in the body. They said it was critical to ensuring my chances of total recovery.

They began imaging studies and other diagnostic tests to determine the location and extent of any remaining cancer cells. When this was complete, my new radiation oncologist developed my treatment plan, which was to begin in late October and run through January 2015.

Well, let me tell you, eating another piece of humble pie was no piece of cake, but I was right back at it with a big shit-eating grin. I informed everyone in my life what was about to unfold. At this point, I had learned that for me to come through this as whole as possible, eating humble pie was the first step, and relying on the humanity of others was the next.

My friends and family, "Team Sharp," came through once again and began immediately supporting me. They even through fundraisers and events to keep my spirits up and help cover the mounting costs associated with my treatment.

As can be expected by now, Sharon put together an exciting event in my honor. She even had T-Shirts printed and managed to pull together a group of people to compete in a kickball tournament to my benefit.

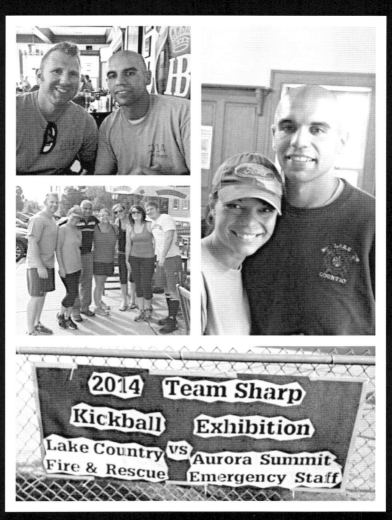

Team Sharp Fundraiser

Team Sharp T-Shirts

LCFR vs. Aurora Summit Emergency Department

Sandy's daughter, Cassie, even offered to take professional photos of me and my son. She was truly amazing, and I am forever grateful for her support. I will always cherish the memories built that day in the sun, draped by Old Glory.

My Son Xavier

Xavier exploring the St. John's Northwestern Field of Flags.

In October, on the cusp of my treatment starting, Sharon again pulled off another impressive stunt with a motorcycle poker ride! It was such a blast, and I needed it so badly. It would be the last hoo-rah before starting radiation therapy.

TEAM SHARP
POKER RIDE

DON'T RIDE? THEN DRIVE!

All proceeds contributing toward the medical expenses of
Jason Sharp who is battling Advanced Stage 3 Lymphoma

As I write, I look back and reflect on every moment, and I remain just as grateful today as I was then. My people came through for me, and the lesson was simple. When others are suffering or going through something extremely challenging or traumatic, the best thing you can do is show up. Just be there, at the very least. My people did that for me, and not only did it save my life, but it also shaped my heart and soul forever.

The poker ride came to a glorious end. We celebrated, we laughed, and some of us even cried. Most importantly, there were no accidents, and everyone went home with ten fingers and ten toes. It was now time to face my reality and get back in the fight. I was ready, and I had my team right behind me.

Radiation Treatment

There I was, sitting on a treatment table with my radiation oncologist next to me. She explained that I would have to have a formed and fitted piece of plastic over me in order to precisely engage with the targeted radiation area. That is, if I moved even a millimeter, they could be radiating my heart instead of the tumor. Bad juju.

They had me lay down on a stainless-steel medical table and laid over me this warm, almost melting plastic that almost looked like a diamond-cut gridiron fence. This warm plastic was then kind of melted over my face and upper chest and then cooled so that my exact facial features and upper body were molded perfectly into it. It had screws all around it, which were then tightened down, so I had zero mobility except for my legs.

This device was my home for the next few months, so I had to get used to it quickly. I never thought I was the claustrophobic type until that device was tightened, and I couldn't even open my mouth.

On the device was a very precisely drawn radiation target area which was meant to be my radiation treatment zone. Again, any digression from this zone could mean some other organ was radiated and not my target area. Almost ten years later and this device still hangs in my garage as an everyday reminder of where I come from and what I've been through. A reminder that whatever battle I face today is too easy and that, ultimately, I will win the fight.

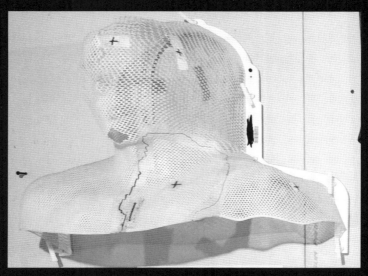

My Custom Radiation Therapy Device

My radiation therapy was delivered using external beam radiation, which involved directing high-energy radiation beams at the cancerous cells from outside the body. After my first treatment, I distinctly remember changing in the exam room and looking at myself in the mirror. I turned around to see my back, which was a little itchy and painful. I had a dark shaded area on my back that roughly mirrored my radiation target area. The radiation left a damn sunburn on my back, at which point I also realized that it had literally burned all the tissue in my body, which is why I had a sunburn-like mark on my back.

"This shit is no joke," I thought to myself.

I turned to look in the mirror again and laughed a bit. The radiation device I was locked into was on so tight it had left marks on my head!

Imprints From My Radiation Therapy Device

This would go on for the next three months culminating in Jan 2015, when I would begin my re-vaccination phase to rebuild my immune system further.

The radiation treatment itself was as brutal and real as it gets. I remember nausea and fatigue from my ABVD cycles, especially my high-dose chemo, but this was different. There was no cumulative effect; it hit all at once and instantaneously. There would be no driving myself to and from treatment this time. On top of that, the long-term complications they described were more real to me as I continued to become an ad hoc expert by experience. Some of these manifest today, like nerve damage, thyroid disease, and even the risk of secondary cancers, which requires me to maintain my regular oncology checkups.

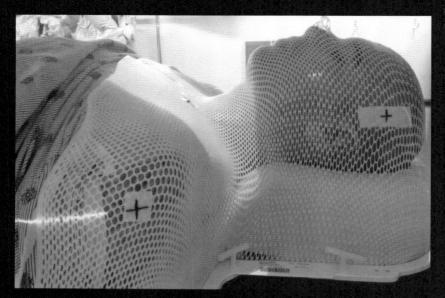

My First Radiation Therapy Treatment

The re-vaccination phase lasted a couple of months by itself. I would go in, and they'd hit me with four immunizations at a time. One in each arm and leg. Some weeks it was fine, and some weeks I could barely move. I knew it was necessary, so I just fought the day's fight and continued.

To be clear, getting all of your lifetime immunizations again after a stem cell transplant can easily be described as a grueling and difficult experience, but I would just call it a pain in the ass.

Of course, I recognized that the process was necessary, given my transplant essentially hit the reset button on my immune system. I lost all the immunity I had ever developed throughout my life. It left me totally vulnerable to a wide range of infections and illnesses that I would normally be protected from.

All that said, it was still a pain in the ass.

Despite all of this, my radiation therapy was, in fact, the critical step in achieving a successful outcome. The treatment did "nail the coffin shut" by destroying the remaining cancer cells. It ensured a full recovery, and, for the most part, I was able to resume a normal life.

Lessons Learned

My diagnosis and subsequent treatment were not just life-altering; they were life-shattering. At the time, it took my career from me, it took my body, and it took my health. Now, as I write, I realize that it gave me so much more than it took. How I live my life post Cancer is dramatically different from how I lived it prior. My Cancer gave me a few gifts. These were the kinds of gifts that kept on giving.

It is often a hindsight issue. You have all heard the phrase, "Hindsight is 20/20". The lesson from that phrase is that it is easier to understand the reasons for past events or decisions after they occurred than to predict them beforehand. This means that we can often see clearly what we should have done or what went wrong in retrospect, but it can be much more difficult or impossible even to anticipate and make the right choices at the moment.

Of course, the phrase encourages us to learn from our mistakes and use the past's lessons to make better future decisions. By acknowledging that hindsight is always clearer than foresight, we can approach decision-making with a humbler and more reflective attitude and be more open to feedback and learning from our experiences.

For me, the lessons learned were not about health or taking care of my body. Yes, all of that is important, but that was never an issue for me. My lessons were about living life itself and having a profound appreciation for certain things.

The Importance of Things

By that, I mean what's actually important to me and what isn't. It's funny how ridiculous things seem after you lay on your deathbed for weeks and months. It's unfortunate that we must be brought to our knees to learn this lesson. I suppose it comes down to the nature of what it means to be human. What I give the power to is up to me. I chose what carries weight in my life and what doesn't.

For example, many of the things that bother us in our day to day are benign and meaningless, but most of us still let them affect our day. One common way people allow meaningless, benign things to impact their day negatively is through the phenomenon of "mood contagion." This occurs when our emotional state is influenced by the emotional state of those around us, even if the cause of the other person's emotion is trivial or insignificant. Like someone losing their shit cause Starbucks did not have their favorite coffee and are in a bad mood for the rest of the day. That negative energy spreads to others and creates a tense, unhappy atmosphere that affects everyone's productivity and positivity for the rest of the day. You have a choice here. You get to choose what is important enough to impact your day.

Another way we can allow meaningless things to impact our day negatively is through rumination or dwelling on small, inconsequential events. For example, if someone receives a curt email from a colleague, they may spend the rest of the day ruminating on the perceived rudeness of the email and allowing it to color their interactions with that person and others. This can lead to a cycle of negativity that affects the person's overall mood and productivity. Instead, it is important to recognize these triggers when our mind is dwelling on things that are not worth our attention. This self-awareness is key to allowing us to focus on more meaningful and positive outcomes in our day. No one ruins my day except me.

Suffering with Eyes Wide Open

Adversity and suffering are quite different, as I have explained. Many of us confuse the two, just as I once did. Adversity hits our doorstep, and we get a choice. We can choose to submit completely and be crushed by its weight, or we can pull our bootstraps up and drive through the obstacles to find success. The difference is soundly distinct. Suffering doesn't come with choices. Suffering we must endure. The lesson then, for me, was that suffering gives us a perfect sense of time. I became aware of every passing second. In so doing, I became aware of the commanding power of time.

Learning to suffer forces us to appreciate time because it helps us to realize that time is an immutable force that cannot be controlled or altered by our desires or preferences. When faced with situations where we must endure suffering, whether physical pain, emotional distress, or difficult circumstances, we may feel powerless and out of control. However, by accepting the reality of the situation and facing our suffering with eyes wide open, we endure with grace and resilience.

Eventually, we come to see that time is not something to be feared or resented but rather a precious resource that we must use wisely and intentionally.

In this way, learning to suffer can help us cultivate a greater sense of gratitude and appreciation for the time we have and inspire us to use that time in meaningful and purposeful ways. This lesson opened my eyes completely and resulted in the third lesson, which ultimately connected with the first.

Eating Shit

I learned whose shit I am willing to eat and whose I am not. By this, I mean that I realized I simply don't have time for nonsense, bullshit, or otherwise non-value-added relationships in my life. Who I give the power to is completely up to me. I make and give time for the people and things which bring joy to my life. Period.

This lesson circles right back to self-awareness. Learning to suffer helps us manage relationships in our lives by helping us develop a greater sense of self-awareness and understanding of our own needs and boundaries. You have to be intentional about it, though. You have to know what is important and what isn't and the value of your life and those around you. When faced with difficult or painful experiences, we are forced to confront our limitations and vulnerabilities, which, if we are intentional about it, can lead us to reevaluate the people and relationships in our lives.

For example, if you consistently suffer in a friendship, personal relationship, or even professional relationship due to the actions or behavior of another person, this should trigger you to question whether that relationship is truly adding value to your life. It is critical that you develop a greater sense of self-awareness and understanding of your needs and boundaries. With this knowledge, you are better equipped to set healthy boundaries and make decisions that are in your best interests.

This lesson is two-fold. Learning to suffer can help you develop empathy and compassion for others too. This, of course, can improve relationships by fostering a deeper understanding and connection with the people you allow in your life. By recognizing and accepting our own vulnerabilities and struggles, we are more open and receptive to the struggles of others, which can help us build stronger, more meaningful relationships.

In this way, knowing whose shit I was willing to eat and whose I haven't helped me manage relationships in my life. It empowered me to make decisions that align with my values and needs while also fostering greater empathy and understanding toward the people around me.

In Closing

When I added up these three lessons, I came away with a powerful mentality. The only person who can ruin my day is me. In the next part of this book, I will dive deeper into that mentality and how it can be built no matter the circumstance.

As Part 1 comes to a close, I think of my life and all the craziness that came with it. I am grateful and happy that I was dealt this hand. It shaped me completely, and I consider myself a better man, father, and husband today than I could have been if I had not experienced what I did.

Looking ahead into Part 2, I will take you on the journey that shaped my path forward in life. I will walk you through how I built an unbreakable foundation for managing the pain of being a human in this world.

CHAPTER 6: Opening Your Eyes: The Ice Age Trail

"The Only Time a Human Being Grows Is When We Leave Our Comfort Zone."

Where do I even begin? Cancer had taken from me all that I had worked so hard to achieve, and I literally had no idea what the hell would be in my next chapter. With bloodshot eyes, lying in my bed, palms sweaty, and my heart racing, I wondered what my future would look like. What the hell am I going to do now?

When I reflected on this, I remembered the many Ranger Instructors who pushed me out of my comfort zone, only to discover afterward that I was perfectly capable of accomplishing it myself. I opened Chapter 5 with a Mark Twight quote, "Bask in the glory and challenge of overcoming difficulties that would crush ordinary people." This was a mantra I lived by, and I knew I needed to do something radical to generate change and fresh ideas. I knew I needed to leave my comfort zone.

The comfort zone is literally the most fantastical escape from all things difficult, challenging, or worthwhile. It can be a great many things for each of us. It's home. It's mom's cooking. It's Netflix binge-watching. It's avoiding crowds or social settings. It's the zone where we feel completely at ease and comfortable — without a single worry in the world. Sadly then, what comes with it is little opportunity or room for growth.

In this zone, we begin to wither away and perish into an inconsequential existence. Lou Holtz once said, "If you're not growing, you're dying." I believe him in every sense of his words. I firmly believe that the only time a human being grows is when we leave our comfort zone.

Leaving the comfort zone means taking risks. It means facing very real anxiety. It means doing what you fear. It means that you will be uncomfortable and out of your element completely. It means that you will be challenged. Most importantly, it means that you will grow.

Accepting the risk, tolerating the anxiety, and facing your fears as you take on the unknown is nerve-wracking, to say the least. The first step toward generating new and different thoughts can be very powerful, however. When you own your outcome, doing things differently equals opportunity.

My "different" was the Ice Age Trail. A 1,000-mile journey across the State of Wisconsin. It was now March of 2015, and in just a few short months, I would be celebrating my one-year anniversary of leaving isolation recovery from my stem cell transplant. Given I spent six long weeks in isolation, I figured, what the hell, why not spend six weeks outside to celebrate my anniversary, eh? This was my chance to put my past behind me, literally one foot after the other. It was on this journey I would re-invent myself.

Hiking the thousand-mile Ice Age Trail across the state of Wisconsin was one of the most challenging endeavors I have ever undertaken. This thousand-mile footpath follows the edge of the last continental glacier in the state. The trail meanders through diverse terrain, including rolling hills, deep forests, and open prairies. The trail is not only a physical challenge, but it would also test my mental and emotional endurance. Again.

It feels like I just did this in Ranger School, "What do I need to prove now?" As I came to realize, this was an opportunity to reflect and figure out how I would carry myself during the rest of my time on earth. I didn't need to prove anything to anyone. It was for me and me alone. I made the decision to press forward and intentionally escape my comfort zone.

"Where do I start?"

"How do I even begin?"

As I explore escaping my comfort zone, I will walk you through how I approached this deeply meaningful and personal initiative.

Recon

If you want to escape your comfort zone, do the homework, and study whatever it is, you're about to get into. This will lessen the fear and anxiety while igniting the motivation and power to achieve your goal.

I went to work researching this "insanity," as some of my friends would call it. I started by picking May 30th as my start date. I began my research about the trail immediately. I read books and articles about the trail and talked to experienced hikers who had completed it. I also researched the weather patterns in Wisconsin, the average temperatures during the time I planned to hike, and the most challenging sections of the trail. None of it mattered, though, cause, as you know, no plan survives first contact. Not to mention that Wisconsin weather is extremely volatile. The recon informed the plan, and that was its purpose.

Planning

Planning is where you write it all out on paper. How are you going to escape your comfort zone and achieve the goals you've set? As I said, no plan survives first contact, but at least you have a frame of reference to adjust your approach. Planning a 1,000-mile hike is a challenging and complex task that requires a significant amount of preparation, research, and logistical skills. If I had to assess this moment, I would say I spent three times the effort to plan for this endeavor than it took to execute.

Of course, I used my research to plan my route, pack my gear, and estimate my resupply needs. I created a detailed itinerary that included the number of miles I planned to hike each day and where I planned to camp each night. Campsites and even primitive camping are significantly regulated in Wisconsin, so my route and miles each day were typically dictated by legal campgrounds and authorized primitive sites. I estimated every single calorie and exactly what resupply I would need and when. Who knew that the calorie-to-weight ratio would become so important in my life?

In Ranger School, I could carry calories for days on end with no problem—we were always starving. Now, I was measuring how much weight I could carry and for how long. Then I had to take that information and try to maximize the calories in each meal: peanut butter packets and macadamia nuts. No shit, those two items were my go-to for the duration of this endeavor. One cup of Macadamia nuts, or about 132 grams, was almost a thousand calories. That's half of an average daily intake. For me, I would need six times that, and I was happy to carry macadamia nuts and peanut butter to pay the bill.

Initial Calorie Count for an 8-Day Supply – 30,000 Calories

As I continued to plan, I needed to define my route. This effort was no walk in the park, to be cliché. A 1,000-mile hike is a long journey, so it was very important that I choose my route and timing appropriately. Ideally, this route would match my fitness level and experience, but for the most part, the Ice Age Trail was well-defined, and I needed to conform. While the route was mainly well-defined, I needed to determine my timeline and daily distance.

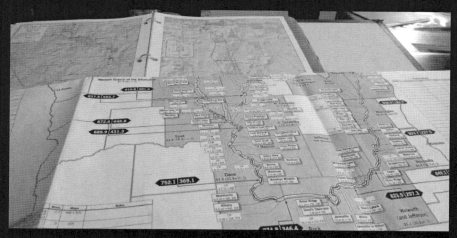

30,000-Foot View Planning Map

Given that the route had been pretty much selected for me, I still needed to figure out how long it would take me to finish. This, of course, depended on my hiking pace, the terrain, and the weather conditions. I tried to set realistic expectations and a timeline that factored in rest days and potential weather delays too. I had other restrictions on my timeline as well. I was asked to come back to the Academy and initiate Summer Youth Programming within the month.

ICE AGE TRAIL THRU HIKE SUMMER 2015

24 MAY - 6 JUNE

SUNDAY	MONDAY	TUESDAY	WEDNESDAY	THURSDAY	FRIDAY	SATURDAY
5/24/2015	5/25/2015	5/26/2015	5/27/2015	5/28/2015	5/29/2015	5/30/2015
PREP	PREP	PREP	PREP	PREP	Trans to Sturgeon Bay	SP from Q Inn NLT 0600 Break Trail NLT 0700
					SP NLT 1200 Arrive 1700 @ Qualify Inn	Sturgeon Bay Seg 13.7
					Final Preparations	Foresville Seg 9.1
					Lights Out NLT 2100	Sleep at Timber Trails Campground **Map 102F** 920-487-3707 $30
						DAY 1 22.8

SUNDAY	MONDAY	TUESDAY	WEDNESDAY	THURSDAY	FRIDAY	SATURDAY
5/31/2015	6/1/2015	6/2/2015	6/3/2015	6/4/2015	6/5/2015	6/6/2015
SP Timber Trails NLT 0700	SP Cedar Valley NLT 0700	SP Tisch Mills NLT 0700	SP Seagull **NLT 0600**	SP Camp ?? NLT 0700	SP Shelter # 2 NLT 0700	SP Pikes Lake NLT 0700
CR to Kawaunee River 14.3	CR to Tisch Mills 25.2	CR to Mischof	Dunes Seg 2.6	La Budde Creek Seg 3.5	Milwaukee River Seg	Holy Hill Seg 6.9
Kawaunee River Seg 11.2	Tisch Mills Seg	Mischof Seg 8	City of Manitowac Seg 7.3	CR to Green Bush 4.5	Wash Cty 6.8	CR to Loew 1.2
		CR to Point Beach 3	CR to La Budde 33	Green Bush Seg 8.8	Kewaukusm Seg 2.1	Loew Seg 4.8
					CR to S. Kawauksum	Monches Seg 3.1
Sleep at Cedar Valley Campground **Map 100F** 920.388.4983	Sleep at DCA In Tisch Mills **Map 98F**	Point Beach Seg 5.3	Sleep @ **Map 90F** Tauschek's B & B 920-876-5087 Res # 7988	Parnell Seg 13.9	S. Kawauksum Seg 2.2	Merton Seg 5.2
		Two River Seg		Milwaukee River Seg (Fondulac) 4.3	West Bend Seg 1.1	Hartland Seg 6.8
					CR to Cedar Lake 6.5	Delafield Seg 2.6
		Map 96F Camp Seagull 920-794-7533 Walk In	$90 W5740 Garton Rd. Plymouth. WI 53073	Sleep @ Shelter # 2 Mil. River Seg 888-947-2757 $22 **Map 87f** Res# 2 36012375	Cedar Lake Seg 5.4	**Sleep @ HOME** Resupply Meet at FD in the AM
					Map 85f 2.8	
					Slinger Seg 1.5	
					Pike Lake 3.3	
					Sleep Pikes Lake DCA	
DAY 2 25.5	DAY 3 28.2	DAY 4 29.1	DAY 5 42.9	DAY 6 35	DAY 7 31.7	DAY 8 23.9

The First 8 Days – Leg 1

I wrapped up route planning and my timeline and now needed to get my gear in order. Carrying all necessary gear and supplies for a 1,000-mile hike is a daunting task. I needed to consider every ounce and every item I brought, such as my lightweight tent, sleeping bag, water filtration system, first aid kit, and of course, appropriate clothing for different weather conditions. I opted for no cooking gear. It was just too heavy, and I knew I could do without it. I relied instead on my peanut butter packets and macadamia nuts. I did bring an ultra-lite jet boil device which required little effort to maintain. Hot coffee in the morning was all I craved, and this was perfect for it.

I only brought items that had at least three uses. That is, if I couldn't use it for three different purposes, I didn't need to carry it. As an example, I brought a trail guide with me. It served as my trail guide, of course, but after I finished sections, I would use the paper to start a fire or even leave notes for those I came across along the way. In doing this, my pack got lighter each day as well.

I initially brought an extra pair of boots but quickly opted to mail them back at the next post office. I opted instead for a change of inserts to keep the bottom of my feet dry, which spared me a lot of weight.

In terms of food, I had no intention of carrying all of the food necessary for the entire journey. As I said, I planned my daily caloric requirements and secured specific resupply points along my path. I literally researched towns, post offices, and other locations where I could send packages to myself for resupply of food, fuel, and other necessary items. More importantly, I needed to determine the distances between these resupply points and plan my daily movement schedule accordingly.

I called at least ten different places along my route and tried to explain my story and why I would need to send them a package to hold for me. Some had no interest at all, and others were excited for the adventure.

While I did have a rock-solid plan in place, we all know that no plan survives first contact, so I had to plan for emergencies. I spent considerable time researching potential hazards and risks along my route and planned accordingly. I decided to go off the grid for this journey, so that meant no cell service. Instead, I opted for a Spot GPS tracking device which sent automatic notifications to my family and friends regarding my location. I programmed it so that if I stopped moving for more than two hours between 6 am and 8 pm, my sister would get an automatic emergency notification with my location.

Of course, I also researched the location of nearby medical facilities and made sure I carried the appropriate safety gear. To prevent drama and other arguments, I carried all necessary permits and documents for the trip as well as a few hundred dollars in cash. You never know when it will become necessary.

I didn't train or condition for this. I figured, what the hell? If I could survive Ranger School, I could survive this. Like Ranger School, this would require maximum endurance, but as you know, I kept up my conditioning post-treatment, so I was confident I had the stamina to accomplish the mission.

			ICE AGE TRAIL THRU HIKE SUMMER 2015 7-20 JUNE			
SUNDAY 6/7/2015	MONDAY 6/8/2015	TUESDAY 6/9/2015	WEDNESDAY 6/10/2015	THURSDAY 6/11/2015	FRIDAY 6/12/2015	SATURDAY 6/13/2015
SP LCFD	SP Shelter # 3	SP Janesville	SP Albany	SP Charltons	SP DA 24	SP DCA Gilbraltar
NLT 0800	NLT 0700	NLT 0700	NLT 0600	NLT 0700	NLT 0600	NLT 0700
Lapham Peak Seg	Blackhawk Seg		Albany Seg 9.4	CR to Cross Plains	CR to Lodi 10.6	
	8	3.5 Janesville Seg	Montciello Seg	IATA Office 8	Lodi Marsh 1.6	CR To Merrimac 2
Waterville 3.8	Whitewater 4.6	10.4	6.5 Cross Plains 2.8	East Lodi Marsh	
CR to Scuppernog	CR to Clover 4.9	Devil's Staircase Seg	CR to Brook 3.8	CR to Table 1.9	3.2 Merrimac Seg 3.6
1.1	Clover Valley Seg	1.7	Brooklyn Seg 3.5	Table Bluff Seg	City of Lodi 1.8	Devils Lake 8
Scuppernog 5.6	1.6	Arbor Ridge Seg	Montrose Seg 7.5	2.5 CR to Groves 2.4	CR to Baraboo 2.5
Eagle Seg 5.6	CR to Storrs 9.3	2.1	CR to Verona 2.9	CR to Indian Lake	Groves/Pert 1.3	Baraboo Seg 4
Stony Ridge 3.1	Storrs Lake 1.9	CR to Albany	Verona Seg 6.4	4.8	CR to Gilbraltar 2.3	CR to Dells 15
Blue Spring Lake Seg	Milton Seg 4.3	19.1	Madison Seg 3.2	Indian Lake Seg	
7.1	Janesville to Milton Seg		Valley View Seg	2.9	Gilbraltrar Seg 4.8	Sleep@Schoenenberger
Blackhawk Seg 3.2	Sleep @ Albany House	1.8		Home in Dells
Map 79f 3.5	Sleep @ Motel 6 Map 75f	Map 70f $80		Sleep @ Indian Lake	Sleep at DCA in	55 Bowman Road
Sleep @ Shelter # 3	390? Milton Ave.	405 S. Mills St.	Sleep @ Charltons!	Park Cabin DA 24	Gilbraltar	CODE:
Resif 2-36012375	Janesville, WI	Albany, WI 53502	Resupply Map 65f	Map 64f	Map 62f	Map D76/77
888-947-2757	608-756-1742 $53	608-862-3636		Resif dcwdcw000036629		Delorme/Gazz
DAY 9 37.8	DAY 10 33.3	DAY 11 33.3	DAY 12 45	DAY 13 22.9	DAY 14 28	DAY 15 35.1
SUNDAY 6/14/2015	MONDAY 6/15/2015	TUESDAY 6/16/2015	WEDNESDAY 6/17/2015	THURSDAY 6/18/2015	FRIDAY 6/19/2015	SATURDAY 6/20/2015
SP WI Dells	SP Adams Inn	SP Mecan River	SP Waupaca	SP Lions Lake	SP Dells of Eauclaire	SP Kettle Bowl
NLT 0600	NLT 0700	NLT 0600	NLT 0700	NLT 0600	NLT 0700	NLT 0700
CR from Dells	Map D69 thru Chaffe	CR to Greenwood	Skunk & Foster Seg	CR to Ringle	CR to Plover River	
CR to Quincy Bluff 2	CR to Chaffe 9.9	0.5	4.4	23.5	3.5	Kettlebow Seg 7.9
25.8	CR to Chaffe 2.8	Greenwood 4.7	CR to New Hope	Ringle Seg	Plover River Seg	Lumber Camp Seg
CR to Chaffe 10.9	Chaffe Creek Seg	CR to Bohn Lake	13.1	9.4	5.7	12
2.5	1.5	New Hope Seg	Thornapple Creek	CR to Kettlebowl	Old Railroad Seg
Sleep @ Adams Inn	CR to Wedde Creek	Bohn Lake 1.2	5.7	3.9	24.1	9.2
2188 Highway 13	0.7	CR to Deerfield 1.8	CR to Ringle	Dells of EauClaire	Kettlebowl Seg	Highland Lakes Eastern
Adams, WI	Wedde Creek 1.2	Deerfield Seg 3.7	5	2.6	2	3.4
Map 76/77	CR to Mecan River	CR to Emmon 14.6			
$67.99		Emmons Creek Seg	Sleep @ Lions Lake		Sleep in Kettlebowl	Sleep @ Highland Lakes
(866) 266 1506	Mecan River Seg	2.6	Camp - MAP 44F		Primitive Site	Primitive Site
		7.2	Hartman Creek 5.6	715-677-4969	Sleep@Dells of Eauclaire	Map 36F	Map 33F
		Waupaca Seg 4.9		Map 40F		
	Sleep at Mecan River			715-261-1566		Resupply @ Summit
	DCA (WS 14)	Sleep @ Waupaca Seg				Post Office
	Map 52f	PW7 - DCA				N9575 County Rd B
		Map 47f				Summit Lake, WI 54485
DAY 16 38.7	DAY 17 27	DAY 18 41.1	DAY 19 28.2	DAY 20 39.4	DAY 21 35.3	DAY 22 32.5

Ice Age Trail Leg 2

The Trail

It was purely up to me to own my outcome. No one else was going to do this for me, and honestly, many tried to talk me out of it. I was responsible for everything, and I was ok with that. This was my choice and my journey. However, I'd be remiss to say that I didn't sometimes pull in friends and family to help hold my feet to the fire. I needed them for moral and emotional support, and I needed them for resupply.

I began my hike in late May, so the weather was still cold, and the trail was wet and muddy too. The first few days were tough, and I struggled to get into a rhythm. Parts of the trail were connected by hardball

200

pavement, and I quickly learned that I moved much faster on the trail than I did on hardball. On top of that, the hardball would beat up my feet much quicker than the trail.

Breaking Trail on May 30ᵗʰ, 2015.

As I hiked further into the trail, I began to find my stride. I hiked an average of 25-30 miles a day, sometimes more, sometimes less, depending on the terrain and the weather. The trail was challenging, with steep climbs, rocky descents, and river crossings. The trail also took me through extremely remote areas, which was truly amazing. I remember I didn't see a single soul for over a hundred miles.

One of the most challenging aspects of this journey was, of course, the trail itself, but also that many segments, usually the more remote and unused segments, were poorly marked. I didn't lose my way, thankfully, but some days did take much longer than I planned. The wildlife made sure I knew they were out there too, but I only had a couple of interesting encounters, which I will get to later.

The physical challenges of the trail were demanding, but it was the mental and emotional endurance that was the most difficult. I hiked alone for most of the trail, and the solitude was both beautiful and intimidating at times. There was never a time that I felt like giving up, but there were times I had to push through the pain and exhaustion to keep going. This was to be expected, and I was well prepared.

Of course, I also had to deal with both expected and unexpected setbacks, such as blisters on my feet, a broken water filter, and even dog attacks. I'll get to that shortly. Each setback tested my resilience and forced me to adapt and overcome. Too easy.

My first night camping was at the Timber Trails Campground, and it was an instant classic. It wasn't too busy, and I had a lot of space and time to reflect. I met a gentleman named Dave, and he was a genuine human. He helped me get everything I needed to settle in quickly so I could rest.

First Campsite – Timber Trails

As I continued my mission the next day toward Cedar Valley, my feet really began to hurt, and I found myself needing my walking stick more and more. I made it to the Cedar Valley Campground, but by the time I arrived, no one was there to check me in, so I wrote a short note and left cash on the door.

The next day was tough. The weather was challenging, and the terrain was very muddy. I passed through a town along the way to Tisch Mills and was finally able to locate a US Post Office to package up some of my gear and ship it home. If I didn't use a piece of gear even once the first few days, I didn't need it.

That night I would cross my first river and make camp on the other side. It was my first deep woods "primitive" campsite on this journey, and it was bliss. No one to be seen or heard for miles. It was just me and my thoughts. This was my purpose. I would reflect, write, heal, and renew on this journey.

At this point, I considered myself a "rootless wanderer," as Stephen J. Nichols put it in his book, *Getting the Blues.* I was intentionally looking to heal and grow at the same time. In the previous chapters, I discussed how the human condition is marked by its frailty and vulnerability. We are mortal beings, subject to illness, injury, and, ultimately, death. Our physical and emotional states are in constant flux, and we experience suffering and pain throughout our entire lives. However, we have the power to overcome these challenges, but it is only achieved through intentional choice.

We can cultivate resilience, empathy, and kindness in the face of adversity, or we can give up. While the human condition is marked by struggle and suffering, our response to these challenges defines us and our legacy. The problem is it's hard. All things like it are hard and, even worse, require us to leave our comfort zone to do it. For many, leaving the comfort zone is as much fun as trying to wipe our asses with sandpaper.

Deep Woods Campsite

One of my most memorable moments was hiking the Point Beach segment. It was beautiful and terrifying at the same time. I'll explain the terrifying part shortly. But it was indeed an unforgettable experience, though. The trail winds through the beautiful Point Beach State Forest, offering stunning views of Lake Michigan and lush forests. As I walked through the segment, I encountered extremely diverse terrain, from the sandy beaches to steep inclines and an array of wildlife. Things got interesting as I hiked along the beach, and the distance between my location and the solid ground grew wider and wider.

Eventually, I realized I was in a fucking swamp, and there was no getting back to the solid ground without going through the damn thing. It was 6 pm, and I was supposed to be at my campsite by 7 pm.

"No fucking way I am making this hit time.", I said to myself.

"I thought I was done with this shit back in Swamp Phase."

"Fuck it, here we go."

Just as it was in Ranger School, this would require perseverance and endurance. Crawling, walking, or running, I would reach the end of this segment and make ready for the next. Upon reaching the end, I made camp and took the time to reflect on what had just happened. It was unparalleled and very different from what I had experienced in the past.

In Ranger School, the RIs push you intentionally beyond your limits so that you eventually establish a new baseline and operate regularly at that new baseline. Hiking this segment was exactly this. This effort reminded me that I was still in charge of myself and what I was capable of. It reminded me that I had the choice to endure or to quit. It reminded me that I alone own my outcome.

I came out to the other end of Point Beach and into the beginning of the Two Rivers segment successfully. While I was proud, I was smoked and beaten up badly. My frog legs didn't do much for me during the cut across the swamp back to dry land, so my feet and boots were jacked up. I would scrub them clean that night and swap out inserts for the next day.

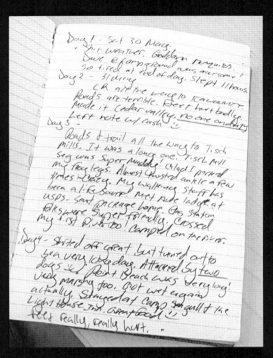

My Journal

The Point Beach segment was a tough experience, but it wasn't done with me yet. Things quickly turned violent. No shit, I was attacked by two dogs as I exited the trail onto the hardball. Without any warning, the dogs lunged at me, their teeth gnashing and growling ferociously as street dogs do. They were relentless, biting and clawing at me with a savage intensity.

At that moment, I knew I had to act fast or risk being torn apart. I used the only real weapon I had available - my walking stick - and swung it with every bit of violence I had in me. They latched onto the end of my stick and ripped off the bottom, but I landed a couple of solid blows, and they finally relented. Unbowed and unscathed, I continued my way down the hardball, walking backward at times to keep an eye on them.

At this point, I was laughing and telling myself, "Fuck the next segment; I'm crashing here tonight." The Two Rivers segment would wait until the next day.

My Walking Stick—A History of My Life

Despite Point Beach and the dogs, what was to come next would take a much bigger toll. It would be one of my longest days, and now add the Two Rivers Segment I carried over from yesterday.

"I hope I don't get behind," I thought.

Additionally, today's segments came with a significant connecting route (CR) that was mostly hardball pavement. No less, I ensured this day's effort would be worth every mile. I planned to stay at Tauschek's Bed & Breakfast in Plymouth, WI, where I could relax in solitude and reflect.

As I made my way to Tauschek's, the terrain was easy except, of course, the hardball CR. I pushed myself hard this day to make it through the hardball and arrive at a decent hour to enjoy Tauschek's. Fortunately, a man driving a small minibus noticed me walking on the side of the road and pulled over to offer me a life. He would take me several miles to my next turning point. This little moment of kindness reminded me of the "Golden Walk" I experienced in Ranger School. He not only saved me time but also reduced the amount of punishment on my feet. I never caught his full name, but I would like to say thank you to him. I am grateful.

I finally made it to Tauschek's, and it was just as glorious as I had imagined. I sat by the fire pit, enjoyed a much-needed glass of wine, and reflected on my life and the direction I wanted to take. I journaled a bit before falling asleep next to the fire.

The Fire Pit at Taushcek's

Eventually, I woke up and moved to the actual bed I was looking forward to. I enjoyed a great night's rest, but to be honest, I had a difficult time getting out of that bed in the morning. As can be expected, these kinds of moments torment the mind, and your brain will surely try to convince you to do everything possible to get as comfortable as possible. I was on a mission, and now was not the time for sleeping in. I got my rest, and it was time to pick up and move out. I was intentional about not letting my mind take over, knowing I had many more miles ahead of me.

I continued into the Milwaukee River Segment, where I'd sleep in shelter #2 that night. The segments leading up to this were chock full of hills and very rocky terrain. I met a helpful trail guide who was able to supply me with additional maps and motivation. Lydia was full of the trail spirit and helped make this segment more enjoyable.

My Ice Age Warrior—Lydia

She was an instant warrior in my fight to find myself. Despite having never seen her again, and probably never will, she deserves my heartfelt gratitude for keeping me motivated that evening on my way to shelter # 2 on the Milwaukee River Segment. I needed every bit of it because it was a pretty shit shelter, but I was a happy man with my jet-boil coffee in the morning.

The Milwaukee River Segment remains special to me to this day. It meant that I was almost home. It was a mixed bag of emotions and physical sensations. As I approached the final stretch of my journey leading to Delafield, I felt both excitement and relief at the prospect of reaching home soon. At the same time, I felt a tinge of sadness that my first leg of this journey was coming to an end.

The terrain of the last 30 miles into Delafield shaped my experience on its own. The trail was steep, rocky, and challenging, but at the same time, I felt energized and motivated to push through so I could see my people.

The most interesting part of those last 30 miles was that I found my mind wandering incredibly. I reflected on my journey so far, and I thought deeply about the challenges I faced, the memories I made, and the things I learned along the way. On the other side of those reflections were both my past and my future. These reflections were a true source of motivation and inspiration as I pushed toward home.

I came through the Monches Segment and approached the Heartland & Delafield segments. I felt a complete sense of accomplishment and pride but also a sense of anticipation for what would come the next day. I had many more miles to go. I was 237 miles in at this point, and fortunately, many of my local friends and family would join me on the Lapham Peak 7.6-mile segment as a farewell of sorts.

The Monches Segment

I arrived home, and I was greeted by the most incredible people. My family and friends welcomed me home, knowing it would be short-lived. I was tired, and I needed to rest. On top of that, I needed to resupply too.

The next morning, we would all meet at Lake Country Fire & Rescue for coffee and a send-off for those who would join me on the Lapham Peak segment. We were at Station 1 in Delafield, WI, where we shared stories and friendships. I was humbled by how many showed up to support me.

Lapham Peak Send-Off Party – LCFR, Delafield, WI

We geared up and moved out. But before we did, Sandy Rosch, one of the main brains at LCFR, offered to take my pack for me and drive it to the endpoint of the Lapham Peak Segment. This was really great as it allowed me to focus on my friends and family who were joining me on this segment. Sandy was one of a kind. She helped me tremendously during my cancer treatments, and now once again, she has come through with her superpowers of kindness and caring.

Send Off by Sandy R.

The crew set off from Station 1, and we hit the trail. It was a little rainy and cloudy, but the mood was great! Most of us had literally hiked the Lapham Peak Segment hundreds of times before. Largely, this was due to the Academy, but it was a local favorite. We hit the trail fast and hard and made our way to the Lapham Peak Tower, where we collected and where they would send me off to move out solo once again.

Entering Lapham Peak Segment – Delafield, WI

Lapham Peak Tower

I departed Lapham Peak Tower and made my way southwest toward the Scuppernong segment. I was rested, motivated, and ready to keep moving. I continued south by southwest, and the trail was mostly welcoming at first.

As I broke trail, a shit storm of weather hit me pretty hard. I promptly put my frog legs on and continued the mission. I made my way through the Scuppernong Segment and straight through the storm onward toward Blackhawk. It was an intense and dangerous thunderstorm and even terrifying at times.

"Should I stop or get out of the wood line?" I thought to myself.

The thunder was so close it was deafening. The blinding flashes of lightning and the torrential rain made it difficult to see, hear, and navigate the terrain. Every step felt uncertain as the ground became slicker and muddier. The risk of slipping and falling was real, but I maintained just fine with my walking stick. I stayed calm and focused as I had no choice but to continue. I was well into the trail at this point and had no real way out. I was in the thick of it.

As I came out of the Black Hawk Segment, I was stopped by a couple of Park Rangers. I thought I was in for it, "What the hell did I do now?" but they were just evacuating folks based on the storm. They said they couldn't allow me to get back on the trail or stay at my planned stopping point, shelter 3, for safety reasons.

"My car is Sturgeon Bay. What do you want me to do!?"

"Hop in the back of the pickup. We'll take you to the next leg."

At first, I thought, "Well, shit. This is not how I envisioned my hike going", but I was grateful. They saved me some time, and I had no choice. They dropped me along the CR between Clover Valley and Storrs Lake, where I'd find a lovely coffee shop to rest and re-fit before moving on. I remember sitting outside the place with my pack minding my own business as I fixed my feet. I'm sure I looked rough at this point, but I also came off as homeless. At least three or four people stopped to drop cash next to me. I tried to stop them and tell them my story, but it was of no use. They just kept walking.

I continued through the Devil's Staircase and into Janesville, where I'd orient the hike north toward Verona and Madison. It was in Verona where I'd link up with a very special family: The Charltons. I don't have nearly enough words to describe the breadth of my love and appreciation for Serena, Patrick, and their family. Almost ten years to the date, they took me in during a time when I had nowhere else to go—stories for another book.

Serena met me with open arms and my equally important resupply. I had shipped it to her several weeks earlier and was so glad that

I could see her along my journey. Unfortunately, no one else was available this day, but Serena and I enjoyed a great night reflecting on the past and all of our old adventures. As usual, I wasn't up late and would later sleep like a rock in my old bed. I could write a whole book exploring this time in my life. Pat, Serena, Harry, Alex, and Emma: I love you dearly, and I am grateful for each of you more than you know.

I would soon leave the Verona area to continue my journey north. I was well-rested and ready to hit the trail hard. I was sad to leave Serena, of course. She was an amazing mother figure, and I'd be careless if I didn't make sure the world knew it. Serena always made me feel like I had a home.

I grabbed my pack, and Serena dropped me off at the trailhead in Valley View, where we said our goodbyes. I hit the trail hard, fast, and full of energy. Later the same day, I would stumble across a real treasure. As before, this discovery reminded me of my golden walk from Ranger School. I was getting good at listening to my soul, and I knew I had to do something with what I just discovered.

I was just coming out of Table Bluff and heading into the Lodi Marsh. As I continue, you should know that this will probably be the last story of the chapter, as I could fill the entire book with this journey. As I trekked through the winding trails, I stumbled upon what seemed to be an abandoned cabin tucked away behind a dense thicket of trees. The forest was silent, it was enchanting, and I couldn't resist opening the door.

My Cabin in the Woods

I certainly had no original plans to stay here tonight, but I looked around and saw no one. I heard no one. My feet were soaking wet and hurting, so I decided this was where I would stay. As I opened the door, I discovered a simple room, but I was completely mesmerized. I felt a sense of wonder and awe wash over me. Finding this unique treasure not only stimulated my soul but also ignited my want and need for reflection and writing.

It was truly sensational. The room had two tables and a wood-burning stove. What else could I ask for? The forest was soaking wet, so it took me longer than I would have liked to find decent firewood. I was supremely focused on starting that fire so I could reflect and write as I gazed upon man's original TV.

Soaking Wet Walking Shoes

It was early. I got the fire started and put my Merrell walking shoes next to the stove to dry out. I sat there for a second and thought about my day. "Life is truly a sliding door event," I thought to myself. Today I chose to walk right through those sliding doors and listen to my soul.

I fixed up the rest of my gear and made ready for the next day before I sat down in front of this epic wood-burning stove. The simplest thing right in front of me brought one of life's greatest pleasures. I sat there for a few moments before pulling out my journal to get to work. I spent more time reflecting than I did writing. It was in this small, unassuming, and unplanned cabin adventure that I truly opened my eyes and came to terms with the sufferings of my life.

A Space to Reflect in Front of Man's Original TV

I was the fortunate one. I was lucky to get the opportunity to deal with such challenging experiences. I questioned myself, "Would I have thrived in a life chock full of luxury and easy paths?" I don't think so. Honestly, I was built to suffer. I was the very definition of the human condition. I could take the hits and help others take the hits too.

Hiking the Ice Age Trail across the state of Wisconsin was an incredible experience. While the trail tested my physical endurance, mental strength, and emotional resilience, it reminded me to embrace discomfort and find strength in adversity. It reminded me that the path of least resistance is never the answer and that I would only grow by doing something different and far outside my comfort zone.

I kept moving after my eye-opening cabin experience. I would come to cross the Merrimac ferry and into Devil's Lake, where I would come to terms with who I am in this world and what I need to do. I needed to do things differently. I needed to take a risk, and like most interesting things in life, different equal opportunity. My difference, in this case, would end up being Kansas City, where I'd be a transplant trying to make a life.

The Ice Age Trail will always hold a special place in my heart, and I hope to return one day to hike it again. I look back and reflect on every mile, every lesson, and every word I wrote.

Lessons Learned

I walked away from my journey with many valuable lessons. The most powerful of which I share below.

This journey was special in many ways, but the opportunity to be away from every kind of distraction allowed me ample time for self-reflection and introspection. Following my cancer, I felt very lost and off track. I didn't even know what track I was on anymore—being alone with my thoughts for hours and days at a time allowed for a much deeper understanding of myself and my values, strengths, and weaknesses. This topic is crucial, so much so that I have discussed it in multiple previous Chapters as well.

Through this reflection, I focused on recognizing patterns of thoughts, behavior, and thinking that were not adding value to my life. This journey, and journeys like it that you may undertake, is one of the most powerful tools for self-discovery.

We must enable our suffering to take us to new levels. We don't know what we don't know, and once brought to a new level, we develop a new understanding of things. At this moment, you can redefine yourself. If you aren't suffering in your life (I find that hard to believe), then again, don't be afraid to seek out pain and suffering.

While the idea of seeking out pain and suffering may seem counterintuitive, there are actually numerous benefits to doing so. By pushing ourselves outside of our comfort zones and embracing discomfort, we open ourselves up to new opportunities for growth and development. You will launch yourself into self-discovery mode.

We become more resilient, more adaptable, and better able to handle the challenges that life throws our way. Additionally, seeking out pain and suffering can help us to develop a greater sense of empathy and compassion as we learn to understand and relate to the struggles of others. Embracing suffering as a means of generating growth will lead to greater personal fulfillment and a more meaningful, purpose-driven life allowing us to stare adversity in the face and punch back when necessary.

As I focused on self-discovery, I was reminded that only I am in charge of myself, but there is another side to that coin—every choice I make can impact everyone around me in powerful ways. As leaders in business or even leaders of families, we must recognize the delicate nature of our choices and the profound impact they can have on ourselves and those around us. Each decision we make is a reflection of our values, ethics, and character and can have far-reaching consequences. We must approach every choice with careful consideration, weighing the risks and benefits and striving to align our actions with our principles.

Moreover, we must recognize that the choices we make can have a ripple effect on our teams, our organizations, our families, and our communities. Our decisions can inspire or demoralize, unite or divide, and shape the direction of our collective future. Therefore, it is crucial that we exercise wisdom, empathy, and foresight in every choice we make.

Ultimately, the delicate nature of our choices demands that we approach everything we do in life with humility and a deep sense of responsibility. We must recognize that our decisions have the power to shape the lives of those around us and strive to lead with integrity, compassion, and purpose. By doing so, we can create a positive impact that extends far beyond ourselves and into the world.

A Risk Taken

During my time alone, I concluded that I would need to take some serious risks if I wanted to leave my comfort zone, improve my life, and grow. It's not that I was cautious in my decisions or avoided anything that posed a risk or challenge. The problem was that I was surrounded by friends and family, and I had a great role at the Academy. This is great, but I was too comfortable, and there was no push or pull factor in my life driving me to grow.

My journey allowed me to realize and accept that post-cancer, I was feeling a deep sense of emptiness and dissatisfaction with my life. I was just good at hiding it from everyone, including myself. Don't get me wrong, I was happy, but I didn't feel like I was growing as a man.

I knew I needed to take a risk and jump outside my comfort zone. I was good at leaving my comfort zone but not in the way I am talking about here. I could push myself and do very challenging things, but to quit my job and move across the country where I had no support structure of any kind? That was a risk taken.

With my newfound sense of courage, I did end up leaving the Academy eventually. I didn't know it at the time, but I would eventually book a one-way train ticket to Kansas City, where I would discover what the future held for me.

Years later, I look back at my decision to take that risk, and I know it was the best thing I could have done for myself and my family. It is when we are willing to take risks and put ourselves in uncomfortable situations that we can truly grow and develop as a person.

Write

I am not a writer by trade. I didn't go to school to learn how to write, and honestly, I never thought I was any good at first, but something changed on my journey. My reflections and my thoughts were intense, and I felt the need to write them down so that I could revisit this experience and hold myself accountable for the decisions I would make.

Writing has been a transformative and healing practice for me. It has the power to unlock our innermost thoughts, feelings, and experiences. Whether through journaling, storytelling, or creative writing, the act of putting pen to paper helps us process our emotions, gain clarity on our values and beliefs, and uncover insights into our personal and professional lives.

Through writing, I have developed an even greater understanding of myself and those around me. It has helped me to foster empathy and compassion along my personal and leadership journey. Ultimately, the lesson here is that writing has vast and varied healing benefits and provides us with a powerful means of self-expression and personal growth.

With this, I put an end to Chapter 6. I will share more with you in the upcoming chapters.

CHAPTER 7 – Embracing the
Human Condition

As we close Part 2 of this journey through the depths of human existence, we arrive at a revelation that transcends the boundaries of pain and suffering. As if reborn from the pits of destruction, emerging with renewed strength and resilience, we have come to understand that suffering, in its rawest form, is not an enemy to be defeated but a profound teacher guiding us toward the essence of our being. In this sacred space of understanding, we unveil the transformative power that lies dormant within our struggles, discovering the extraordinary beauty that blossoms when we dare to embrace the untamed terrain of our own vulnerability.

With newfound wisdom etched into our souls, we step into the final chapter of our story, ready to embrace life's symphony of joy and sorrow, for we have learned that even in the depths of suffering, a beacon of hope will forever illuminate our path—*if we allow it.*

While profoundly difficult, keeping our eyes wide open is crucial to facing every challenge, obstacle, and suffering this life has to offer. For years I only dreamt of writing about my journey and the lessons it gave me, but thanks to Johnnie Blue Hands, I found the courage to put pen to pad and bring my story and experiences to life. I opened my eyes and realized what needed to be done—*write about suffering and the lessons it brought me.*

I started this book with the story of my life, where I came from, where I've been, and the suffering I've endured. All of these offered uniquely precious lessons, which I've carefully curated chapter after chapter.

Learning to Suffer Is About Reflection and Growth

As we are expected to do so, I have grown over the years through my experiences, successes, sufferings, joys, and setbacks. With each passing year, I grew stronger and wiser by keeping my eyes wide open. As I wrote in Chapter 1, learning to suffer means we learn to be comfortable with being uncomfortable. When we have an executive session or gut check, we open our eyes to everything we are afraid of or running from, and we face it. Anytime something wasn't going "my way" or "to plan," I forced myself to have a gut check and understand exactly where my failures were. From there, I would course correct, learn, grow, and move forward.

Self-awareness provides the keys to our kingdom and helps us become the best version of ourselves. As you learn to suffer, forcing the gut check while intentionally embracing your circumstances, you'll find that the concept of self-awareness holds invaluable benefits. For example, you will have better control of your outcomes, better perspective on your circumstances and those of others, and you might build better relationships.

All roads to success began with knowing myself, accepting my circumstances, and figuring out what to do next. The only other option was to let my circumstances control me, succumb to the norm, and, if I was lucky, live a mediocre life at best. As my eyes opened, I became aware of my true, raw potential and what I was capable of. That I was capable of taking the punches. That I could take every hit in stride and figure out to take that energy and do something great with it. The key, of course, was the constant gut check. Regular and honest assessments of myself so that I could move forward in the right direction. With each passing day, I tried to remember the limitless possibilities my future held. By figuring out what I was truly capable of, I was able to move my life forward one day at a time, taking every hit with my eyes wide open.

Learning to Suffer is About Empathy and Connection

I spent most of my life in a hardened defensive posture. My walls were tall, strong, and impenetrable. Because of this, I never built any truly meaningful relationships in my young life or even during early adulthood, for that matter. Only a select few were allowed inside my walls, and that really started with Yael. She didn't force her way in but instead built up my trust and confidence slowly. Her being present in my life enabled me to see past the proverbial walls, embrace change, and take risks.

My barrier walls were built during my childhood, but it would be many years later before I learned to tear them down completely. My emotional detachment, while flawed by nature, actually allowed me to thrive independently. When I was young, I didn't have anyone in my life to truly be emotionally dependent on, so this path was my only recourse until Yael came along.

Over the years, I learned how important empathy and connection are in the face of suffering. When we share our suffering, we gain a deeper understanding and compassion for others who are also enduring hardships.

A few months after Justin was born in 2001, my mother went missing again. The difference this time was that Justin was with her. My sister went looking for her, and, not surprisingly, she was with our aunt Sandy. Along with the rest of the house, she was drugged up beyond recognition. My sister took Justin from my mom that night and went to live with her boyfriend at the time, Fito.

I discussed this memory with my sister recently, and she put it like this, "Jason, I remember crying to you about it. That I needed you to help me save up some money for a security deposit for an apartment on Lawndale. And you came through. I don't know how, but you did. It was just me and the kids for a few years, and you somehow managed to get money while you were at St. John's. Even though you couldn't help me physically with both of them at the time, you definitely sent me money often to help us out. You always looked out for us even while you were at the Academy."

Shared suffering has a unique power to forge unbreakable bonds and nurture the strongest relationships. When we face adversity together, whether it be physical, emotional, or psychological, we experience a deep sense of empathy and understanding for one another. In these challenging moments, vulnerability and authenticity emerge, creating a safe space for genuine connection. I look back at Jodi's memory, and it superiorly reinforces the concept of shared suffering for me. Like my childhood, Ranger School did the same, except now it has been sewn into the fabric of my existence.

Through shared suffering, we witness each other's resilience, courage, and unwavering support, instilling a profound trust and reliance on one another. The mutual experience of hardship cultivates a profound sense of unity, allowing relationships to transcend superficialities and thrive on a foundation of shared strength and compassion. Together, we navigate the stormy seas, finding solace, comfort, and companionship in the knowledge that we are not alone in our struggles. In this crucible of shared suffering, the bonds that are formed become unbreakable, representing a profound testament to the power of human connection and the strength that arises from enduring hardships together.

Empathy is the essential quality that allows us to understand and relate to the experiences of others. However, there are moments when we unintentionally (or, for some, intentionally) fail to recognize other people's problems as real problems. As was my case many times over the years, including the stolen cheese sticks, if you recall. We may be quick to dismiss or invalidate other people's struggles because we cannot fully comprehend or relate to their circumstances.

As with the cheese sticks, I learned how important it is to acknowledge that everyone's reality is unique, and what may seem insignificant or trivial to me can be deeply significant to someone else. Often, we fail to see the real root of their problems, overlooking the underlying emotions and complexities that make their challenges genuinely impactful. As was the case with the cheese sticks. It wasn't that his cheese sticks were stolen from the employee lounge fridge but that he was feeling deeply disrespected and undervalued by his co-workers.

This was precisely when I learned how crucial it is to approach others with an open mind and heart, recognizing that their feelings are valid and their experiences matter, regardless of how they might differ from our own. I have to say, though, that I remain allergic to "bullshit" and continue to practice tactical empathy on a case-by-case basis. That said, I do seek to understand first before placing judgment in every situation.

Learning to Suffer Is About Acceptance and Surrender

In the face of adversity, I have discovered that learning to suffer goes hand in hand with acceptance and surrender. This profound realization has taken root within me throughout my life, from Chicago to Ranger School and all the way through my journey with cancer. My childhood circumstances were what they were. I accepted that very early and surrendered to the fact that I needed to be the owner of my future. No one else was going to do it for me. I surrendered to the fact that I needed to do something bold. That life is a series of sliding door events and that when the time came, I needed to have the courage to jump through.

When I was diagnosed with cancer, I recall that at first, the news struck me like a thunderbolt, engulfing my world in shockingly loud fear and uncertainty. I grappled with anger and resentment, questioning why such a cruel fate had befallen me. I was 26 years old and looking down the barrel of my own mortality. But as time passed, I came to understand that resisting the inevitable only intensified my suffering.

Acceptance became my refuge—a sanctuary of inner peace as the storm raged before me. It meant acknowledging the reality of my condition and the uncertainties that lay ahead. It meant embracing the pain, both physical and emotional, as an integral part of my existence. Instead of fighting against it, I began to see suffering as a companion on this path, teaching me invaluable lessons about strength, resilience, and compassion.

Surrendering became my liberation—a release from the burden of control and resistance. At first, I refused to surrender. I refused to show any weakness, and because of that, I only suffered more, except in this case, it was the kind of suffering that didn't make me stronger. Surrendering meant relinquishing my desire to manipulate the outcome, to defy the natural order of things. I realized that surrender was not synonymous with defeat but rather an act of profound courage and wisdom. It meant relinquishing the illusion of power, allowing life to unfold with its own rhythm. In surrender, I found solace, for I no longer carried the weight of the world upon my shoulders.

Through acceptance and surrender, I discovered the profound beauty hidden within the depths of my suffering. It was a transformative process that shattered my preconceived notions of resilience. True resilience, I learned, does not lie in steeling oneself against pain but rather in embracing it as an essential aspect of the human condition. It is the ability to find strength in vulnerability, to seek solace within the cracks of our brokenness.

In embracing my pain and finding peace within myself, I became a messenger of a powerful truth: the key to true resilience lies in accepting and embracing the hardships we face. Through my journey, I have experienced the blossoming of a newfound inner strength—a resilience that emerges from the depths of surrender. It is a resilience that does not deny or suppress suffering but rather walks hand in hand with it, acknowledging its presence while refusing to let it define my spirit.

As I continue along my path, I offer my story as a testament to the transformative power of acceptance and surrender. I hope it can serve as a guiding light for you, illuminating the way to embrace your own suffering, find peace within, and discover the immeasurable strength that lies within the depths of our souls.

Learning to Suffer is About Finding Meaning and Purpose

In the face of adversity and suffering, we experience a profound transformation that can lead to the discovery of a greater sense of purpose and meaning in life. Amidst my suffering, I searched for a path forward. I searched for meaning and purpose. My journey across the Ice Age Trail serves as a powerful example of discovery, resilience, inner strength, and a newfound perspective on life.

Embarking on my solo journey was a physically and emotionally demanding endeavor that I knew would carry me to the next stage of my life. The solitude of the trail presented a unique opportunity for self-reflection and introspection. As the miles passed by and the challenges intensified, I was reminded of the raw reality of struggle and discomfort.

A welcome reminder of the cards I was dealt as a child and, of course, my Ranger School struggles. Each step I took became a testament to my endurance, my resilience, and my unwavering determination to keep moving forward.

It was within this crucible that I developed a deeper understanding of myself, and the world began to emerge. My mind, stripped of distractions and preoccupations, became attuned to the essence of existence and the human condition. I came to realize that my personal suffering was but a small part of the grand tapestry of life and that meaning is found only in the shared experience of overcoming adversity.

Through the trials and tribulations of my journey, a newfound perspective on life took root. The challenges faced on the trail became metaphors for the struggles encountered in everyday life. The trails walked, and the valleys traversed became symbols of personal growth, resilience, and the ability to overcome obstacles. Like with Ranger School and my cancer, I developed a profound appreciation for the small joys and wonders that had previously gone unnoticed—a simple cigar, that first smell of coffee in the morning, or just sitting next to a fire with old friends.

This newfound perspective instilled a sense of purpose and a desire to share the lessons learned. Whether through inspiring others to embark on their own journeys of self-discovery or by dedicating myself to causes that promote resilience, healing, and compassion, my sense of purpose expands beyond the boundaries of our personal experience.

As We Learn to Suffer, We Learn to Open Our Eyes

In the realm of learning to suffer, we are challenged to keep our eyes wide open, embracing the full spectrum of human experience with unwavering courage. It is a call to abandon the instinct to shield ourselves from pain and to resist the temptation of closing our eyes to the harsh realities that surround us. For when we dare to keep our eyes open, even amidst the darkest moments, we open ourselves to profound growth, transformation, and ownership.

To keep our eyes wide open means confronting the depths of our own suffering head-on, refusing to turn away or deny its existence. It is a willingness to sit with discomfort, to explore the tangled web of emotions that accompany our most intense trials. Through this unwavering gaze, we cultivate a profound sense of empathy, not only for ourselves but for the collective human experience.

In keeping our eyes wide open, we witness the intricate tapestry of life—the moments of bliss and the moments of despair, the threads of joy interwoven with threads of sorrow. We begin to understand that suffering is not an anomaly but an integral part of the human condition. It is through this recognition that we find solace in our shared vulnerability, connecting with others on a level that transcends words.

By keeping our eyes wide open, we also unveil the invaluable lessons that suffering has to offer. We learn that pain holds the potential for profound growth and wisdom, and within the depths of despair lie the seeds of resilience and transformation. We discover the power of surrender, of releasing our resistance and embracing the lessons that suffering has to teach us.

Keeping our eyes wide open demands a relentless commitment to self-awareness and introspection. It necessitates a willingness to face our own demons, to confront our fears and insecurities without flinching. In this act of courageous self-examination, we unravel the layers of our being, peeling back the masks we wear and embracing our authentic selves.

Ultimately, to keep our eyes wide open as we learn to suffer is to embark on a pilgrimage of the soul. It is an invitation to embark on an odyssey of self-discovery and growth, to embrace the fullness of our humanity, and to walk hand in hand with the profound and transformative nature of suffering itself.

The Contrarian Mindset

In a world that often seeks solace in comfort and avoids the turbulent waters of adversity, we embark on a journey that challenges conventional wisdom and embraces the contrarian mindset. These final words delve into the profound intersection of learning to suffer and the power of embracing a contrarian perspective. As we navigate the depths of our own discomfort and confront the harsh realities of life head-on, we discover that the contrarian mindset becomes a beacon of strength and resilience. It dares us to defy the status quo, challenge societal norms, and find wisdom and growth in the very act of embracing suffering. I challenge you to embark on a transformative exploration of how the contrarian mindset can become your guiding light on the path toward mastering the art of enduring, learning, and, ultimately, triumphing through the crucible of suffering.

My journey took me to places emotionally, mentally, and physically. My journey allowed me to visit my soul, and it opened my eyes to the fact that when it comes to my mental state—I am in charge.

After taking some serious time to explore why, I concluded that the way I live my life now is dramatically different from the way, I lived it before I learned to suffer. In previous chapters, I explained my philosophy on this concept that no one is allowed to ruin my day except me.

Let me ask again, who was the last person to ruin your day? As you wrap up this book, I hope your answer has undergone a profound and meaningful transformation. While sorting through my garage, I stumbled upon an old sign intended for display. It bore the words, "Close your eyes and breathe," seemingly designed to aid in navigating challenging times and promoting a slower pace when managing those times. Although this method might prove effective for some, it failed to resonate with me. I took the liberty of amending the sign by crossing out "close" and substituting it with "open" while replacing "breathe" with "make a decision." Open your eyes and make a decision! Confront life head-on with eyes wide open. Embrace your ability to endure with unwavering motivation and drive.

- This is how we retain our strength in this existence.
- This is how we make intentional decisions about our happiness.
- This is how we decide what kind of people we allow in our life.
- This is how we decide who and what has access to our power.
- This is how we decide what makes our hearts sing.

As this chapter draws to a close, I hope my words ignite a flame within your soul and carry some essence of wisdom not otherwise known.

From the moment we take our first breath, we become eligible for death. I'll say it again, we are all born some kind of broken, and our vast existence is spent healing in some way. To that end, suffering weaves its intricate threads, entwined with joy and resilience. It is in the crucible of adversity that our true mettle is forged, where we discover the untapped reservoirs of strength residing within us. It is through suffering that we uncover the essence of our being, unearthing depths of character we never knew we possessed.

Embrace the hardships that come your way. For they are not roadblocks but stepping stones on the path to self-discovery. Do not avert your gaze; instead, let your eyes remain wide open, unflinchingly confronting the trials that beset you. It is in this unwavering gaze that you will find the transformative power to endure.

Let suffering be your teacher, guiding you toward growth and self-improvement. In its embrace, you will unearth compassion, empathy, and a profound understanding of the human condition. Every scar etched upon your heart becomes a testament to your resilience, a badge of honor earned through the crucible of experience. As we say in the Army, "Another ribbon across!"

Remember that life's challenges are not meant to break you but to mold you into a person of profound depth and wisdom. Embrace them with an open heart, for it is within the depths of suffering that the seeds of greatness are sown.

So, as you turn the final page of this journey, carry with you the realization that suffering is not a curse but a gateway to profound transformation. Embrace it, learn from it, and let it shape you into a beacon of strength and inspiration.

With eyes wide open, venture forth into the world, ready to face life's tempests head-on. Let suffering be your companion, and through its trials, may you discover the boundless power that resides within. Remember always: in the tapestry of life, it is the interplay of light and shadow that creates the most breathtaking masterpiece.

May your journey be filled with purpose, resilience, and an unwavering commitment to thrive, for it is in learning to suffer that we truly learn to live.

The Contrarian Mindset

The contrarian mind is bold and free,
Challenging the status quo with glee.
It sees the world in a different light,
And questions what we assume is right.

In times of strife and hardship too,

The contrarian's strength comes shining through.

For when the winds of change do blow,

It adapts and thrives and learns to grow.

Through trials and tribulations faced,

The contrarian finds a hidden grace.

With resilience born of a restless mind,

It overcomes what others leave behind.

So let us learn from the contrarian's way,

And dare to challenge what others say.

For in the face of life's great tests,

It's the contrarian who finds true success.

PART THREE:
Beyond the Classroom

As we embark on the last and final part of this book, we delve into the profound depths of learning to suffer and the transformative power it holds. Part Three brings us to the forefront of non-cognitive skill development, where we unlock the untapped potential within ourselves and others. Part Three is for the business leader, the educator, the youth non-profit director, and all those looking for real work applications. This part of the book focuses on practical applications where we explore the intricacies of programming techniques for businesses, schools, camps, and other organizations that have emerged as crucibles for resilience and personal growth. Moreover, we venture into the realm of execution techniques, where the lessons learned through suffering find practical application, allowing us to thrive amidst the challenges that await. In this part, we embrace the wisdom gleaned from the story laid out in the pages before. Here, we pave our path toward mastery and embrace the indomitable spirit that resides within us all as we learn to suffer.

Through the lens of suffering, we gain a unique perspective on the mastery of executive function skills. While traditionally associated with cognitive abilities, we explore how these skills extend beyond the realms of intellect and manifest in the crucible of adversity. We unveil the profound influence of executive functions on the ability to endure, adapt, and thrive amidst life's most daunting trials.

Drawing on my journey, we unravel the intricate interplay between suffering, executive function skills, and personal growth. As we progress through the following chapters, we will explore practical strategies and techniques that can be applied to cultivate these skills in the face of hardship, fostering resilience and empowering individuals to overcome the most formidable challenges.

CHAPTER 8 – Nurturing Grit:
Unleashing the Power of Executive Function Skills

Of all the things I learned and discovered in my life, the need for non-cognitive skills is top of the list. Let me tell you why as we continue to discuss the path forward.

As someone who grew up in the rough streets of Chicago and experienced poverty first-hand, I have come to appreciate the importance of non-cognitive skills in achieving success. My personal experiences have shown me that non-cognitive skills such as grit, resilience, and emotional intelligence are often the true determinants of success.

During my years of developing young leaders, I have seen firsthand the transformation that can occur when non-cognitive skills are emphasized and nurtured. I have seen young people who were struggling with self-doubt and insecurity develop the confidence and resilience necessary to achieve their goals. I have seen students who were struggling academically thrive once they learned how to manage their emotions and develop a growth mindset.

It is my belief that by focusing on the development of non-cognitive skills, we can help individuals overcome the obstacles and challenges they may face in their lives. This is why I am so passionate about discussing the importance of non-cognitive skills and their role in achieving success. By prioritizing these skills, we can empower individuals to reach their full potential and lead fulfilling lives.

While cognitive abilities such as intelligence, knowledge, math, and English are essential for success in life, business, and family, non-cognitive skills are equally, if not more, critical. You've heard me say that we can get all "As" in school and still flunk life. This is because non-cognitive skills, such as empathy, communication, resilience, and self-control, enable us to navigate complex social situations, build relationships, manage stress, and adapt to change.

Looking back at my Ice Age journey, I was fortunate to have the training and knowledge necessary to build and execute a plan. However, if it weren't for my base of non-cognitive skills, I wouldn't have had the existing relationships or the ability to build new ones to get through successfully.

Even in today's fast-paced world, where technology and automation are rapidly transforming the job market, those of us with strong non-cognitive skills will be better equipped to succeed in the workplace, lead teams, and manage our personal lives effectively. I am specifically addressing non-cognitive skills in this chapter because I firmly believe that all successful outcomes in our lives are rooted in them.

As we think about the path forward and how we truly learn to suffer, non-cognitive skills are paramount among all things. This is, of course, my opinion which is rooted in my personal experiences and sufferings. I am not sure there is any evidence that exists today to convince me otherwise.

There are many terms for non-cognitive skills, such as soft skills or socio-emotional skills; some are accepted more than others, depending on your school of thought. For me, these skills come down to one thing—grit. Non-cognitive skills, or as I call them, grit, are extremely important when it comes to learning to suffer because they help us develop resilience and cope with adversity.

When faced with difficult situations, those who possess strong non-cognitive skills are better able to regulate their emotions, maintain a positive attitude, and persevere through challenges. As we discussed, someone who has developed self-awareness, self-control, and empathy may be better equipped to handle the stress of a setback or failure than someone who lacks these skills. Every morning I drink my coffee, and I wonder how these skills are not on the priority curriculum list for schools.

Non-cognitive skills help us develop a growth mindset, which is the belief that challenges and failures can be opportunities for learning and growth. This mindset helps us view suffering as a necessary and valuable part of the learning process rather than a sign of inadequacy or failure. The bottom line is that these skills help us build the mental and emotional resilience needed to cope with the ups and downs of life, including the suffering that often accompanies learning and personal growth.

Political Correctness

There is a lot of discussion about what term/phrase to use for these skills. I will discuss some of the history shortly, but for now, I want to highlight some differing views. In large part, these skills are labeled "non-cognitive" skills as equally important but opposite to cognitive skills.

They are very different types of abilities that we possess. Cognitive skills are related to our brain's ability to process information, analyze data, and make decisions. They include skills such as problem-solving, critical thinking, and logical reasoning. Non-cognitive skills, on the other hand, refer to personal qualities and characteristics that are not related to cognitive abilities, such as emotional intelligence, communication skills, and social skills. While cognitive skills are necessary for academic success, non-cognitive skills are equally and sometimes more important for personal and professional success, as they help us interact with others, manage our emotions, and navigate different situations.

I've had this discussion many times at various conferences and over many different dinner tables. Some do take issue and have a valid argument against the terms used to describe these skills. There are many terms, including one of the originals, which is non-cognitive skills. Others include soft skills, life skills, social skills, and personal skills.

Soft skills generally refer to a set of personal attributes that enable us to interact effectively with others, including communication skills, teamwork, problem-solving, and adaptability. Social skills focus specifically on our ability to interact with others in a social setting, such as making friends, empathizing with others, and expressing ourselves appropriately. Life skills refer to the ability to manage one's personal life effectively, such as time management, financial literacy, and decision-making skills. Personal skills are a broad category that includes both cognitive and non-cognitive skills, such as self-awareness, motivation, and resilience. Each of these terms reflects a different aspect of non-cognitive skills, but they all emphasize the importance of personal qualities and interpersonal abilities for success in life.

I've just described the CEO of my life, my soul, my mind, my everything. I personally continue to use the term "non-cognitive skills" when trying to explain the concepts to others, but for the most part, I have come to call these important skills "Executive Function Skills." The Chief Executive of my existence manages these skills daily and enables me to employ them when needed.

Interestingly, I recently read an article in Forbes Magazine titled, "It's About Time We Abandoned the Term' Soft Skills" where the author, Dan Pontefract, introduces the term "Professional Skills." Dan argues that "there is no such thing as a 'soft skill.'" Pontefract continues to say that these skills have long been mislabeled as "soft" and that they are, "in reality, the bedrock of effective leadership. It's high time we abandon the outdated and derogatory term 'soft skills' and embrace their true essence: professional skills."

I don't disagree with Dan when it comes to our professional lives, but it does beg the question, "How can the act of my three-year-old sharing his toys with other kids at the park be considered a professional skill at this point?" Recognizing that Dan's article is entirely focused on business and our professional lives, it demonstrates the vast and varied opinions on terming this skill set. It also gives credence to the fact that these skills are truly non-cognitive in nature and that they may develop into professional skills/abilities later in life. This is why I call them "Executive Function Skills."

The very day we are born, we become eligible for death, and, in my experience, it's our executive function skills that help us manage our lives from the cradle to the grave.

A Short History

I want to take a brief step back and recognize the history behind non-cognitive skills and the role our very own US Army played in developing the concept.

In the early 20th century, the United States Army recognized that traditional measures of intelligence alone were not sufficient predictors of soldier success. Thus began the exploration of non-cognitive skills, such as leadership, resilience, and adaptability, which could not be measured by intelligence tests.

During World War II, the Army developed a training program called "Leadership, Education, and Training" (LET), which aimed to teach soldiers non-cognitive skills. This program became the precursor to modern-day leadership training in the military.

In the 1950s, the Army began to recognize the importance of emotional intelligence, which includes self-awareness, self-regulation, empathy, and social skills. These skills were incorporated into military training and became an essential component of successful leadership.

In 1974, Ronald G. Downey of the US Army Research Institute for the Behavioral and Social Sciences wrote, "The concept of leadership in the US Army of the 1970s has been changed by a variety of new environmental pressures. The movement to an all-volunteer force has placed increased pressures on the leaders to attend to the concerns of the individual Soldier in ways which were not as crucial in the past." This meant we had to start giving a shit about Soldiers and each individual problem they had. The bottom line: it was crucial to mission success that we cared for every Soldier and each unique problem they faced.

Today, the US Army continues to invest in the development of non-cognitive skills, recognizing their importance in modern warfare and in civilian life. The Army's leadership training programs are models for many civilian organizations, and the importance of non-cognitive skills is increasingly recognized in fields ranging from business to education. The history of non-cognitive skills is a testament to the importance of these skills in all aspects of life.

Non-Cognitive Skills Are Not Innate.

Non-cognitive skills are not innate abilities but are instead learned over time from birth through adulthood. As we grow and develop, we acquire and develop these skills through various experiences and interactions with our environment, including family, school, work, and society.

In Part 1, I described how lucky I was to have the childhood I did, despite the challenges. I also said that I considered myself to be at an advantage over most others, especially those who've never been brought to their knees by the school of hard knocks—hunger, thirst, homelessness, drug addiction, or otherwise.

I became good at smiling. I never had the perfect teeth for it, but I managed. I figured out how to talk to people and drive a good hustle. I knew how to build friendships and partnerships, but more importantly, I knew how not to burn bridges. Those around me who didn't figure out how to manage people burned their bridges pretty quickly. Some even dug a hole, buried that bridge, and poured concrete over it. I developed critical executive function skills out of necessity, of course, but also through the early teachings of my parents.

Our parents play a crucial role in the development of our executive function skills. My parents played a very critical role in my development despite the cards we were dealt. Albeit indirectly, they taught me to be unafraid of people and the circumstances around me. That meant that I had no issue engaging with every walk of life, no matter the situation. My parents, while challenged with life's circumstances at best, taught me how to flex in every situation I was in. To adapt and to survive. Isn't that what relationships are all about? Adapting and being flexible to ensure the relationship or situation stays alive.

I look back at my parents, and I am pretty sure that is all they taught me. Each of our situations is unique & different, but ideally, our parents provide a nurturing and supportive environment that encourages the development of our social and emotional skills, such as empathy, communication, and self-regulation. Parents are supposed to model positive behaviors and provide opportunities for us to learn and practice these skills. This is how we help our children develop a strong foundation for success in life.

Like me, many of you were born into challenging circumstances or had parents who struggled to be positive role models. All of which is ok. It has to be ok. If it weren't, you wouldn't be reading these words right now.

Challenging circumstances are natural; sometimes, we are simply dealt a bad hand. It doesn't mean we can't take that hand and play the best damn game possible—we can own our circumstances. Usually, though, the problem for young people is that they don't even know it's possible to do that. This is where educators and mentors come in to pick up the ball.

Outside of the home, educators and mentors play the next most crucial role in developing our executive function skills. In schools, camps, youth organizations, and other educational settings, an educator's mandate is to help young people develop important executive function skills such as teamwork, problem-solving, and leadership through group projects, discussions, and extracurricular activities. Our mentors, both in our personal and professional lives, are meant to provide guidance and support to develop these important skills.

Finally, society plays an essential role in shaping the development of our executive function skills. Cultural norms, social expectations, and institutional structures can all influence how we learn and practice these skills. By creating a culture that values and rewards the development of executive function skills, society can help us acquire the skills we need to succeed in life.

The Social Media Culture of Today

On the topic of cultural norms and social expectations, social media has become an integral part of people's lives, especially young people. Its impact on their development of executive function skills cannot be ignored. While social media can provide opportunities for communication, learning, and creativity, it also poses a significant risk of hindering the development of vital executive function skills. One of the significant challenges is the impact of social media on communication skills. Young people spend a considerable amount of time texting, messaging, or posting on social media, which can limit their face-to-face communication skills. Because of this, they may struggle with empathy, active listening, or conflict resolution skills, which are crucial executive function skills necessary for success in personal and professional life.

Furthermore, social media can lead to the development of negative self-image and low self-esteem in young people, which affects their emotional regulation and resilience skills. The constant exposure to unrealistic beauty standards, body shaming, and cyberbullying on social media can cause stress, anxiety, and depression, which can hinder their ability to manage emotions and cope with stress. For instance, studies have shown that young people who spend more time on social media platforms, such as Instagram and Snapchat, have higher rates of anxiety and depression than those who spend less time on these platforms.

While social media has its benefits, it is essential to be aware of its impact on young people's executive function skills and take proactive steps to mitigate the risks. When I think about my childhood, we suffered, yes, and we starved at times. But the kind of suffering that comes with social media is a different kind of suffering. It is vast, varied, and hugely significant in today's world. While my childhood was tough, it galvanized me to stay strong and survive. The kind of suffering we see from social media today has the opposite effect and tends to drive mental and emotional states into a downward spiral.

Not that anyone invited me to parties, but if they didn't, I would have never known I wasn't invited. Nowadays, when your son or daughter isn't invited to something, they know it instantly as they view the images of their so-called friends hanging out and having fun without them. Of course, these are all assumptions they develop and are not necessarily rooted in facts. Nonetheless, the damage has been done, and this happens multiple times a day, thus the issue our young people face with social media today.

Cyberbullying, online harassment, and exposure to unrealistic beauty/fitness standards, and body shaming can negatively affect young people's self-esteem, confidence, and emotional well-being. Furthermore, excessive use of social media can lead to addiction, reduced attention span, and decreased motivation, which can impact academic and personal growth.

To proactively mitigate these risks, parents and educators can take several steps. First, they can teach young people about the importance of digital citizenship and online safety. This includes setting guidelines and boundaries around social media use, monitoring their online activity, and discussing the impact of social media on their mental health and well-being. Second, parents and educators can encourage young people to engage in offline activities that promote executive function skill development, such as sports, volunteering, and arts. This can help young people develop communication, leadership, teamwork, and problem-solving skills, which are essential for personal and professional success.

Third, parents and educators can teach young people to focus on their strengths and real abilities rather than their appearance or perceived abilities. They can also encourage them to speak out against online bullying. This isn't to say that they should censor or silence anyone, but rather speak up against those who would cause real harm for no other reason than for their own pleasure.

Lastly, parents and educators can provide resources and support for young people who may be struggling with mental health issues or addiction to social media. This includes seeking professional help, therapy, or support groups. At the end of the day, they need real human contact and engagement.

By proactively addressing the risks associated with social media use, parents and educators can help young people develop the executive function skills they need to succeed in life.

The Case Against Executive Function Skills

The interesting thing about executive function skill development, aka non-cognitive skills, is that some think it to be derogatory all together, not just politically incorrect. It reminds me of the phrase "remedial training," which was often used in the US Army up until recent years. That phrase, too, apparently had a derogatory essence to it. According to the

Oxford Dictionary, the definition of remedial is "giving or intended as a remedy or cure." The fact that a soldier was remedial meant they needed to be cured? Or that they were somehow inferior to their fellow man?

While many argue that executive function skills are important for success in life, there are some who question the value of focusing on these skills over more traditional measures of intelligence and achievement. Here, I'll offer a few arguments against executive function skill development:

- ✓ **Focus on "hard skills":** Some argue that executive function skills, aka non-cognitive skills, are less important than "hard skills" such as math, science, and technology. They believe that prioritizing executive function skills over hard skills may lead to a workforce that lacks the technical expertise necessary for innovation and progress.

- ✓ **Difficulty in measuring:** Unlike cognitive skills, non-cognitive skills can be difficult to measure and assess objectively. This lack of standardization and quantification can make it challenging to determine the effectiveness of non-cognitive skill development programs and their impact on individual and organizational outcomes.

- ✓ **Overemphasis on individual responsibility:** Some argue that the emphasis on non-cognitive skills places too much responsibility on individuals to improve their own outcomes. They argue that systemic issues such as poverty, discrimination, and inequality cannot be solved by individuals alone and require broader social and policy solutions.

- ✓ **Lack of evidence:** Despite the growing interest in non-cognitive skill development, there is still limited evidence to support the effectiveness of these programs. Skeptics argue that without rigorous scientific research and empirical evidence, it is difficult to justify the time and resources invested in executive skill development.

While these arguments against executive function skill development may have some merit, it is important to note that non-cognitive skills are not mutually exclusive with hard skills. Both are important for success in life, and individuals and organizations can benefit from developing both cognitive and non-cognitive skills. That said, I've always maintained the idea that one can get all "A's" in school and still flunk life. Executive function skills, while equally important to hard skills, will dictate all outcomes.

Beyond Intelligence: The Role of Non-Cognitive Skills
in Developing Resilience

While intelligence is undoubtedly important for academic success, it is not the only factor that determines our ability to cope with adversity and bounce back from setbacks. Non-cognitive skills, or as you've heard me call them, executive function skills, such as grit, perseverance, and emotional regulation, play a critical role in developing resilience and overcoming challenges.

Recall that resilience is defined as the ability to bounce back from adversity and recover from setbacks. While intelligence can help individuals navigate challenges, it is not enough to develop resilience. Executive Function skills, such as grit, perseverance, and emotional regulation, play a critical role in developing resilience. For example, research has shown that individuals with high levels of grit are more likely to achieve success in academics, sports, and business. Additionally, emotional regulation skills, such as mindfulness and self-awareness, can help individuals manage stress and bounce back from setbacks.

Resilience is critical not only for coping with adversity but also for personal and professional growth. Individuals with high levels of resilience are more likely to succeed academically and professionally, as well as have better mental health and well-being. For example, a study conducted by Connor & Davidson in 2003 on college students found that those with high levels of resilience had higher GPAs and were more likely to graduate on time than those with low levels of resilience. Similarly, a study by Fred Luthans in 2006 showed that employees with high levels of resilience are more likely to perform well under pressure and be promoted to higher.

Executive Function skills can be cultivated through a variety of strategies, including mentorship, extracurricular activities, and mindfulness practices. Mentorship programs can provide young people with role models who can teach them essential non-cognitive skills, such as leadership, teamwork, and perseverance. Extracurricular activities, such as sports and music, can help young people develop grit and resilience by providing opportunities to overcome challenges and setbacks. Finally, mindfulness practices, such as meditation and yoga, can help young people develop emotional regulation skills and increase self-awareness.

When SFC T and I developed Raider School for the Academy, we had many objectives and goals for our program, but when we defined what success looked like, it wasn't high performance or first-place finishes. We would consider our program successful if our Raiders walked away more resilient than when they arrived. Success for us meant solid grit and mental toughness earned through a series of intense challenges and obstacles. Our

Raiders learned to suffer. I will talk at length about programming in the next chapter.

As we've discussed, learning to suffer is an essential aspect of personal growth and development. It involves facing challenges and setbacks head-on so that we learn to stay in the fight and maintain hope. However, the development of executive function skills is not without its challenges. In fact, the process can be likened to a double-edged sword.

On the one hand, the development of executive function skills is critical in fostering the capacity to suffer. The capacity to suffer refers to the ability to tolerate unpleasant emotions and experiences. This is an essential skill that allows individuals to persevere through challenging situations, adapt to change, and ultimately thrive in their personal and professional lives. The development of executive function skills can help individuals build the resilience and emotional regulation needed to endure and overcome difficult situations.

On the other hand, suffering itself can be a catalyst for the superior development of executive function skills. When we experience adversity, we are forced to adapt, problem-solve, and exercise self-control. These experiences can enhance our executive function skills and help us to become more resilient in the face of future challenges.

However, it is important to recognize that not all suffering leads to superior development of executive function skills. Chronic stress, trauma, and other forms of adversity, if not managed well, can hinder executive function development and lead to a range of negative outcomes, such as anxiety and depression.

Therefore, it is important to foster the development of executive function skills in a healthy and supportive environment. This can include providing opportunities for individuals to practice problem-solving, decision-making, and self-regulation in a safe and controlled setting. It is also essential to prioritize self-care and stress management techniques to mitigate the negative effects of chronic stress and trauma.

As I said, the development of executive function skills is a double-edged sword. On the one hand, executive function skills are critical in fostering the capacity to suffer. On the other hand, suffering can be a catalyst for the superior development of executive function skills. However, it is important to recognize that not all suffering leads to positive outcomes, and fostering the development of executive function skills requires a healthy and supportive environment.

In conclusion, executive function skills play a critical role in developing resilience, bouncing back from setbacks, and learning to suffer. While intelligence is important, it is not enough to develop resilience. Skills such as grit, perseverance, and emotional regulation, can be cultivated through mentorship, extracurricular activities, and mindfulness practices. The impact of resilience on personal and professional growth cannot be ignored, and it is essential to cultivate executive function skills in young people and growing leaders to help them thrive and succeed in life.

In the next and final chapter, I will discuss programming techniques and tactics I've developed to cultivate these skills in others as well as other evidence-based programming, such as social-emotional learning.

CHAPTER 9 – Translating Theory into a Resilient Reality

The phrase "everyone wants to go to heaven, but no one wants to die" is a metaphorical expression that highlights the human tendency to desire success, achievement, or happiness without being willing to go through the challenges, hard work, or sacrifice required to attain them. The phrase suggests that while people may have lofty aspirations and goals, they may not be willing to endure the necessary difficulties and challenges that come along with pursuing those goals.

In essence, the phrase means that people often desire the end result but are unwilling to put in the necessary effort to achieve it. It is a reminder that success and achievement come with a price and that it takes courage, determination, and a willingness to endure hardship and struggle to reach one's goals.

In today's world, the concepts and phrases I've discussed, such as "grit" and "mental toughness," are sometimes seen as buzzwords, and there isn't any real depth behind them. The question I always get is, "But what do these terms really mean, and how can they be applied in the real world?"

At the heart of these concepts lies the idea of learning to suffer or developing the ability to face challenges and setbacks with resilience and determination. In this chapter, we will explore the real-world application of learning to suffer, drawing upon the foundation of grit, resilience, and mental toughness. We will examine how individuals, teams, and organizations such as schools and businesses can use these concepts to overcome obstacles, achieve success, and build exceptionally strong minds able to navigate personal and professional setbacks with grace.

At its core, learning to suffer is about developing the ability to face adversity and overcome challenges. It involves cultivating qualities like perseverance, determination, and grit. These skills can be applied in a variety of settings, from personal goals to professional pursuits. By embracing the idea of learning to suffer, individuals can approach difficult situations with a sense of purpose and resilience. Teams can work together to overcome obstacles and achieve shared goals. Organizations can foster a culture of resilience and mental toughness, empowering employees to tackle challenges with confidence and determination. In the following sections, we will explore these concepts in more detail and provide real-world examples of how they are applied.

I concluded Chapter 3 of this book with an introduction to my leadership philosophy. As I begin to discuss real-world applications for these concepts, I offer below the details of my leadership philosophy so that it may serve as a framework for you to reference in this chapter.

- ✓ **Leaders who reach the end of their rope have no choice but to make more rope.** You signed up for this. You agreed to be a leader, and therefore you agreed to be of service. An old quote by Andre Malruaz is often held over newly appointed officers in the military, "To command is to serve, nothing more and nothing less." As leaders, we have a responsibility to make more rope. We have an obligation to achieve the objective though you be the lone survivor. It is this commitment that we signed up for, and when you've run out of options, out of rope, out of road, you have no damn choice but to start laying hardball to pave the way. No choice but to start weaving more rope.

✓ **Leaders must have a vision: Where are we going, who's coming along, what are we doing, and for what purpose?** This goes back to the definition of a leader. As we grow, we tend to forget about the shoulders we stood on to get there. We have a responsibility as leaders to develop our perfect replacements. In this, we ensure continuity of effort in the organization, and we develop the next generation of leaders. It is said that the higher we soar, the smaller we appear to those who cannot yet fly. It is those we must bring with us. Strategically choose those who will serve the organization best and bring them with you all while ensuring everyone around you understands "the why" of the organization. This will help them develop and connect their personal "why," enabling them to be completely bought into the common goals.

✓ Leaders must know how to fail. More importantly, leaders must allow their people to fail without necessarily becoming a failure. This part of my philosophy is probably the most important. When you are determining how to resource load your projects and deploy your people, you have an obligation to set them up for success. Time, urgency, and complexity. When deciding who does what task or if I may have to execute it myself, I always think of the time available, how urgent the issue is, and how complex the problem is, or how complex the potential solution will be. In this, I am more likely to find success. As you know, however, no plan ever survives first contact, and things will go wrong. When they do, obviously, you must find a solution, but more importantly, how do you create a teachable moment for your team or point of failure? You want others not to make mistakes because they don't want to disappoint, not because they fear being fired. It's that shame you felt when your father or mother looked at you, shaking their head in disappointment. In that moment, you learned, and you never wanted to let them down again. Their failures are exactly the experience needed to build strong, cohesive teams. Let them fail, but don't let them become a failure.

✓ **Leaders will never know as much as their people on the ground; empower them to make decisions.** This is simple, really. Think of the manufacturing CEO who has never actually seen what's going on in the plant or on the plant floor. He never talks to the ground-level leaders and never reads the reports. Then, that CEO goes and tries to formulate a plan to "improve" operations, or they release a seriously unrealistic requirement that will surely result in failure. This is unacceptable leadership. There is a fine line between being disconnected completely and micromanaging your team. However, that doesn't prevent us from getting our boots on the ground to understand what is happening. Developing your leaders to make decisions on your behalf means you've ensured they're aware of what they can and can't decide singularly without your input. Then, leave them to it, assess, and redeploy.

Planning and Execution Techniques

In this section, I will walk you through techniques I use when leading and developing programs for individuals, teams, and organizations. There are a number of planning and execution techniques that can be used to cultivate executive function skills, including the following.

Set challenging goals: No matter what programming I initiate from individuals to groups, I start by setting challenging goals for both my staff and program participants. In this way, I can push others outside of their comfort zones in order to develop the necessary resilience and determination needed to accomplish meaningful goals. It's important to set goals that are achievable but also require intense focus, effort, and persistence to accomplish.

Set meaningful goals: Meaningful goals are those that align with our values and aspirations and require effort and persistence to achieve. These are the kinds of goals that make your hair stand up when you think about them. When setting goals for my staff and program participants, I aim for a balance between challenge and attainability, as goals that are too easy or too difficult can lead to boredom or discouragement, respectively. Meaningful goals should make the heart sing.

Self-reflection, mindfulness, and after-action reviews: In all things we do, from our professional lives to programming to our personal endeavors, there must be time for reflection. Plan it into your daily schedule. In the military, we use a simple model after every training event, major planning cycle, and every mission.

➢ What was supposed to happen?
➢ What actually happened?
➢ What went right?
➢ What went wrong?
➢ How do we improve?

I encourage my teams to always be mindful. I urge them to take a tactical pause when necessary, look in the mirror, breath, and then make a decision about the very next thing they should be doing. These practices can help us stay focused and present, even in the face of challenging situations.

Encourage positive self-talk: Ever talk to yourself? If not, you should. An optimistic inner monologue can help us develop a sense of grit and determination. In the Army, we tell our soldiers to "hunt for the positive," and in this case, the goal is to focus on your strengths and to use positive affirmations to build confidence and resilience.

The Growth Mindset

From planning to preparation and execution, develop and maintain a growth mindset culture: On an individual level, a growth mindset can drive you to develop your abilities through hard work and perseverance.

In a growth mindset culture, teams and organizations are more likely to view challenges as opportunities for growth and learning rather than as roadblocks. This can lead to a more resilient, innovative, and cohesive team, as individual contributors are more willing to take risks and try new approaches. Additionally, a growth mindset can promote a culture of continuous improvement, where people are motivated to seek out feedback and develop new skills. Tenets of a growth mindset include:

Refusing To Be Scared: As leaders in our personal and professional lives, it can be tempting to give in to fear and uncertainty. Whether it's facing a challenging project, making a tough decision, or taking on a new responsibility, fear can be a powerful force that holds us back. But refusing to be scared is an essential component of effective leadership. When we choose to face our fears head-on, we demonstrate courage and resilience and inspire those around us to do the same.

Refusing to be scared also means embracing uncertainty and taking risks. As leaders, it's important to be willing to take calculated risks and try new approaches, even when the outcome is uncertain. This requires a willingness to embrace ambiguity and to be comfortable with the unknown. By modeling this behavior, we encourage those around us to take risks and be more innovative in their thinking and problem-solving.

For me, this meant embracing the unknown anytime I developed a new program or brought new ideas to life. Especially when facing pushback from peers or stakeholders who didn't necessarily support the effort. They would carry enough fear in of themselves to account for all of us.

Refusing to be scared is about demonstrating the courage and resilience that are essential for effective leadership. By embracing uncertainty, taking risks, and facing our fears head-on, we can inspire those around us to be more innovative, creative, and successful in their personal and professional lives.

No Feeling Sorry for Yourself: When we face adversity and setbacks, it can be easy to fall into a pattern of self-pity and victimhood. We may feel sorry for ourselves, dwelling on our misfortune and blaming others for our struggles. However, this mindset is incredibly destructive and prevents us from taking responsibility for our situation and taking steps to move forward.

Instead, we should strive to avoid feeling sorry for ourselves and focus on taking action to overcome the challenges we face. This requires a shift in mindset from one of victimhood to one of empowerment. As leaders, it is your mandate not to let your team feel sorry for themselves. This takes us directly back to my leadership philosophy—no one becomes a failure on your watch.

We must recognize that while we may not be able to control the circumstances we face, we can control our response to those circumstances. By taking ownership of our situation and focusing on solutions rather than dwelling on problems, we can develop a more positive and resilient mindset.

Not feeling sorry for ourselves also means recognizing that setbacks and failures are an inevitable part of the journey toward success. Rather than seeing these experiences as a reflection of our inherent worth or abilities, we should view them as opportunities for growth and learning. By adopting a growth mindset and focusing on the lessons we can learn from our setbacks, we can develop the resilience and mental toughness we need to overcome any obstacle.

<u>Build A Support Network</u>: Having a support network can help us maintain focus and stay the course. As leaders, we must connect with our peers and our mentors and ask them to keep us accountable for what we say we are going to do. As leaders, we must also encourage our teams to connect with their peers, mentors, and coaches who can provide support and encouragement during challenging times.

We need the kind of people in our lives who are unafraid to tell us the truth and keep us locked into reality. They will always give you a "no bullshit" answer when asked. This level of accountability is invaluable in both our personal and professional lives.

If you are a parent, take a second look at every technique I outlined above except from the perspective of a father or mother. They each apply in unique and specific ways as it relates to your circumstances. As a father, I strive every day to embrace these techniques, and as I grow, I find it more fulfilling with each passing day. Now don't get me wrong here; I don't sit my kids down and have an after-action review! I do, however, sit down with my wife, and we talk about what's working, what isn't, what we can do better, and if there are any new ideas.

Programming Techniques

In order to truly develop the skills of grit, resilience, and mental toughness, that is to say, learning to suffer, individuals and organizations must have a structured plan in place. This section explores programming theories and techniques for learning to suffer, with a focus on teams, schools, camps, and businesses.

Teams: In a team setting, cultivating a culture of accountability and communication is crucial. By holding each other to high standards and providing feedback and support, team members can help each other develop the necessary skills to be mentally strong. Additionally, creating opportunities for team members to step outside of their comfort zones and take on new challenges can help them develop these skills in a supportive environment.

I maintain a regular approach with every team that I am part of. Whether I am talking to those I lead or those who lead me, I use two phrases with precision. The first is, "Would you be open to feedback?" This allows the individual a moment to take a bite of some humble pie and breath. This approach actively prevents them from becoming defensive and consequently destroying the relationship. It's important to note that this is never done in a group setting unless absolutely necessary, and all other options have been exhausted.

The second phrase, "Is there something about what I just that you didn't like?" This forces the conversation and clears the air immediately, as opposed to allowing whatever it is to stew and have a negative impact on someone's day. This path is direct and makes the other think about their emotions and the facts of the situation.

In my programs, staff are taught to use these techniques and maintain tact. The last thing you want to do is ruin relationships. It should be a top priority to build the team, not destroy it. Same team, same fight.

Schools and Camps: Programming for schools is an intensely challenging topic and warrants an entire book of its own. Multiple books, for that matter. Public schools specifically are regulated beyond recognition and offer very little creative liberties for programming. I am a product of the Chicago Public School system, but I would argue that I survived it and was made whole at St. John's Northwestern.

Some private schools have managed to retain their programming autonomy but are often driven by overbearing parents. That said, I know many private schools that have managed to maintain their soul and, thereby, their programming. While I am biased, St. John's Northwestern Academies is one of those private schools. Even through exceptional financial challenges, St. John's Northwestern has managed to maintain focus on developing sound leaders capable of dealing with life's challenges.

From my perspective, camps (summer, day, overnight, etc.) have the most creative autonomy and fluid programming options. Some camps have given in to intense regulation and programming based on political drivers, major donors, and other agendas but, for the most part, maintain independence from convoluted and politically driven regulation. The camping environment is probably the last true place where young people can experience real education in terms of executive function skills.

No matter the type of organization, it is paramount to implement experiential learning opportunities. This is the most effective way to help students develop executive function skills. Outdoor education programs, adventure courses, and team-building activities provide opportunities for young people to face challenges, overcome obstacles, and build meaningful relationships in a supportive environment. Additionally, promoting a growth mindset inside and outside the classroom can help students develop the resilience and mental toughness they need to succeed.

Every summer camp and program I developed, including Raider School, was the embodiment of these concepts. Our focus was 100% experiential. In that way, we drove young people to be successful in every situation they found themselves in.

I am often asked, "How exactly do you find success developing these skills in young people?" My response is the same for anyone who asked me in the past as it is now. As educators and leaders, the most impactful technique is to praise effort as opposed to only praising outcomes.

From my chair, praising effort instead of outcomes holds maximum benefit when it comes to developing young people to be resilient and mentally tough. When effort is praised, it reinforces the idea that hard work and perseverance are valued over innate talent or ability. This can lead to an increase in motivation as individuals become more invested in the process of learning and improving rather than just achieving a certain outcome. Additionally, praising effort helps to create a growth mindset, where individuals believe that their abilities can be developed through dedication and hard work.

My Raiders have a great many requirements, day in and day out. The two requirements that were an absolute "no fail" event were as follows:

➢ <u>Requirement 1</u>: No matter the situation, circumstance, or question, you had to provide a SWAG idea or SWAG answer. SWAG = Sophisticated Wild Ass Guess. At the very least, you had to put some effort into critical thought and problem-solving.

➢ <u>Requirement 2</u>: Crawling, walking, or running, you cross the finish line. At this point in their development, it wasn't about who came in first place. It was about crossing the finish line under your own power, no matter how long it took.

These requirements enabled my instructors to focus on effort as opposed to outcomes, and we were successful because of it. Praising outcomes leads to a fixed mindset, where individuals believe that their abilities are predetermined and cannot be changed. This is detrimental to developing resilience and mental toughness, as individuals may give up easily in the face of challenges or setbacks if they believe that success is solely based on innate talent. Furthermore, praising outcomes also leads to a fear of failure, as individuals may be more concerned with achieving a certain result than with the process of learning and growing.

Praising effort fosters a culture of resilience and mental toughness, where individuals are motivated to work hard and persevere in the face of challenges. This is how I create a growth mindset, where individuals believe that their abilities can be developed through effort and dedication.

<u>Business</u>: From a corporate or even small business perspective, providing opportunities for employees to take on new challenges and learn from setbacks helps them develop grit, resilience, and mental toughness. This can include stretch assignments, cross-functional projects, and leadership development programs. Additionally, fostering a culture of

innovation and experimentation can help your employees develop these skills by encouraging them to take risks and learn from failure.

Recall that my leadership philosophy dictates a decision matrix of time, urgency, and complexity. When making task organizing or making decisions about who does what and when, I consider the time available, how urgent the issue is, and how complex the problem is or how complex the potential solution will be.

From an entrepreneurial perspective, learning to suffer is the first disclaimer you signed. It's absolutely critical that your risk tolerance is high, that you are comfortable with failure, and that you have the perseverance and energy to push past failure mode after failure mode.

Overall, programming theories and techniques for learning to suffer are essential for individuals and organizations looking to develop the skills needed to thrive in the face of adversity. By implementing these planning and execution techniques, teams, schools, camps, and businesses can cultivate a culture of resilience and mental toughness, allowing them to overcome obstacles and achieve their goals with confidence and purpose. The most important outcome is the exceptional growth of executive function skills within the individual, the student, the camper, and the employee.

Programming Tactics

Realizing that I haven't differentiated between tactics and techniques, I will do so now before moving on. Tactics refer to the specific actions or steps taken to achieve a particular objective. They are often short-term in nature and are used to accomplish specific goals within a larger strategy. Tactics are generally more concrete and practical than strategies, and they can be adjusted or changed as needed to achieve the desired results.

Techniques, on the other hand, refer to the methods and procedures used to perform a particular task or accomplish a goal. They are more focused on the process or methodology used to achieve a desired outcome. Techniques can be used as part of a larger strategy, or they can be applied independently to achieve a specific objective.

In summary, tactics are specific actions taken to achieve a goal, while techniques are the methods or procedures used to perform a task or achieve an objective. Both tactics and techniques are important components of a successful strategy, and they should be chosen and implemented carefully based on your goals and objectives.

Imposed Stress

The most important programming tactic I deploy is imposed stress. Imposed stress is a concept that has been used to train the US Special Operations community for decades. The idea is to intentionally create stressful and challenging situations for soldiers during training in order to better prepare them for the physical, emotional, and mental demands of real-world combat situations. These stressors can take many forms, such as sleep deprivation, physical exertion, and simulated combat scenarios. By subjecting soldiers to these stressors, they can learn to perform under pressure and make better decisions in high-stress situations.

While imposed stress is often associated with military training, the concept can be applied to other areas of life as well. For example, camps, schools, and businesses can incorporate elements of imposed stress into their training and development programs. This might include simulated emergency scenarios, high-pressure performance evaluations, or intense physical challenges. By exposing individuals to these stressors in a controlled environment, they can develop the skills and resilience necessary to perform well under pressure in real-world situations.

Under pressure is the operative word. Everything about life is under pressure, especially if you want to be successful and have a meaningful impact on your family and community. I imposed stress in every program, every business, and every personal endeavor I embarked on.

How Do Individuals Impose Stress on Themselves?

There are several ways that individuals can impose stress on themselves to develop grit and resilience. One common technique is something we've already discussed, to set challenging goals that push us outside of our comfort zone. This can include setting a difficult physical fitness goal or taking on a challenging work project. By setting challenging goals and working towards them, we develop perseverance and grit.

Another tactic is to intentionally put yourself in uncomfortable or unfamiliar situations. This involves trying new experiences, such as traveling to a foreign country or taking on a new hobby. By putting ourselves in new and uncomfortable situations, we can build resilience and learn to adapt to change.

Additionally, individuals can intentionally expose themselves to stressors and then work to manage their response to them. This includes mindfulness & reflection, which can help to build resilience to stress and anxiety. I chose to impose stress when I hiked the ice age trail, and the vast emptiness of the trail enabled me to reflect often and take action on the outcomes of my thoughts.

How do you impose stress within your camp or school?

274

Recognizing that I previously placed camps and schools at the opposite ends of the regulation spectrum, I think it's important to co-exist in this case. Camps and schools (both public and private) can impose stress within their programming in a variety of ways to develop executive function skills. Here are some specific programming examples:

Challenging Outdoor Activities: Summer camps and schools can offer a range of challenging outdoor activities, such as hiking, rock climbing, and kayaking races. These activities require physical endurance and mental toughness, as participants need to push themselves beyond their comfort zone to succeed.

Team-Building Challenges: Team-building activities, such as problem-solving challenges and obstacle courses, can help to develop grit and resilience by forcing participants to work together to overcome adversity. These challenges can be designed to require persistence and mental toughness to complete. Remember, it's paramount to praise effort first and foremost. Recognizing outcomes, in this case, is important as well as those who went above and beyond really do deserve recognition for their effort as well.

Service Projects: Volunteering for service projects, such as cleaning up a local park or participating in a community garden, can be a great way to develop grit and resilience. These projects require participants to work hard and persist through challenges while also developing a sense of responsibility and purpose. In my programs, I often required that we develop and agree upon a group project for the semester or the year. Getting input from every contributor was vital to our success.

Mentally Stimulating Workshops: Schools can offer workshops that challenge students' intellectual and emotional capacities, such as a philosophy or debate workshop. This, of course, is premised on the faith of each student that their views and speech are not censored or otherwise persecuted. These activities expose young people to new ideas and ways of thinking, which can help them develop a growth mindset and become more resilient.

Controlled Adversity: Schools and camps can create controlled adversity, such as sleep deprivation, food deprivation, or exposure to extreme weather, to help participants develop resilience and mental toughness. These experiences can be designed to be challenging but safe, with the goal of teaching participants how to cope with difficult situations and build their resilience. I will expand on this tactic in the next section, Optimal Deprivation.

Combatives

This tactic makes my heart sing. When looking to civilize the mind but make savage the body, nothing is more effective than ground fighting combative training. When was the last time you fought someone at full speed in the sand, knowing you would have to fight at least ten or fifteen more times that night? I remember every fight and every lesson.

Often, our young people deal with major emotional swings, and in schools today, violence continues to be the default remedy. Just as I once did, our young people see it as a means to preserve their honor and their dignity. There is no other way in their eyes, especially if you are the bully's bully.

Because of this, I began to implement combatives training as a daily programming requirement. Simply put, it is a powerful tool for building grit, resilience, and mental toughness in young people. My design and thought process was rooted in my military experience, specifically Ranger Training. My philosophy with these programs targeted emotional and mental regulation as the paramount goal.

Principles of My Combatives Programming:

➤ Don't fight to win. Instead, fight not to lose.

➤ Generally, when we lose, it is because we made a mistake, and our opponent capitalized on that mistake.

➤ We make mistakes when we are overly aggressive and allow our emotions to take control. This is what happens when we fight to win.

➤ Achieve leverage in all things, from breathing to positioning to the timing of every decision you make.

Of course, we all want to win the fight, but with my programming, the goal is not to lose. This forces the fighting pair to listen to each other, to pay attention to their surroundings, hand movements, etc., and to hear their own heartbeat while feeling that of their opponents. This encouraged the fighter to stay calm and to think clearly about where they are positionally and where they should target next. I call this tactical patience, which I will discuss in detail later in this chapter.

I would start every new program with a review of UFC (Ultimate Fighting Championships) 1-10. Interestingly, most UFC enthusiasts have never watched UFC 1, much less UFC 10. In the beginning, these tournaments were martial art against martial art. The purpose of the UFC in these early years was to determine the best martial art in the world. I will offer a brief history for you, much the same as I do for my programs.

In 1993, the UFC held its first event in Denver, Colorado. At the time, the UFC was seen as a showcase of different martial arts styles, as fighters from different disciplines, such as boxing, wrestling, kickboxing, and karate, competed against each other in a no-holds-barred format. The early UFC events were controversial and attracted criticism for their brutality and lack of rules.

One family that made a significant impact on the early days of the UFC was the Gracie family, who brought the Brazilian Jiu-Jitsu (BJJ) style to the United States. The Gracie family, led by Helio Gracie, had been promoting BJJ in Brazil since the 1920s and saw the UFC as an opportunity to showcase their style to the world. In the early UFC events, Royce Gracie, one of Helio's sons, dominated the competition with his BJJ skills, winning three of the first four UFC tournaments.

As the sport evolved, the UFC began to introduce more rules and regulations, and fighters began to develop a hybrid style that incorporated different martial arts disciplines. This marked the transition from the early days of the UFC to what is now known as Mixed Martial Arts (MMA).

It was also during this time that the US Army Rangers began a review of at hand to hand combat training methods. In the early 1990s, the Rangers began to seek out new training methods to improve the effectiveness of our soldiers in close-quarters combat situations. This search led them to Brazilian Jiu-Jitsu.

The Gracie family had developed Brazilian Jiu-Jitsu as a way for smaller individuals to successfully defend themselves against larger opponents in real-world situations. The Rangers recognized the potential of this martial art for their own training and began to incorporate it into their combatives program. The Modern Army Combatives Program was developed in the late 1990s as a way to teach soldiers the most effective techniques from a variety of martial arts, including Brazilian Jiu-Jitsu.

The program was a success, and many soldiers credit their training in the Modern Army Combatives Program with saving their lives in combat situations. Today, Brazilian Jiu-Jitsu is a core component of the Army's combatives program and is taught to soldiers across all branches of the military.

Getting back to my programming, I would often dictate the required outcomes of a select fight. That is, I would tell the fighters that the only way they could claim victory was by placing their opponent in a rear naked choke or an arm bar or some other requirement.

This approach was the key to enabling my students and campers to achieve a level of emotional regulation consistent with that of successful adult citizens of our community. It forced each fighter to be hyper-focused on their movements and breathing while also dialing in that of their opponents. You had to control your aggression if you were going to control the outcome.

Finally, I would focus on the "tap out." This enabled instructors to concentrate on the effort and not the outcome. Let me explain. Anyone can land a lucky punch. The smallest and weakest among us can land a knockout punch. Is that a true indicator of skill? I don't think so. A true indicator of skill, focus, and determination is when you force your opponent to tap out. At this moment, your opponent admits that you are more skillful and determined than they are. There are two wins after a "tap out," and both deserve recognition.

The first win is, of course, forcing your opponent to tap out. That meant you were able to control your aggression, your emotional state, and your breathing. The second win belongs to the losing opponent. That fighter has to swallow a nice chunk of humble pie and admit that there is more work to be done.

After each fight, I would conduct an after-action review with the entire program. We studied every move and every mistake in order to enable maximum knowledge gain for everyone, even if it wasn't your fight.

Other key benefits of incorporating this type of training in schools and camps include:

- ➤ Confidence and self-esteem: Learning how to defend oneself and engage in combatives training empowers young people. As they develop their skills, they gain confidence in their abilities and improve their self-esteem. I reiterate the need to praise effort here.

- ➤ Teamwork and communication: As I described above, combatives training involves working with partners and in groups to practice techniques and drills. This helps young people develop their teamwork and communication skills, which are critical executive function skills.

- ➤ Discipline and focus: Combatives training requires discipline and focus to master techniques and improve skills. By practicing this type of training, young people can develop their ability to stay focused and disciplined, which can help them in other areas of their lives, such as academics or other extracurricular activities.

Imposing stress in a safe and controlled way can help camps and schools develop grit and resilience in their participants. By providing challenging activities and experiences, young people can learn to push beyond their comfort zone, develop a growth mindset, and build their resilience for the challenges of the future.

How Do You Impose Stress Within Business and Corporate America?

Incorporating stress-inducing training programs helps leaders and individual contributors develop grit and resilience, which leads to better outcomes when dealing with serious setbacks, whether rooted in the supply chain or the customer. Below, I will outline some programming examples as experienced in my career:

Leadership development programs: Executives can offer leadership development programs that challenge participants with difficult assignments and high-pressure situations. These programs can simulate real-world business challenges, such as managing a crisis, leading a team through a difficult project, or handling unexpected situations. By practicing and learning how to handle these types of situations, participants can build the necessary resilience to thrive in any situation.

Role-playing exercises: Role-playing exercises can help individuals develop their ability to handle difficult or confrontational situations. For example, participants can practice negotiating, giving and receiving feedback, or dealing with difficult customers or clients. These exercises can be stressful, but they can also help build mental toughness and resilience.

Cross-training and stretch assignments: Companies can offer cross-training and stretch assignments to their employees to help them build resilience and confidence. These assignments expose employees to new challenges, which can help them develop new skills and perspectives. For example, an employee who is trained in one department can be given a stretch assignment to work in another department or function, which can help them develop adaptability and mental toughness.

Incorporating stress-inducing training programs can help leaders and individual contributors develop grit and resilience. These programs provide opportunities for participants to face difficult and stressful situations, learn from them, and become more mentally tough and resilient.

It's important to note that imposed stress concepts should be used carefully and appropriately. There should be significant study, planning, and preparation to mitigate risk and injury. Too much stress can be harmful and counterproductive, leading to burnout, injury, or other negative outcomes. The key is to find the right balance of stress and challenges that can help individuals and organizations grow and develop without overwhelming them.

Optimal Deprivation

"Hard times create strong men, strong men create good times, good times create weak men, and weak men create hard times." The quote from the postapocalyptic novel *Those Who Remain* by author G. Michael Hopf sums up the historical pendulum of the circumstances of men.

In today's society, the focus on comfort and convenience has led to a lack of resilience, grit, and mental toughness among many young people, junior leaders, and of course, adults. It is vital for individuals to learn how to handle adversity, develop mental strength and resilience, and build grit. We end up with stronger, more capable minds that can manage setbacks, rejection, failure, and any other number of life's challenges. When we think about the mental health crisis in this country, we need to pay attention to schools and youth organizations and what we're doing to build exceptionally strong minds. We must focus on programming for our children and young adult.

This section will explore the concept of optimal deprivation and its role in building mentally strong minds.

What is Optimal Deprivation?

Optimal deprivation is a term used to describe a deliberate and controlled experience of discomfort or deprivation. It involves exposing individuals to controlled and manageable levels of adversity in order to build resilience, grit, and mental toughness. Optimal deprivation is not about pushing individuals to their limits or creating harmful situations but rather about finding a balance that challenges individuals without overwhelming them. The goal, of course, is to move the needle a little bit each day. Eventually, new baselines of expectations and performance are established.

Optimal deprivation and imposed stress are two different approaches to developing resilience and grit but are complemented by each other.

Optimal deprivation is the intentional removal of certain comforts or conveniences without causing undue harm or distress in order to build a person's resilience and adaptability. It involves experiencing temporary discomfort or inconvenience that is within the person's control and can be stopped at any time. For example, going without technology or electricity for a certain period of time or intentionally choosing to sleep on the ground instead of a comfortable bed. The goal of optimal deprivation is to teach individuals to appreciate what they have, become more self-reliant, and learn how to cope with difficult situations.

On the other hand, imposed stress is the deliberate application of stressors that are designed to push a person beyond their current physical, mental, or emotional capabilities. This stress is typically delivered by an external source, such as a drill instructor, coach, or mentor, and may involve exposure to physically demanding or psychologically challenging situations. The goal of imposed stress is to teach individuals to develop mental toughness, overcome adversity, and persevere in the face of difficulty.

Both approaches are effective in developing resilience and grit, but they differ in their methodology and the level of control the individual has over the stressor.

<u>Benefits of Optimal Deprivation.</u>

Optimal deprivation has a range of benefits. Firstly, it can help us develop resilience and grit, which are paramount when learning to suffer. By exposing ourselves and those we lead to adversity, we can learn how to bounce back from setbacks and build the mental strength necessary to overcome future challenges. Secondly, optimal deprivation helps individuals develop mental toughness.

By facing controlled levels of adversity, individuals can learn how to manage stress and perform well under pressure as they slowly raise their baseline. Finally, optimal deprivation can also help to develop a sense of perspective and appreciation for what we have as we learn to overcome challenges and thrive in spite of adversity.

Applying Optimal Deprivation to Young People and Junior Leaders.

Optimal deprivation can be applied to young people and junior leaders in a variety of ways. As mentioned previously, it could involve outdoor activities such as camping or hiking, where individuals are forced to deal with discomfort, weather conditions, and other challenges. In this case, you wouldn't add extra miles or extra weight to the pack but instead, remove comforts such as sleep and food.

Additionally, optimal deprivation could be applied in educational settings by challenging individuals to step outside of their comfort zones and take on new tasks or projects that require perseverance and determination.

We can challenge our students and promote personal growth by putting them in situations where they are forced to adapt and overcome. Some examples include:

> Outdoor education programs: Students can be taken on outdoor trips where they are deprived of certain comforts like electricity,

running water, and cell service. This can teach them survival skills, promote teamwork and communication, and develop their resilience.

➤ Classroom activities: Teachers can design activities that intentionally create a sense of deprivation. For example, they can challenge students to complete a project using only limited resources or to work on a task with a tight deadline. This can teach students to be resourceful, adaptable, and resilient in the face of challenging situations.

➤ Service projects: Students can participate in service projects that involve working with communities that are deprived of certain resources like food, shelter, or clean water. This can help students develop empathy, build resilience, and learn problem-solving skills while helping those in need.

Optimal Deprivation and Parenting.

As parents, the last thing we want to do is deprive our children in any way. Rightfully so, most parents want to give their children the world, myself included. The problem is that when we shelter and shower them, we aren't doing anything to build up their ability to handle life's challenges, including all of the setbacks and all of the failures.

With these concepts, we can help our children develop resilience and adaptability. Here are some examples:

➤ Limiting screen time: Parents can set limits on screen time for their children, such as no screens during meal times, before bedtime, or on certain days of the week. This can help children learn to entertain themselves without relying on technology and develop other skills like creativity, communication, and problem-solving.

➤ Chores and responsibilities: Giving children age-appropriate chores and responsibilities can help them learn self-sufficiency and independence. For example, children can be responsible for making their own beds, doing their own laundry, or cooking simple meals. In my house, we have two kinds of chores. The kind of chores because you live here, such as garbage day, vacuuming, etc., and the kind I will pay you for, such as cleaning the car or organizing the garage. Other responsibilities we invoke on our children include managing the weekly dinner menu and choosing what evening and weekend activities to do. This can help them learn important life skills and build confidence in their abilities.

➤ Outdoor activities: Encouraging children to spend time outdoors independently, even in less-than-ideal weather conditions, can help them develop resilience and adaptability. "Independent" is the operative word here. Going for a hike in the rain or camping in the cold can help children learn to push through discomfort and challenges while developing a sense of accomplishment from overcoming obstacles.

➤ You've heard it many times, "What happened to coming home when the streetlights come on?" That's what I remember, and I'm sure many of you do as well. Nowadays, parents are intensely afraid to let their children independently navigate the neighborhood or anything else for that matter. Today, we never see a child outside of the arm's reach of an adult. Even worse, we don't encourage them to manage their own problems. Instead, we tell them, "If you have a problem, come find me," or "If you're having trouble, go find the teacher."

➢ This, unfortunately, doesn't foster problem-solving or critical thinking, and we end up with teenagers who cannot manage themselves when no adult is around to manage them directly. Optimal deprivation, in my experience, is a powerful tool for building resilient, capable, and mentally tough young people. By exposing individuals to controlled levels of adversity, they can learn how to manage stress, overcome challenges, and develop the mental strength necessary to succeed in a variety of settings.

It is important to remember that optimal deprivation should always be approached with care and consideration for individual needs and capabilities, but when used appropriately, it can be a valuable tool for building resilience and grit.

Tactical Patience

This is an all-out battle between decisiveness and knowing when to take a knee. Yes, it is important to be decisive and take action at times, but does that constitute every decision you make? No, it doesn't. Suffering with your eyes wide open will help you to understand the difference. Know when you play your hand and when to fold. Know when to take the tactical pause.

One of my pet peeves in life has traditionally been watching people at work or in training move as if they had nothing to accomplish that day; no sense of urgency whatsoever. I recall often telling people they're moving like a snail stuck in peanut butter.

Serving in various leadership capacities throughout my career, I came to realize that as a leader, we sometimes must choose to move that slowly. It becomes a tactic deployed to achieve a specific outcome. When we learn to make the conscious choice to move like a snail stuck in peanut butter, we learn the value of what's called tactical patience. Some definitions and context below for reference:

> The term tactical is generally used militarily and is defined as relating to or constituting actions carefully planned to gain a specific end result. These are tactics, techniques, and procedures (TTPs), which, if deployed consistently, can increase your likelihood of success in a given situation.

> Patience can be defined as the capacity to accept or tolerate delay, trouble, or suffering without losing grip on the situation at hand.

> The essence of pausing is to interrupt an activity briefly to gain more information or wait for something else to happen before continuing. Thus, tactical patience is a deliberate pause deployed to glean more information or gain an advantageous position so as to increase your chances of being successful with whatever it is you're engaged in.

I have personally failed at this many times throughout my career. I'll give you a recent example that isn't too embarrassing. I received a Friday afternoon phone call from a talented engineer on another team I worked closely with. She asked for my help to resolve a software issue as part of a test program I helped to write.

At first glance, and from her description, it sounded exactly like something my team had previously worked on, so I went into immediate recall, identified what I thought was the solution, and began work. Not only that, but I also immediately agreed to have my team resolve the issue before departing for the start of the weekend. Sure enough, the issue ended up being the complete reverse of what I conceptualized, and my hasty over, aggressive approach caused me to stay that Friday evening until almost 9 PM to solve this issue.

I certainly wasn't going to ask anyone else to bear the burden I aggressively agreed to shoulder. Had I taken a step back and watched the situation evolve as more and more information became available, I may have saved multiple hours of unnecessary rework for my team and myself. Nothing like starting the weekend with a 15-hour workday.

What happened that Friday got me thinking again about tactical patience and the lessons I learned several years ago when studying Helio Gracie and his ground-fighting theories. We know that 90% of fights go to the ground and that Brazilian Jiu-Jitsu, his family's ground fighting martial art, proved to be exceptionally powerful.

I strongly believe that Helio's martial art holds its foundational concepts in tactical patience. When we discussed implementing imposed stress tactics, I outlined my programming philosophy for a combatives program. The lessons below are the basis for my philosophy.

> Lesson 1: Don't fight to win. Instead, fight not to lose. Every time I say that to someone, they look at me with a "What the hell does that mean?" face. This lesson will make more sense when combined with lessons two and three.

> Lesson 2: Do not become overly aggressive. Ties into lesson one. When you become overly aggressive, you stop thinking clearly. When you stop thinking clearly, you make your most grave mistakes. Generally speaking, you lose the fight because you made a mistake. You made a mistake because you became overly aggressive and forgot to breathe.

> Lesson 3: Make calculated decisions based on your opponent's mistakes. This is where it all comes together with tactical patience. From a combatant standpoint, you capitalize on your opponent's mistakes and thereby gain the tactical advantage. This

is called leverage. Atlas, a Titan condemned to hold up the celestial heavens for eternity, is known to have said, in a variety of reported ways, "Zeus, you can keep my strength. Give me leverage, and I will move the world."

So, what does it all mean from a leadership application perspective? A business application perspective? We have opponents in life and in business all the same. The difference is that these opponents are more in line with strategic opponents vs. hand-to-hand combatant opponents. Our lesson from a leadership and business point of view is what we've been talking about all along - tactical patience. The deliberate pause. Simply put, it's invaluable. Gaining the tactical advantage and employing leverage over a given situation will be the difference between what could be your success or that of your opponent's if you allow them to capitalize on your aggressive mistakes.

Tactical Empathy

"...You 'feel' just as much as anyone, Jason; you just process it differently. You don't lack empathy; you're just very frugal with it..." – Dr. Yael Cidon.

I spent quite a bit of time at the Bloch School of Management as part of the University of Missouri-Kansas City, where I earned my EMBA or Executive Master of Business Administration in 2020. During one of our on-site weekends, I spent the entire day with my EMBA Cohort focused on emotional intelligence, which is sometimes known as EQ (Emotional Quotient). We found ourselves in a relatively heated debate involving stolen cheese sticks, my "bullshit button" (like the easy button), and rotting flesh—yep, it went just like that. The entirety of our engagement had me reflecting heavily on my roots and the decisions leading up to the primary reason I joined the Bloch School EMBA.

At this point, you know my story. For those that are just getting caught up, I grew up on the streets of Chicago with a drug-addicted yet loving mother and a father who spent most of my young life in prison. I was broken, we suffered, but we survived thanks to people believing in us. I survived cancer and beat odds unthinkable to me at the time. Even now, I firmly believe we're all born broken and spend the rest of our lives healing. All of this and more established a deep-rooted foundational identity I live within today. It also guided the development of my moral compass and, yes, my greatest character flaws.

In Chapter 2, I talked about how I learned not to trust—people most of all. I learned at a young age that what may be true tonight most likely won't be real in the morning. I became cold with decision-making. It was me, myself, and I. It was survival. Almost flawlessly, I developed a serious lack of empathy for others, especially those "suffering" from first-world problems. This is where the stolen cheese sticks took the stage. For context, I once had a co-worker who continued to have his cheese sticks stolen from the employee lounge fridge. He was always angry and complaining, of course, and I'm over here like, "Please just shut the fu** up already; it's not that serious." "Really, cheese sticks ruin your day?" I thought to myself.

In my mind at the time, stolen cheese sticks or the long line at Starbucks doesn't qualify as a reason for me to suffer anyone's ridiculous inability to manage even the slightest discomfort. This is where my "bullshit button" usually took over.

A very dear person in my life messaged me that night, and I mentioned this very topic as she caught me in the middle of my writing. Yael continues to be my greatest mentor, confidant, and friend. We talked for more than an hour over the phone, discussing all of this in depth. I

291

carefully explained how the conversation with my cohort unfolded. As I spoke, I could sense her passion for the topic. I began explaining the message I aimed toward my cohort, and what she said next completely shattered the stillness of an otherwise quiet night. She interrupted and said, "You 'feel' just as much as anyone, Jason; you just process it differently. You don't lack empathy; you're just very, very frugal with it." This really got me thinking about Tactical Empathy.

As I explained, the term tactics and tactical is generally used militarily and is defined as relating to or constituting actions carefully planned to gain a specific end result. I've defined some of these terms previously, but tactics, techniques, and procedures (TTPs) have proven to increase the likelihood of success in a given situation.

Mr. Daniel Goleman was the first to bring the term "Emotional Intelligence" to a wide audience with his 1995 book of the same name. He defines Empathy simply as the ability to consider other people's feelings, especially when making decisions. The part that strikes me the most is "especially when making decisions."

Later, he goes on to say that the ability to understand the emotional makeup of other people is paramount to not just good but great leadership. Further, he explains that the skill of treating people according to their emotional reactions can, in fact, be learned. Thus, I argue that it can certainly be deployed as a carefully planned, deliberate tactic to achieve a more positive result when dealing with people and making decisions.

I'm not at all suggesting that you shouldn't genuinely care for people's feelings or emotional reactions, but let's be real here—some stuff is just plain old ridiculous, outlandish, and frustrating. My time is very important to me, and I know it is for you, which is why these situations can be tricky. What I am suggesting here is an exercise in Tactical Patience followed by the deployment of Tactical Empathy.

Can this be learned? I found out firsthand that it most certainly can. However, it requires a lot more than just reading an article or book. It requires hands-on, active, intentional practice to break bad habits and engage in situations with real people who are ready and willing to give you real feedback. I suggest you start by taking a high-level look at what emotional intelligence is. Daniel Goleman identifies five distinct components of EQ as it relates to organizations and employment. In this section, we are focusing on empathy, but we have already addressed the other components in previous sections and chapters.

➢ Self-Awareness: Again, we revisit self-awareness as it is paramount to our growth. As a reminder, it is the ability to recognize and understand your moods, emotions, and drives, as well as their effect on others. Find a confidant, mentor, or even a trusted co-worker and employ them to be your eyes and ears. Ask them to tell you, without filtering, everything they see and hear when you engage with others at meetings.

➢ Self-Regulation: The ability to control or redirect destructive impulses and moods. This is Tactical Patience! To think before acting.

➢ Motivation: A passion to work for reasons that go beyond money or status. Pursuing goals with energy and persistence. If I asked you what you thought the most important thing in life is, what would be your response? As you know, for me, it is motivation. Without it, no idea, no goal, no dream can ever come to fruition.

➢ Empathy: The ability to understand the emotional makeup of other people. Master the skill of treating people uniquely according to their emotional reactions. This is where I struggled the most personally, but I forced myself to grow, and it all started with a gut check. Know your weaknesses.

➤ Social Skill: Proficiency in managing relationships and building networks. Focus on finding common ground and building rapport. I recently wrote a case study response discussing how to build personal, political, social, and cultural capital. Having social skills leads to social capital. Why would anyone want to do you a favor? Why would anyone want to come to your housewarming party? It all starts with building friendships and emotionally meaningful relationships. This can be exceptionally challenging in new environments.

I like to deploy a 2 x 10 rule when building the foundation for a new relationship. Spend two minutes a day for ten days in a row talking to this new person in your life about anything at all that isn't related to the reason you know each other. For example, if you met at work, don't talk about work. If you met at school, don't talk about school. Get this person to tell you their story. Stories are powerful, and you'll appeal to their emotional makeup.

"People do not care how much you know until they know how much you care. By establishing a relationship first, you qualify yourself to speak truth into their lives, even when it may hurt." - John C. Maxwell.

It takes a lot of focused effort and practice. I didn't try to become this new person overnight. Instead, I focused on moving the needle just a little more each day. As I grew, I realized that my co-worker's anger had nothing to do with the stolen cheese sticks. It had everything to do with other people not valuing or respecting him enough to leave his lunch alone. He felt deep sadness, and this, as I discovered, was the root cause of his anger and lack of motivation. Again, not because of the stolen cheese sticks but because no one cared enough even to try and understand where he was coming from emotionally.

It's important to note that all of this is hands-on practice with engaging feedback from trusted peers, friends, and family. Each day I strive to be a better leader, father, neighbor, and citizen of humanity.

Other Notes on Programming for Schools and Youth Organizations

We have addressed several programming tactics and techniques for schools, youth organizations, and businesses but below are a couple more thoughts on the topic. All of which apply to individuals as well.

<u>Structure independence and problem-solving into daily instruction, daily life, and everything else in between:</u>

Structuring independence and problem-solving into programming is crucial because it sets our children up for success in the long run. By encouraging children to think for themselves and take responsibility for their actions, they become more self-sufficient and better equipped to handle challenges as they arise.

For example, instead of simply telling a child what to do when they encounter a problem, a parent or teacher can encourage them to brainstorm possible solutions and make their own decisions. This helps the child develop critical thinking skills and become more confident in their ability to solve problems on their own. This approach isn't just for academics but for every other facet of school life, from the cafeteria to the schoolyard, to the bully. They must be given the opportunity to resolve very real issues on their own with the right tool set, guidance, and support.

Additionally, encouraging independence helps children develop a sense of autonomy and ownership over their lives. They learn to take responsibility for their own decisions and actions, which can lead to greater self-esteem and a sense of purpose.

Most educators are great at implementing this concept in school assignments or projects. Instead of simply providing all of the necessary information, teachers encourage students to seek out answers on their own and think critically about the material. That's great but what about everything else? What about the classmate they had a serious disagreement with or the teacher who they think is targeting them unfairly? Did any teacher encourage that student to go and be forthcoming about their feelings and their position? Probably not.

In short, structuring independence and problem-solving into every teachable moment is essential for long-term success and development. It helps our children become more self-sufficient, confident, and capable of handling challenges as they arise.

<u>Do away with meaningless, ineffective emotional programs for life:</u>

Abraham Maslow was an American psychologist who developed a theory of human motivation known as the hierarchy of needs. Maslow's hierarchy of needs theory proposes that human needs are organized into a hierarchical order. At the base of the hierarchy are physiological needs, such as the need for food, water, and shelter. Above physiological needs are safety needs, followed by the need for love and belonging, the need for esteem, and finally, the need for self-actualization.

According to Maslow's theory, individuals must satisfy their lower-level needs before they can progress to higher-level needs. For example, a person who is hungry and thirsty is unlikely to focus on love and belonging until their physiological needs are met.

As we progress up the hierarchy, we are expected to become more self-directed and self-actualized, but if these needs are not met, painful emotions and outcomes show their ugly face. Depression, anxiety, humiliation, fear, anger, and even shame consume us. Most of us, me included, tend to shove these emotions down deep into the heart of our souls, preventing us from truly facing our challenges with eyes wide open.

As I said, we are supposed to graduate our responses and self-regulate as we grow into adulthood, but instead, we end up making them life programs and requirements for instant gratification. Instead of growing and re-evaluating our needs and motivations, we just keep thinking of bigger and better ways to do the same stupid things. We get more security, we seek more approval, and we take more power and control.

Because of this, we tend to build programs for happiness during our young lives that simply do not work as adults. We end up putting too much energy into ill-fated programs for happiness that do not enable success when real-world problems bring us to our knees.

Seeking validation from others:

As children, we often seek approval and validation from our parents, teachers, and peers. While validation is important, it is equally critical that we learn to manage rejection and become comfortable loving ourselves. If we don't, we end up seeking validation from others in our adult lives, which can be problematic because we may not always receive the validation we seek. As witnessed time and time again, this leads to low self-esteem, anxiety, and depression.

Avoiding discomfort:

As children, our parents, teachers, and caregivers protect us from discomfort and pain. Of course, this is the right thing to do in most cases. However, if no opportunities are offered so, young people are exposed to adversity (imposed stress and optimal deprivation), it leads to a habit of avoiding discomfort in our adult lives. This becomes problematic because discomfort and pain are necessary for growth and learning. Avoiding discomfort leads to stagnation and a lack of personal development. The only time we grow is when we leave our comfort zones.

<u>Pursuing external markers of success:</u>

As children and young adults, we may be taught that success is measured by external markers such as grades, degrees, job titles, and salary. This leads to a habit of pursuing external markers of success in our adult lives, which can be problematic because these markers may not align with our values and may not lead to true happiness or fulfillment.

Of course, I think some external markers are important, but in my experience, they don't always lead to successful outcomes as we transition to adulthood. This is especially true if schools and youth organizations maintain an "everybody wins" philosophy and have a legitimate budget for participation trophies. My philosophy remains to praise effort and recognize legitimate outcomes.

My Raider program averaged 60-75 participants at a time. We had five awards, and everyone knew what it took to be earned. That said, we recognized effort on a daily basis, especially when someone crossed a threshold of personal performance that they weren't successful at the previous day or week.

<u>Comparing ourselves to others:</u>

As children and young adults, we tend to compare ourselves to our peers and feel pressure to conform to societal norms. This leads to a habit of comparing ourselves to others in our adult lives, which can be problematic because it can lead to feelings of inadequacy, jealousy, and a lack of self-worth. This, again, warrants mentioning the potential negative effects of social media if we don't have the right mental toolset available to manage it properly.

We need to focus on our own progress and growth instead of comparing ourselves to others. I encourage all young people and anyone I coach or mentor to set meaningful and challenging goals and track their own progress with the help of others, such as parents, teachers, coaches, and mentors.

Emphasizing the importance of self-acceptance can also be beneficial, as it teaches them to value themselves for who they are rather than how they measure up to others. Additionally, it is very important that we teach young people to appreciate the strengths and accomplishments of others without feeling threatened or envious. This cultivates a positive and supportive network and team.

The last thing I will mention here is touched on briefly already. I reiterate the importance of teaching them to recognize and challenge negative self-talk. By focusing on their own progress and growth, valuing themselves for who they are, and cultivating supportive relationships, young people can learn to be strong and avoid feelings of inadequacy or jealousy.

It is important to recognize these emotional programs and work to restructure them in a way that is more conducive to happiness and fulfillment in our adult lives. This may involve seeking therapy, practicing mindfulness and self-reflection, and developing a strong sense of self-awareness. We own our outcomes.

SEL – Social Emotional Learning

Definitions, history, and urgency:

Social-emotional learning (SEL) is an educational approach that focuses on teaching children and young people the skills they need to manage their emotions, build positive relationships, and achieve their goals. Basically, everything that we have been talking about except now with a buzzword name. I am not a certified SEL expert by any means, but I chose to discuss it here, given its relevance to educational standards as they exist today.

The history of SEL can be traced back to the early 20th century when John Dewey, an American philosopher, advocated for a more holistic approach to education that emphasized the social and emotional well-being of students. However, it wasn't until the 1990s that the term "social-emotional learning" was coined, and the concept gained wider recognition in the field of education.

The need for social-emotional learning has become increasingly urgent in recent years, as research has shown that students who have strong social and emotional skills are more likely to succeed academically, have better mental health outcomes, and are less likely to engage in risky behaviors. Additionally, as the COVID-19 pandemic has disrupted traditional school settings, the need for social-emotional learning has become even more pressing. The pandemic caused stress, trauma, and isolation for many students, and SEL can potentially provide a framework for supporting their emotional well-being during these challenging times.

While issues of this nature have existed and impacted young people throughout history, the pandemic highlighted the need for trauma-informed practices in schools. Trauma-informed approaches recognize that many students have experienced significant stress and trauma in their lives from broken homes, abusive parents, hunger, and, yes, even the recent covid pandemic. These experiences can impact their ability to learn and engage in school and in life. By incorporating SEL into their practices, schools and youth organizations can provide students with the tools they need to cope with stress and trauma, build positive relationships, and achieve academic success.

<u>SEL Programming:</u>

SEL is a crucial component in the development of young people, providing them with the skills and tools needed to build resilience, manage emotions, and achieve success in various areas of their lives. SEL programs promote the development of self-awareness, self-management, social awareness, relationship skills, and responsible decision-making. These skills are necessary for individuals to thrive in academic, personal, and professional settings. I have addressed most of these skills and benefits in previous sections and chapters, but I find it necessary to mention them again here.

According to a study by the Collaborative for Academic, Social, and Emotional Learning (CASEL), schools implementing SEL programs reported increased academic performance, improved attendance, and a reduction in negative behaviors such as bullying and substance abuse. SEL has also been shown to have long-term benefits, with individuals who participate in SEL programs reporting increased employment rates, higher salaries, and better overall health and well-being.

SEL can be implemented in various settings, including schools, youth organizations, and businesses. In schools, SEL programs can be integrated into the curriculum and classroom culture to promote academic success, positive behavior, and social-emotional development. Youth organizations can use SEL programs to foster positive youth development and support the social-emotional growth of their participants. In businesses, SEL can be used to develop aspiring leaders, promoting emotional intelligence, empathy, and effective communication.

One example of a successful SEL program is the RULER program, developed by the Yale Center for Emotional Intelligence. The RULER program provides schools with a framework for integrating SEL into the school culture, providing training and support for educators to promote emotional intelligence, improve relationships, and foster academic success. The program has been implemented in schools across the country, resulting in improved academic performance, decreased behavioral issues, and increased overall well-being of students and staff.

In summary, SEL can be a powerful tool for building resilience and success in young people, promoting emotional intelligence, effective communication, and responsible decision-making. By implementing SEL programs in schools, youth organizations, and businesses, we can provide young people and aspiring leaders with the skills and tools needed to navigate life's challenges and achieve their full potential.

Conclusion

Via my planning, execution, and programming techniques, the combination of imposed stress, optimal deprivation, and social-emotional learning can help individuals and organizations build resilience, grit, and mental toughness. Imposed stress involves exposing individuals to challenging situations to help them build skills and confidence. Optimal deprivation involves depriving individuals of certain comforts or privileges to build appreciation, self-discipline, and resourcefulness. Social-emotional learning involves teaching individuals skills such as self-awareness, self-regulation, empathy, and relationship-building to help them navigate relationships and manage emotions effectively.

When applied in real-world scenarios, these concepts can lead to positive outcomes. For example, schools can implement social-emotional learning programs to teach students the skills needed to succeed academically and in life. In addition, summer camps can use imposed stress and optimal deprivation techniques to help campers build resilience and grit. Businesses can incorporate social-emotional learning and imposed stress techniques into leadership training to help managers and executives develop the skills needed to lead effectively during challenging times.

In the current world climate, the application of these concepts is more important than ever. The COVID-19 pandemic has caused significant disruption to education, work, and daily life, leading to increased stress, anxiety, and mental health issues. By incorporating imposed stress, optimal deprivation, and social-emotional learning, individuals and organizations can develop the skills and resilience needed to navigate these challenges effectively.

Epilogue

Learning to suffer is like being the eternal Sisyphus, forever pushing the boulder of adversity up the mountain of life. Each time we stumble, we must rise again, find strength in the face of struggle, and continue our uphill journey. Just as Sisyphus's burden seems relentless, our suffering becomes our teacher, shaping our character, resilience, and wisdom. Embracing the struggle, we transform ourselves into resilient conquerors, relentlessly pushing forward, undeterred by the weight of our challenges. Through the eternal act of pushing the boulder, we discover that true growth and triumph emerge from within the depths of our struggles as we learn to find meaning in the process of overcoming.

We have come to the end of this transformative journey of learning to suffer with our eyes wide open. Let us remember that the true power lies not in the avoidance of suffering but in our ability to embrace it with unwavering courage and unwavering hearts.

Armed with the wisdom gained from our experiences, we can step forward into the world, ready to face life's challenges head-on. Let us approach every moment, every setback, and every trial as a profound opportunity for growth and transformation.

May we cultivate resilience in the face of adversity, drawing strength from within as we navigate the storms of life. Let us keep our eyes wide open, aware of the beauty that exists even amidst the darkest of times. May we extend empathy and compassion to ourselves and others, knowing that we are all united in the shared human experience—we are all broken in some way, and we spend our lives healing.

As we embark on the next chapter of our lives, let us remain committed to continuous learning and self-discovery. Let us be intentional in our pursuit of personal and professional growth, applying the lessons learned from our suffering to forge a path of purpose and fulfillment.

Together, let us inspire others to learn from their own suffering, to open their eyes to the lessons that surround them, and to embrace the transformative power that lies within each and every one of us.

In the vast tapestry of existence, there are those who walk among us, bearing the scars of battles fought in the shadows. They are the resilient souls who have learned the art of suffering, their spirits tempered by the searing fires of life's most formidable challenges. Our journey has led us through the depths of extreme poverty, military academies, the hallowed grounds of Ranger School, the unforgiving clutches of cancer, and thousand-mile odysseys of self-discovery. We stand now, weary yet triumphant, at the summit of an epic saga—a testament to the indomitable human spirit and the power of learning to suffer.

In the heart of Chicago's concrete jungle, we witnessed the raw and relentless face of poverty. It clawed at our dreams, tested our resilience, and forged within us an unyielding determination. We emerged from the depths of deprivation, armed with a hunger for change and a refusal to succumb to the limitations that life had imposed upon us. Through the darkness, we glimpsed the flickering flame of possibility, and we grasped it with a relentless grip.

The crucible of military boarding school awaited its rigid walls echoing with the footsteps of discipline and sacrifice. We learned to navigate its treacherous corridors, honing our minds and bodies and battling adversity at every turn. Amidst the rigidity, we discovered the seedlings of resilience, character, and leadership—foundations upon which we would build our indomitable spirits.

Then came the ultimate test, the grueling crucible of Ranger School. In the sweltering heat and bone-chilling cold, we faced physical and mental trials that pushed us to the very brink. It was here, amidst the crucible's flames, that we were forged into warriors of unwavering determination. We learned that suffering was not a foe to be feared but a companion to be embraced—a guide leading us toward the inner strength we never knew we possessed.

Yet, life was not finished with us, for destiny had one final battle to wage. Cancer, a relentless adversary, sought to claim our bodies and shatter our spirits. We stood toe-to-toe with mortality, facing the depths of fear and uncertainty. But in the face of this monstrous adversary, we summoned a resilience that defied the odds. We fought, we endured, and we emerged from the crucible of illness with a profound appreciation for life's fragile beauty.

In the aftermath of our trials, we embarked upon a pilgrimage of the soul—a journey of self-discovery. With each step, we shed the weight of our past, unraveling the layers of pain and suffering that had defined us. We walked amidst the grandeur of nature's embrace; our souls intertwined with the majesty of the world. It was here, amidst the awe-inspiring expanse, that we grasped the true meaning of our journey—the revelation that learning to suffer is the most masterful accomplishment in our lifetime.

For in the crucible of suffering, we unearthed the deepest truths of our existence. We discovered that resilience blooms from the darkest soil, that courage is forged in the fires of adversity and that the human spirit is an unstoppable force when faced with the trials of life. Through the anguish, we found wisdom, compassion, and an unquenchable thirst for life's untamed beauty.

As we turn the final page of this extraordinary tale, let it be etched upon our souls that embracing suffering with our eyes wide open is the true essence of mastery. We, the survivors, the warriors, the masters of our own destinies, stand as a testament to the indomitable spirit that resides within every human soul. May this journey inspire others to embrace their crucibles, to walk through life's fires with unwavering courage, and to emerge from the depths of suffering as beacons of resilience and hope.

And so, let us venture forth, carrying the lessons learned through the crucible of suffering, forever transformed by its alchemical touch. For we are the living testament to the extraordinary power of embracing life's challenges, eyes wide open, hearts ablaze with the unwavering determination to thrive amidst the most formidable storms.

Now, with our hearts open and our spirits ignited, let us go forth and create a life of meaning, resilience, and joy. The world awaits our awakened presence, our unwavering determination, and our boundless capacity to learn, grow, and flourish. Embrace suffering, learn with eyes wide open, and let your journey continue to unfold with grace and strength.